# The Legend of Dell Briggers

*A novella and two short stories by*

## Joe Hilley

## Dunlavy + Gray
HOUSTON

Dunlavy + Gray ©2020 by Joe Hilley

Library of Congress Control Number: 2019957862

ISBN: 978-0-9997813-3-3

E-Book ISBN: 978-0-9997813-4-0

# Table of Contents

# The Legend of Dell Briggers

## *A Novella*

Dell Briggers was born in Vidalia, Georgia—or so he said—and I believed him, too. Back when we were growing up, he was my best friend and we told each other everything. So naturally, when he said he was from Vidalia, I took it as the truth. It wasn't until the weekend of his funeral that I learned he was actually from Hot Springs, Arkansas; that his father was a writer and not a civilian who worked for the Navy at a top secret nuclear submarine base; and that his mother had never even been to Hollywood, much less acted in movies or been mentored by Tallulah Bankhead.

The weekend of his funeral was also when I found out Dell had a brother. Well, a stepbrother, but I suppose that counts when you're deciding in retrospect just how well you knew someone you thought you knew better than you knew yourself. After the funeral, though, I wondered whether I ever knew him at all. And I wondered just how much of a friend I had been to him. I mean, he came to see me when I was sick with scarlet fever, even though the doctor said I shouldn't see anyone. And when I needed money for lunch at school or to buy a Coca-Cola at the store in the afternoon, he always gave me some and never let me repay him. I don't think I ever gave him anything except a birthday present once or twice when my mother reminded me. And in spite of being closer to him than anyone, it turned out I didn't even know the place where he was born. Not the real place.

*1*

Or the truth about his family. Not the real truth. A friend who knew him like I thought I knew him would have known those things and more.

Dell and I first met when we were six years old. That year my mother held a birthday party for me at my grandfather's farm. Dell showed up wearing a cowboy outfit with real leather chaps, double holsters, a hat the size of a peach basket, and a pair of cap pistols that were the envy of every kid at the party. Later that day, when I opened my gifts, I found he'd given me an outfit exactly like his.

After that party, Dell and I were inseparable. We went through elementary school together, graduated from high school in the same class, and went off to college together. We roomed together, talked our way backstage at a Bob Dylan concert together (twice), even had coffee with the president—former president actually but that counts, I think. And I was with him when the engine in the car he was driving ran without a battery. Those stories weren't just Dell's stories. They were my stories, too.

So naturally, when Dell told me he once had a cat that could talk and that the birds outside his bedroom window awakened him every morning as regularly as an alarm clock, I said, "Wow. Nothing great like that ever happens to me." Then Frank showed up at the funeral with all that Hot Springs and "he's my brother" talk and poof! Just like that, my whole childhood vanished. Most of college, too. Well, not college. Like I said, I was there for every minute of that. All of those stories were true.

The funeral was also where I met Dell's partner—his life partner—Steve Atterbury. And that's when I found out Dell was gay. Knowing that about him wasn't a problem for me. I'm not saying I'm a cosmopolitan guy. I'm just saying, it didn't change my sense of devotion to Dell to know that he was in a committed relationship with a man. The thing that bothered me, that scratched me at a place I couldn't reach, was the sense that Steve had invaded my space. And it wasn't merely a passing thing but remained as a conflict in my mind even after the funeral—the notion that Steve was an interloper and shouldn't have been a part of Dell's life, followed by the unsettling implication that I should have been the one living with Dell. Which was odd considering the way our lives had opened up.

Dell and I lived through a lot together—childhood, high school, college—then he left Tenaca, moved to Chicago, and had an exciting career in advertising. I stayed right there in that tiny little town in Alabama where we grew up, took over the family construction business, and married Babs Oliver from New Market, North Carolina.

In spite of the distance between our two locations, Dell and I stayed in touch through phone calls and letters, then emails and texts. I didn't use social media and he never suggested I try, but we visited two or three times a year at first, usually in cities where he traveled on business—New York, Cleveland, Cincinnati, Atlanta, places like that. Once we met at a cabin on the Michigan peninsula and spent three days fishing. Spent a weekend in Indianapolis for an automobile race—one of his clients sponsored a car. And we met in Louisville one May for the Kentucky Derby. Then Babs and I had children and the visits with Dell became less frequent. Gradually, the excitement in my life shifted to coaching Little League, attending dance recitals, and hosting cookouts for the Sunday school class— we still had Sunday school back then, though not so much now. Dell and I still talked regularly by phone, sent each other emails and texts, and we exchanged gifts on birthdays and Christmases, but the interaction was not as intense as it had been.

After Dell's funeral, Babs wanted to stay in Chicago for a few days and see the city. Steve found out about it and asked us to stay with him, then he offered to show us around the city. We spent two days together, much of it in the house where Dell and Steve had lived together. The house was a two-story craftsman on North Beacon Street. Built in the 1920s, it was a house that we would describe as having "a lot of wood," which meant it was solid. The kind of solid you noticed when you entered it for the first time and the kind no one would pay to build today. I liked it.

On the first floor, Dell had a study that opened to the left of the main hallway at the front of the house. To the right of the doorway were two large, double-hung windows that afforded a view of the street and allowed natural light to fill the room most of the day. A desk sat near the windows with the chair positioned in a way that allowed the light to fall over it from behind. Bookcases lined the wall facing the desk. The other wall—the one directly opposite the door—held photographs, most of them in black and white and taken at various events, presumably involving Dell's clients. Two or three of the photos were of him with celebrities. As I studied the pictures, Steve entered the room. "This one was his favorite," he said.

When I turned to see what he was taking about he was standing beside the desk, pointing to a photo in a gold frame at the corner of the desktop. The picture was of Dell and me standing together behind my grandfather's barn. We'd been fishing in a pond in the pasture and my mother made us pose for a photograph. For more than one reason that was a special place for me and the sight of being there with Dell brought tears to my eyes.

"I remember that day," I said. "My mother took that photograph. I didn't realize he had a copy."

"Two, actually," Steve replied. "He had another one just like it on his desk at the office. Dell always smiled when he talked about it. Said you liked to fish so he went fishing."

"Ha," I chuckled. "I never knew he didn't like it. We went there several times and he always made us stay at the pond until he caught more fish than I did."

Steve laughed and ran his hand lightly over my shoulder. "He was like that to the end."

Once or twice while we were there it seemed as if Dell was with us, too. Not in a mystical way but I heard him in Steve's voice and saw him in Steve's mannerisms—the way he said a word or the look in his eye or the things he found to be funny. Hearing and seeing that, I realized how much I missed Dell and the relationship I had wasted in not staying close to him after he moved away. I could have come to visit him more often. We could have gone for walks together and talked about everything, or anything, or nothing at all. Each enjoying the presence of the other the way we did when we were younger and life was full of possibilities. Now, that was impossible and there was no way to get him back. More than once I had to turn away so Babs wouldn't see the tears in my eyes.

When the time came for us to go I didn't really want to leave Chicago, or Dell's house, but we had no choice. The business back in Alabama wouldn't run itself. We said our goodbyes and Steve promised to sort through Dell's belongings and send me anything that he thought might be a reminder of the past. I doubted I would ever hear from him again but appreciated the gesture all the same.

The trip up from Tenaca to Chicago had taken ten hours. We drove it straight through without stopping. Babs didn't want to do that for the ride back home and insisted we spend the night in Indianapolis. Stopping there made the drive easier, but added an extra day to the trip. It did, however, give me more time to think, which I very much needed to do.

My confidence in Dell and the person I had known him to be had been shaken by the things I'd learned that weekend. Not by the fact that he was gay but by the other things—that he wasn't really from Georgia, that he had a brother named Frank, that his father and mother weren't at all the people Dell had said they were—and I wondered how that could have been true and I not know it. The longer ride home gave me time to process some of that.

Later in the week, after we were back home and I was sipping coffee with Babs on the back porch just before dark, my faith in Dell seemed to right itself a little—but only just a little. Like I said, the part about what we did in college—the twins and Bob Dylan and the president—was true. I was there and knew that those things happened just as surely as I knew the fan blade from Dell's Chevrolet flew off the front of the engine, sliced through a crow in midair, and planted itself in the wall of Winston Green's barn. I was there when it happened—the fan blade went right by my ear. Whap, whap, whap. Like the sound of a helicopter.

But the stuff he said and did before then—all those stories Dell told when we were still in the sixth grade about being from Georgia and where his father worked and his mother's career—all of that was hanging in limbo. Especially the one about the birds waking him up every morning instead of an alarm clock. Of all of the stories Dell told, I was disturbed the most to think that one might not be true.

And that's when I decided to do something about my crisis of faith. That's when I decided to find out just exactly who Dell Briggers really was.

# 2

Getting our business straightened out after the trip to Chicago took longer than I expected, but two weeks after Dell's funeral I finally had a few minutes to spare at the end of the day so I decided to stop by the Tenaca library on the way home from work. I left Daddy with the crew to clean up the job site and started for town in the pickup truck.

While we were in Chicago I became interested in knowing the facts about Dell's life and while we were driving home from the funeral it seemed like a good idea to find out which of the two versions of his life were true—the one from Dell or the one I'd heard from Frank—but that Monday afternoon as I drove toward town I began to doubt whether I had the energy for it. The closer I got to town, the more I thought it might be better to let him lie in the grave in peace and add the things I'd learned from his stepbrother to the Dell story. Fold them into the fabric of my memory and say, "Well, that's just like Dell to go out with a mystery," and laugh off the incongruities.

Nevertheless, the library was on my way home and I had a few minutes that afternoon and by then I could already see the sign out front. So, I turned from the street into the parking lot and brought the truck to a stop in a space next to the front steps.

The town's library was located in a house that once had been the home of Clarissa and Morgan Alspaugh, longtime Tenaca residents who died before I was born. When Dell and I were in the seventh grade, my father won a contract from the city to renovate the building. It was a big deal for the town and a big deal for us. I liked the building as an example of his work, but libraries were never my place. Not my most favorite place, or my least favorite place, just not my place at all. During my entire time in high school I only went there once and that was under duress. We had to write a term paper for English class and Mrs. Stennis said we had to cite something other than an article from *World Book* encyclopedia.

So going to the library to find information about Dell now, after all the years that had passed, seemed more than a little out of place and as I made my way around the truck to the front steps it seemed really out of place. Still, I had heard about people who wanted to research their family history and how the library had been a place for them to start so, like it or not, there I was, at the library to begin my search for Dell. The real Dell.

It was late in the day by then and, it being Monday, I knew the library would close soon. That meant I wouldn't have much time, but it also meant I wouldn't be trapped there with Mrs. Smith—which was exactly what I hoped to avoid. Just enough time to get started, figure out what a Dell Briggers project might entail, and determine if I wanted to see it through.

As I came to the steps I glanced up at the building and saw Mrs. Smith staring back at me through a window that looked out onto the parking lot. She was standing at the circulation desk and from the expression on her face I knew she was as surprised to see me as I was to be there. Feeling more than a little awkward and by then very much out of place, I made my way up the steps, pushed open the door, and went inside.

"Billy Thomas," she said as I entered the building, "I haven't seen you in here since the eighth grade."

"Actually," I replied, "it was the tenth, Mrs. Smith."

"Yes," she said slowly. "I believe you're correct. Mrs. Stennis made y'all write a term paper that year."

"She made her class write one every year."

"For a few years," she agreed. "Then they switched that assignment up to the eleventh grade." She was right. I had forgotten that point. "So," she continued. "What brings you in here today?"

"Dell Briggers," I replied.

Her expression turned somber and she looked away. "He was so young," she said in a mournful tone. The tone of her voice seemed odd to me—a little over done for someone who, as far as I knew, never had anything to do with him. The age implication was also disconcerting. Dell and I were the same age and I often thought we looked quite youthful, even after college. Mrs. Smith's comment suggested she thought otherwise about me and after a moment she looked up in a way that suggested she realized it, too. "You know." She attempted to recover. "You're here and he's not."

We were getting off to a bad start. "Yes, ma'am," I replied.

"What about him brings you here?"

"I was wondering what I could find some information about him. Where he came from and all."

"Georgia, I think." Her eyes darted away as she spoke and for a moment I saw something that looked like anger.

"Well," I said, "that's what he always said. But now I'm not so sure about that."

She looked in my direction again. "You think he wasn't from Georgia?"

"That's just it. I don't know."

"Why the sudden doubt?"

"I met his stepbrother at the funeral."

"Stepbrother?" Mrs. Smith frowned. "Dell Briggers didn't have a stepbrother."

"That's what I always thought but there he was, right there at the funeral. And Dell's mother didn't deny it."

Mrs. Smith looked surprised. "Dell's mother was as the funeral?"

"Yes. Why? You thought she was somewhere else?"

Mrs. Smith had a disapproving look. "Dell's mother has Alzheimer's. She's over in the home at Bright's Mountain."

Now I was the one with a frown. "The woman I saw at the funeral was his mother. I've known her since forever."

"The woman you've known since forever was Dell's aunt."

My mouth fell open. "His aunt?"

"Yes. And the man you knew as Dell's father was his uncle. The aunt's husband."

"He was raised by his uncle and aunt?"

"Yes. The aunt was his mother's sister."

"But they seemed just like a family."

"Yes. Quite so."

Her response left me frustrated but I kept going. "And Frank? The guy at the funeral who said he was Dell's stepbrother. Who is he?"

"The son of the aunt and uncle."

"Mr. and Mrs. Briggers?"

"Yes."

"So, he is—"

"Dell's cousin."

"But I've never seen him before."

Again her eyes darted away as if something about the topic made her uncomfortable. "That's because he was born out of wedlock and raised by his grandparents."

"This is a little confusing."

"More than a little. And imagine how Dell must have felt."

"How do you know all of this?"

"I'm a librarian. I know things." She glanced away and her voice became even more officious than before. "Come on. What you need is over here."

Mrs. Smith came from behind the desk and led the way to the opposite side of the room. Behind a row of bookshelves we came to a closet and she opened the door, then pointed to the top shelf. "Take that down." A cardboard box sat on the shelf. I grabbed it, slid it out until the end of the box rested against my chest, and stepped back.

"Set it over here," she said. I followed her between the rows of books to a table and placed the box on it. "This box," she said, "has copies of the Tenaca Times from 1968. Look through it and find the issues for June. I don't remember the exact date you need, but there's an article in here from sometime in June. Look through the papers from that month for an issue with a headline about an explosion over at Bright's Mountain."

"An explosion?"

"At a coal mine," she explained. "Doesn't have anything to do with what you're looking for but that's the issue you need. The one that begins with that headline. The article you need to read is inside that issue."

Tenaca was bounded by mountains to the east, the last vestiges of the Appalachian foothills. Of those in our county, Bright's Mountain was the tallest. It was riddled with seams of coal, the mining of which had been the area's largest source of employment for many generations. Much of that coal had been mined out and only a few active mines remained, but back in the day it was a booming business. The article to which Mrs. Smith directed me was about an incident that happened in 1968. A spark from one of the mining cars set off an explosion. The resulting cave-in trapped a dozen miners deep inside the mountain. Rescuing them required at a two-week operation that included expansion of an air shaft, then cross-tunneling to their location. Two of the miners died before they were reached, but the remaining ten survived. People still talked about it even now.

Having been raised to be a good little boy, I did as Mrs. Smith said and sorted through copies of the newspaper. They were musty and once or twice I stopped to sneeze, but it didn't take long to find the newspapers from June and rather quickly after that I located the one she was talking about. Across the top of the page, in big bold letters, was the headline, "Coal Mine Explodes."

"Here it is," I said.

Mrs. Smith returned to the table where I was seated. "Okay," she said. "Now, look on the last page of the first section."

That issue of the paper wasn't very thick, about twenty pages total. Finding the end of the first section was only a matter of turning two pages. As I spread the newspaper flat on the table, Mrs. Smith reached over my shoulder and tapped an article with her finger. "Read that," she said. The article was entitled, "Local Man Arrested."

According to the article, a man named Odell Norton from Tenaca was arrested in Atlanta that month while participating in an anti-war protest. He faced several charges and was set for trial later that year. "Okay," I said. "Odell Norton was arrested in Atlanta. What about it?"

"The case was delayed but they tried him the following year. You won't find anything about it in newspapers from around here, but that's what happened. He was convicted and spent a year in prison."

"Okay."

"Apparently, prison wasn't as bad as it's been made out to be because Odell had a lot of time on his hands. To pass the time he started reading. When he was released, he moved to Florida and began writing."

Suddenly I understood what she was saying. "Wait. Odell Norton?"

"Yes."

"The writer?"

"One and the same."

Odell Norton was a bestselling author of Southern fiction. I wasn't an avid reader but I had read several of his books and found them enjoyable. Apparently other people liked them, too, because he was very well known, though until that moment I never knew he had a connection to Tenaca.

"I never knew he was from around here."

"I don't doubt it. Mrs. Stennis didn't care for him and didn't require her students to read his work. And some others didn't like him, so no one else made a fuss over him."

"Some others?"

"Powerful people." She had a dismissive tone. "Never mind about that."

"I've read some of his books."

"Really?" Her voice indicated she had serious doubts.

"Is he still alive?"

"Yes. Getting up in years, but I think he's still alive."

"Where does he live?"

"Last I heard, he was still somewhere down in Florida."

By then, the moment caught up with me and I became suspicious. "Why are you telling me about Odell Norton?"

Mrs. Smith scowled at me. "Haven't you been paying attention?"

"Yes ma'am."

"Odell Norton," she repeated. The tone in her voice suggested the name was supposed to mean something special to me now.

"Yes," I replied, still bewildered. "The writer."

"And what was Dell's name?"

"Dell Briggers," I said.

"All of it," she snapped. "What was his whole name?"

I thought for a moment, then slowly shook my head. "I don't know," I replied. And that was true. I knew what he wanted on a hamburger. Knew the kind of books he enjoyed reading—he was a much better student than I. Even knew his favorite color—which was blue, by the way. But I was clueless about his formal name.

Mrs. Smith placed both hands on her hips and glared at me. "You don't know?"

"No, ma'am."

"All these years you've been his friend—maybe even his best friend—his best friend in the entire world—and you don't know his full name?"

She seemed more worked up about it than the moment required. "No, ma'am," I said meekly. "I don't think I ever heard it."

"And you didn't think to ask him?"

"No, ma'am. I never did." I was feeling guilty about it now but not sure why, except that I already felt guilty about not knowing the things I'd recently learned about him—the brother, Arkansas, his relationship with Steve—and this just added to the list.

Mrs. Smith stood up straight, still staring down at me like a disgruntled school teacher. Her eyes focused squarely on mine and for a moment she seemed ready to keep them fixed on me permanently. Finally, in a firm, even voice, she said, "His full name—the one they gave him—the one he would have told you if you'd ever thought to ask—was Odell Norton Briggers." She stressed the Norton when she said it.

Suddenly I realized what she was trying to say. The writer, Odell Norton, was Dell's father. "Damn," I whispered.

Mrs. Smith was startled. "What did you say?"

I ignored her reaction. "I had no idea Odell Norton was Dell's father."

"That's what I've been trying to show you." She picked up the newspaper and folded it along the creases. "Did you get a passing grade on that term paper?"

"Term paper?" I looked at her again with a blank expression.

"The one you wrote for Mrs. Stennis when you were in school. The one that brought you in here the only other time you've ever been here. Did you get a passing grade on it?"

"Yes, ma'am," I replied. "I got an A- on it."

"Well." She stuffed the folded newspaper into its place in the box. "It's a wonder you even completed the task."

Her words were insulting and I saw no need for it. I'd come in there on an honest search for information about my friend. If I'd already known it, I wouldn't have been there. And the fact that I didn't know it should have made me a prime library customer. Instead, the librarian was beating me up because I didn't know ahead of time what I came there to learn. "Why do you say that?" I asked, making no attempt to hide my disdain.

"You don't pay attention, Billy."

"Pay attention? To what?" My voice was more argumentative than she liked.

"To the people around you," she railed. "To life. To things happening right in front of you." She gestured to the box. "Put that box back on the closet shelf. It's time for me to close up."

Mrs. Smith disappeared in a huff behind the bookshelves. I returned the box to its place on the shelf in the closet, closed the closet door, and made my way past the circulation desk to the front entrance. Without a goodbye or a thank you, I pushed open the door and stepped outside. The truck was right there at the bottom of the steps and I plopped my way down to it in a slack-jointed jaunt, then got in behind the steering wheel and backed away from the building.

"The very idea," I mumbled to myself. "Talking to me like that—as if I were still a student in school. I paid attention. Especially to the things that mattered. And I paid attention now. No one could stay in business very long if they didn't pay attention."

And I paid attention to other things, too. I knew Babs' birthday was September ninth and her favorite color was red and her favorite food was ice cream, though she didn't want anyone to know it. And I knew to ask her when it seemed like our children's birthdays were coming up. And okay—I put business first and Babs second and the kids were always there but the details often escaped me.

Still, I didn't like being talked to the way Mrs. Smith did that day and it bothered me. She didn't know me well enough to talk to me that way.

And on top of that, I forgot to ask her for Dell's mother's name.

I hate it when people treat me that way.

# 3

By the time I got home from the library I had calmed down a little, but only a little. Being scolded by the town librarian—or by anyone else for that matter—wasn't something I normally experienced and enduring it brought up all kinds of emotions from the past. Getting that sorted out and put back in place took a little longer than the drive home from the library. I still was aggravated when I arrived at the house.

"Right on time," Babs said as I came through the mudroom to the kitchen. That's when I noticed the smell of coffee. Babs made good coffee and I took a deep breath, allowing the aroma to sink deep inside. That always helped, no matter what the day had been like.

As I came past the refrigerator, Babs moved closer and gave me a kiss—the kind that let me know she was interested in more than a kiss if we still had the house to ourselves after drinking our afternoon coffee. The suggestion of what that meant pushed the episode at the library further to the back of my mind, but it didn't remove it completely. I still felt tense.

Babs filled our coffee cups, then I took mine from the counter and followed her out to the porch. We had a screened porch on the back of the house and every afternoon at about six we sat out there and sipped coffee together. Even in the summertime, we drank coffee on the porch and if it was hot that day we turned on the ceiling fan. Well, the ceiling fan ran all the time unless it was winter and even then unless it was a particularly cold day.

"You didn't look too happy when you came home," she said. "Something wrong?"

"Not really," I sighed.

"That's convincing." Her voice had a skeptical tone. "What happened?"

"It's nothing," I replied. "Really."

"And that kind of nothing is almost always something."

The coffee was particularly good that day so I took two sips before I said, "Mrs. Smith. Over at the library. That's what's wrong."

"Mrs. Smith?" Babs had a perplexed expression. "You were at the library?"

"Yes."

"What on earth for?"

See, I wasn't lying when I said I hadn't been to the library since high school. That was the truth and just about everyone who knew me knew it. Except for those Odell Norton books I mentioned earlier, reading for pleasure wasn't something I did. Most of the information I sought was related to work and the kind of information I needed for work didn't come from a book published ten years ago, which is the kind of books they had at the library. The kind of information I needed for work had to be up to date and I got most of it from online sites, trade journals, the building code, and product information sheets included with the products and appliances we used and installed. The rest of what I needed to know I picked up from trial and error.

"I wanted to find out about Dell." I was sure I told her before I left the house that morning where I was going. "That's why I was at the library."

"What about him?" she asked.

"Where he came from and who he really was. That sort of thing."

"You've known him since first grade. I'm still not sure what more there is that you want to find out."

"I knew him," I corrected. "I knew him since the first grade."

"Right," she acknowledged. "It doesn't really seem like he's gone." She took another sip of coffee. "But why go to the library?"

"I don't know." I had a frustrated tone and an exaggerated shrug to go with it. We'd talked about this several times since the funeral and I wasn't sure why she was being difficult about it now.

"They have books." I sounded more exasperated than I intended. "I thought they might have something that would tell me a little about him."

"About Dell? In the library?"

"Yeah. You know. All of that genealogy stuff you hear about."

"Frank really bothered you, did he?"

"Yes," I said. "He did."

She took another sip. "I wouldn't worry too much about Frank and what he said at the funeral. People make up stories about their life all the time."

"That's just it. I don't think Frank was lying."

"You think you were around Dell as much as you were and you still didn't know him?"

"Seems like it," I replied.

A moment passed and I heard a dove coo from a branch on an oak tree in the back yard. An airplane passed to the south of us. It was several miles away by the sound of the engine. And a car went by on the road out front. Finally Babs asked, "What did Mrs. Smith have to say?"

"She told me that Dell's mother wasn't really his mother."

Babs glanced in my direction. "He was adopted?"

"Not legally—I don't think—not that it makes any difference. The woman who raised him was the woman he knew as his mother—and the woman I knew as his mother. But Mrs. Smith said the woman who raised him wasn't the woman who gave birth to him."

"Did she know who did?"

"She said the woman who gave birth to him is in the home over at Bright's Mountain."

"Mountain View?"

"Yeah."

"So she's still alive?"

"Yes."

"What's her name?"

"She didn't say." I paused to take a sip before adding, "And I forgot to ask."

"You got mad."

"Yeah." I took another sip of coffee. "I got mad."

"What about his father? What's his name?"

I held the edge of the cup against my lip and rubbed it gently from side to side. The porcelain felt smooth and the steam from the cup rose up against my face. "His name is Odell Norton," I replied.

"The writer?"

"Yes."

"Don't hear much about him anymore."

"Not too much."

"Isn't he from Georgia?"

"No," I said. "He's from here."

"Here?"

"Yeah. Grew up right here in Tenaca."

"I never knew that."

"Apparently not many people do."

"Where is he now?"

"Mrs. Smith said he lives in Florida."

"Florida."

"Um hum." I was thinking about Odell Norton and Florida and wondering what he would have to say about Dell. And about Mrs. Smith and the condescending tone in her voice when she talked to me at the library.

Babs glanced in my direction again. "What are you thinking?"

"About that," I said.

"About Florida?"

"Yeah."

"You want to go down there and talk to him?"

"Yes." I took a drink from my cup. "But not yet."

"Not yet? What else are you wanting to do?"

"I need to find someone else to talk to. Someone who knew Dell when we were really young. Maybe someone who was around before he was born."

"And what would that do for you?"

"Maybe help me find out a little more about what really happened before I drive all the way to Florida to talk to Odell Norton. I wouldn't know what to ask him right now. Not much, anyway."

"That sounds like a good idea."

"Yeah."

"Think Odell Norton would talk to you if you went down there?"

"I don't know." I took a long sip from the cup. "I really don't know."

Neither of us spoke for a while. We just sat there drinking coffee and not saying anything. Then Babs said, "It bothered you when you met Dell's partner at the funeral, didn't it?"

A lump formed in my throat and my eyes filled with tears. I hadn't expected that question from her, or from anyone else, and it took a moment for me to catch myself. "Yes," I said weakly. "It bothered me."

Babs seemed not to notice my distress or if she did, she showed me the kindness of not mentioning it. Instead, she said, "Did it bother you because you found out Dell was gay or because you found out he was living with someone else besides you?"

That wasn't the first time I had considered the issue but hearing it from her was different. The question hit me hard and I didn't really know what to say. I never thought of Dell as my lover, but I did feel jealous when I found out he'd been with Steve all that time. Not because I wanted to be with Dell, necessarily, but because I knew Dell had been talking to him and doing things with him that we used to do together. Telling each other things we never told anyone else. Thinking each other's thoughts without having to be told what they were. Feeling each other's feelings before they became obvious. That was the part that made me jealous. He was that way with Steve and not with me. I also was angry with myself.

Intimacy is difficult for a man to achieve. True intimacy. Real intimacy. Especially intimacy with another man. Not the kind that involves physical acts, but genuine intimacy that gets beyond the obvious. For most men, the mere mention of the word intimacy in the context of another man is unnerving, never mind getting to know someone well enough to share your deepest thoughts. And to think that I had that with Dell, from a young age all the way through college, and then allowed it to slip away, left me sad in a way that I hadn't realized before. It also left me aggravated, too, which is part of the reason I reacted to Mrs. Smith the way I did.

But I couldn't say that to Babs. Not right then, maybe never—just to Dell, if he still was alive. Instead, I shook my head and said, "It mostly just made me curious."

"About Dell?"

About a lot of things, but again, I couldn't tell her that. Not yet. "Yes," I said instead. "About who he really was."

"Well." From the tone of her voice I knew she was trying to be supportive. "Who can you talk to about him?"

"I'm not sure."

"Your mother, maybe?"

"Maybe." I nodded my head slowly. "But I need to know a little more before I talk to her, too."

"She's not an easy person for you to talk to now, is she?"

"It's gotten harder over the years."

"Age."

"Yeah. That's part of it, I guess." Babs knew the part to which I was not referring. She knew the whole story with Mama, she was just being nice. "I'll talk to her about it eventually. But right now, I need to find someone else."

"Your dad?"

"Nooo," I said. "Not about this."

"Why not?"

"You know why not. Men. Gay. Jealous." I cut my eyes in her direction. "Too many code words for him."

"I think you underestimate him."

"Maybe so. It might be worse than I think."

"Not that." She reached over and popped me with a backhand on the shoulder. "He's a nice man."

"He's usually polite," I conceded. "But I don't think he's changed his mind about anything since I was born."

We fell silent again and I listened to the birds in the trees and the traffic going by on the road in front of the house. In a few minutes, though, Babs finished the coffee in her cup and stood. "Well," she said. "I'm going inside." As she moved past me, she ran her fingers over the back of my hand and leaned down, placing her lips next to my ear. "Maybe you want to join me." She raked her teeth across my ear lobe and a tingle ran down my back. "Not sure how much talking we'll do." She kissed my ear. "But I think you'll like it just the same."

There was a little coffee remaining at the bottom of my cup, but I wasn't thinking about that right then. I stood, holding the cup with my right hand, and leaned close to kiss her but she backed away and avoided my lips. "Come on," she said. "There's plenty of time for that where we're going."

# 4

Later in the week I put aside my attitude about the way Mrs. Smith treated me and began thinking again about who Dell's mother really was and how I could find her name. Mrs. Briggers—the woman who raised him—probably knew her name, depending on the nature of their relationship and how she came to have Dell in her care, but I didn't feel right about barging into her life again. Other than seeing her at the funeral, I hadn't talked to her in quite a while, even though she lived only a few miles away. And I wasn't interested in going back to Mrs. Smith again. Not after what happened before. No way. And if she ever—

Well, I suppose I wasn't as much over the things Mrs. Smith said to me as I thought. I still was interested in learning about Dell, though. So I began to think of other ways I could uncover the details of his life—about which it now seemed I had been oblivious, even though he was my best friend.

After working through a mental list of the people who might know something about what happened when Dell was born—which, by the way, was the same time I was born—I remembered Gladys Haywood. I should have thought of her first. She was older than my mother but younger than my grandmother and one of the oldest people I knew in Tenaca who was still alive. I had known plenty of people who were older than she but they all had died. And Mama—by the time I calmed down from the way Mrs. Smith acted toward me and came around to thinking about Dell again, it was Friday. Talking to Mama on Friday about anything serious was never a good idea.

With talking to Mama not an option, and my grandmother not available, and with going back to see Mrs. Smith never even a consideration, Gladys was the next best thing. Friday afternoon, after we finished with the new kitchen at the Autwells' house and satisfied everything on the punch list, I decided to pay her a visit. I should have called first, but I was already on the way when I thought about it so I decided to just stop by and see if she was home.

Gladys lived in a white two-story house on Sixth Street near the center of town. It had a wrap-around porch that was deeper than most living rooms I'd ever seen and a huge oak tree in the front yard with branches that sprawled over the top of the house. Back in the day, her father had been a lawyer and her mother came from a family with good taste. They were comfortable but never had as much money as everyone thought. Yet with her eye for style and his penchant for negotiating costs, they built the house as a showplace and lived in it all their lives. When they died, they left the house to Gladys. She never had lived anywhere else.

Traffic on the street was light so I parked the pickup truck at the curb in the shade of the oak tree and walked up to the front door. Gladys saw me coming and met me as I stepped onto the porch.

"Billy?" She was grinning from ear to ear. "Is that really you?"

"Yes, ma'am," I replied.

"I haven't seen you in months." She shopped at the same grocery store where we shopped and I was sure I'd seen her more recently than she thought, but I was there to ask for her help so I let the comment pass. "It's been a while," I said.

"Well come on in here." She pushed open the door and held it while I stepped inside. "I've got some iced tea I made at lunch. You want a glass?"

"I would love some."

"I bet you would." She closed the door behind us and led the way toward the kitchen. "It's been hot today."

"Yes, ma'am. It's been hot every day."

"I saw your daddy at the post office the other day. He said business was good."

"Yes, ma'am," I said. "We're busier than we've ever been."

From the front door, a hallway ran through the center of the house and I followed her down it to the kitchen. "Have a seat," she said. A table sat in the center of the room between the sink on the back wall and the stove on the front. I sat down and waited while she prepared two glasses of tea. She set one in front of me, then put hers at a place across from me and sat down.

"I know you didn't just drop by for a visit," she said. "What's on your mind?"

"Well," I said, not sure where to begin. "I wanted to talk to you about Dell Briggers."

"Uh huh." Gladys had a knowing tone in her voice. "I wondered how long it would be before you came around asking about him."

That comment caught me off-guard. "You did?" My voice was less controlled than I'd hoped.

"Yes," she said. "I did."

"Why was that?"

"I heard he passed away and your daddy told me you and Babs went up to the funeral. You and Dell were best friends and I had a feeling you would come back from that funeral with more questions than answers." She paused to take a sip of tea. "And here you are."

"I asked Mrs. Smith about him. But she—"

"Mrs. Smith over at the library?"

"Yes."

"Oh my." Gladys shook her head and sighed. "I wish you had come to me first."

"Why?"

"That lady has a lot going on in her head."

Her comment forced me to explain. "I only went there because it was the library. Not to see her. I was looking for information. The library seemed like a good place to start."

"And what did Jenny Smith tell you?"

"Jenny?" I said with a frown. "That's her name?"

"Yes." Gladys nodded once again. I knew from the look in her eyes that there was more to the story than that. "What did she tell you?"

"She told me that Dell Briggers wasn't really Dell's name."

"What name did she say was his?"

"Odell Norton Briggers."

"She told you Odell Norton was his daddy?"

"Yes, ma'am. Odell Norton the writer."

"What else did she tell you?"

"That the woman I knew as his mama wasn't really his mother. She was actually his aunt."

Gladys frowned. "I'm surprised she told you that much."

"That much? You mean there's more?"

"Oh, yeah," she said. "There's a lot more."

"So, what's the rest of it?"

"Well to begin with, everything she told you is true. I mean, I don't know all she said but what you just told me—about Dell Briggers wasn't Dell's real name, the woman who raised him didn't give birth to him, and his daddy being Odell Norton the writer—all of that is true. But the whole story is a little more complicated."

"Okay," I said. "Then tell me the whole story."

"I'll do my best." Gladys reached behind her, took hold of the tea pitcher by the handle, and set it on the table. "But we might need some more tea before this gets done."

"I'm fine for now." My voice had an insistent edge. "Start talking."

"Okay. Jenny told you Odell Norton was—"

"Wait. Back up a little. You called her Jenny several times. I never knew that was Mrs. Smith's name."

"You never had a reason to know."

"I guess not."

"People don't think about that part of it," Gladys continued.

"Which part?"

"You can't learn something unless you want to know it. Or need to know it. You got to want to know something before you can learn it."

"I never thought about that."

"Nobody ever does."

"So, Mrs. Smith only told me part of the story."

"Yeah. She told you the part about Odell Norton was a young man from Tenaca, went off to Atlanta, got involved in some kind of protest, got arrested, and went to prison."

"Yes."

"While in prison he started reading, then got interested in writing, and became a writer."

"Yes."

"And after that he never had much to do with Dell or the woman who gave birth to him."

"That's not what happened?"

"No," Gladys said with an emphatic tone. "Like I said, the part about Dell's name, him being raised by a woman other than his mother, and the name of his father was correct. Most of what she told you from that point on was nonsense. And I don't know why they're still telling it."

"But I thought you said that what she told me was true."

"Odell Norton—the writer—really was from here. He was born in a house about three blocks from where we're sitting. And he got Dell's mother pregnant. But he wasn't arrested in Atlanta."

"And he never went to prison?"

Gladys shook her head slowly. "No. Someone else used his name. Created a big mess. Odell hired a lawyer in Atlanta who straightened it all out. Odell never even appeared in court."

"There was an article in the newspaper about it."

"I know. But that's just part of the story. You'd have to know the people running the Tenaca Times back then to understand."

"So, why did Mrs. Smith tell me that about him getting arrested?"

"Okay. Let's begin at the beginning, at least as far as Dell is concerned."

"Okay."

"The woman Odell Norton got pregnant was named Lucy Johnson."

"So Dell's mother was someone named Lucy Johnson?"

"Yes."

"One of the Johnsons from here?"

"Yes. Her father was Harold Johnson. Lived where all the other Johnsons live now. Up toward Quimby."

"I remember Harold. I never knew about a daughter named Lucy. Or any of his daughters, for that matter."

"I don't expect you did. That was a long time ago and whatever part of it you might have known you were too young to hear. Hearing is a lot more than just knowing."

"Like learning," I said, following her train of thought.

"Now you're with me," Gladys said with a grin.

"What's the rest?" I asked. I wanted her to keep talking.

"So, Lucy Johnson went off to college at the University of Arkansas. A friend of hers from the high school here in Tenaca was accepted up there and Lucy went, too. Odell Norton was teaching there and Lucy had him for a class. They started seeing each other and she got pregnant."

"And to think that actually happens," I said sarcastically.

Gladys frowned. "To think what actually happens? People getting pregnant?"

"No. A college teacher with a student. You see it in movies all the time. You would think they'd realize what was going on and one or both of them would avoid it."

"Lot of things seem obvious when you aren't in the situation," Gladys opined. "Not so much when you are in the midst of it."

"So, Lucy Johnson was pregnant with Dell?"

"Yes."

"That would have been in the 1970s."

"Right. Dell was born in 1973. Lucy was twenty-one."

"And then they came back here?"

"Yeah," Gladys said. "But not like you think."

"What do you mean?"

"Lucy and Odell stayed together most of that first year and the next, but about the time Lucy graduated, Odell took a job at a school in Tennessee. Said he would send for her when things got settled but after he got over to Tennessee, he found someone else. Ended things with Lucy in a telephone call."

"Wow," I replied.

"Yeah. And her with that little boy."

"What did she do?"

"She wanted to come home—back here to Tenaca—but her father said no. Said the family had a reputation to take care of and she'd made her decision and had to deal with the consequences. I think her mother might have let her come back but her father wouldn't agree."

"Seems rather heartless."

"That's the way Harold Johnson was." She gave me a questioning look. "Do you really remember him?"

"Tall. Rawboned. Always a stern look on his face."

"Yep," she nodded. "That was him."

"He and my grandfather were friends."

Gladys glanced away. "They did business together," she said. "I'm not sure they were that good of friends."

My grandfather was an enigmatic sort of person, but I could hear stories about him from my father any day of the week. I wanted Gladys to tell me about Dell. "Where did Lucy and Dell go after they couldn't come back here?"

"Lucy had a friend in Savannah, Georgia. She and little Dell went there. The friend helped her get a job teaching school in Valdosta. Lucy did that for about four years, then she had a nervous breakdown. I'm not sure what set it off. Nobody seemed to know. Doctors over there diagnosed her as schizophrenic, I think. That's what people said, anyway."

"Mrs. Smith said she had Alzheimer's."

Gladys had a disgusted expression on her face and made a dismissive gesture with a wave of her hand. "That's just Jenny being Jenny."

"Dell's mother doesn't have Alzheimer's Disease?"

"No. She has many problems, but that's not one of them."

"What happened to Dell?"

Gladys leaned away from the table. "I'll have to back up in the story a little to tell you that."

"Okay." She looked over at me. "You want some more tea?"

"No, ma'am," I replied. "I'm good."

She rested her hands in her lap. "This all came to light about Lucy because one day she didn't show up to teach her classes."

"Over in Valdosta?"

"Yes," Gladys replied. "Someone at the school—a teacher she'd made friends with—went to see about her. They found her at the house, sitting in the corner. Not doing nothing. Just sitting there, staring blankly into space. Little Dell was in the kitchen on the floor eating crackers and pickles."

That made me smile. "Crackers and pickles," I repeated softly.

"That means something to you?"

A lump formed in my throat. "He used to eat that for a snack."

"Well, that's what he was eating when they found him. Whoever the person was that came and found her knew about the friend in Savannah and they got in touch with her. That lady called Lucy's parents but they still didn't want nothing to do with her."

A frown wrinkled my forehead. "Not even then?"

Once more Gladys shook her head. "Not even then," she sighed. "I think it was her father who said that. But Jenny found out about it and—"

"Who?"

"Jenny. Her sister."

"Jenny?" Suddenly my eyes opened wide. "Jenny Smith?"

Gladys smiled and nodded. "Jenny Smith at the library."

My mouth dropped open. "They were sisters?"

"Yes."

"Mrs. Smith was Jenny Johnson?"

"Yes," Gladys said. "Before she married Grant Smith, she was Jenny Johnson."

"That means she was Dell's aunt, too?"

"Yes," Gladys replied. "The woman who raised him was Alice Johnson Briggers, his aunt. And Jenny Smith at the library was his aunt."

I leaned away from the table and ran my hands through my hair as I struggled to make sense of what Gladys had told me. How could I have been Dell's friend and not known this? How could I have lived in Tenaca all of my life and not know this?

"When Mrs. Johnson—Alice and Jenny and Lucy's mother— when she found out what happened to Lucy, and that Harold wasn't going to let Lucy come home, she went to see Jenny."

"About helping her anyway?"

"Yes."

"I bet that went over well with Harold."

"We'll get to that part."

"Okay."

"After they talked, Jenny and Mrs. Johnson went over to Valdosta and picked up Lucy and Dell."

"What did Harold say when they came back?"

A troubled look came over Gladys. "There was a terrible fight. But I'll get to that in a minute."

"Okay."

"So, the short version is, Jenny and Mrs. Johnson couldn't bring Lucy to the Johnson's house because Harold didn't want anything to do with her or Dell or the whole situation, so they brought both of them to Jenny's house until they could get Lucy into the home over at Bright's Mountain."

The facility she was talking about was a place for the elderly. "They take psychiatric patients over there?"

Gladys arched one eyebrow. "They took Lucy."

"Okay," I said. That part was totally believable. Things like that happened all the time in Tenaca, if you were the right person, or knew the right person, or paid the right person.

"Harold Johnson had a lot of sway in the county back then. Most of the people were afraid of him."

"But you said he didn't want her here."

"No. He didn't. But the Johnson girls knew how to use his name to their advantage. Which is why they developed the explanations like Jenny told you."

"That's how they kept him from knowing?"

"I don't know if he knew where Lucy was living or not. But it's how they presented her to the town. And once they put Lucy on the right medication, she was coherent and able to function with a little help, so that part wasn't a challenge. She couldn't live by herself but she could make it through the day if she took her medicine."

"And she's alive now?"

"Yes."

"And she's still like that now? She's able to function?"

"As long as she gets her medication on time."

"And you know her?"

"Yes," Gladys said. "I know her."

"Where was Dell after they put her in the home?"

Gladys paused to take a sip of tea, then said, "Dell was one of the big worries. They were worried about Lucy but people kept saying, 'What about that little boy?' He stayed with Jenny a week or two while they got Lucy situated, then the oldest sister took him."

I felt another frown wrinkle my forehead. "Mrs. Briggers?"

"Yes." Gladys grinned. "For someone who's lived here all their life, you really don't know much do you?"

"I think I know less than everyone around me," I sighed.

"Alice Briggers—the woman you've known all your life as Dell's mama—was Alice Johnson before she married Charlie Briggers."

With that, my mind reached a saturation point and gave up for the moment. I leaned forward and rested my head on the table-top while memories of my childhood swirled around my head. With those memories came the overwhelming realization that the things I didn't know, the things I didn't remember were the most important things of my past. And I had missed them.

The things I knew, the things I remembered from my child-hood—that Lonnie Jones was Mary Well's nephew, even though they were in the same class at school, that Billy Simms liked Eliza-beth Thompson but wouldn't ask her out, that Dell and I sneaked a taste of whiskey from the bottle under the sink when we were in the sixth grade—none of that mattered at all. I had noticed the trivial. Reveled in it at the time. Relished it in the years that followed. As if those moments were the ones that mattered, that defined us, and made us the people we became. All the while, I was floating in a sea of really important things I never noticed and even worse, never knew existed.

Gladys reached over and rubbed my head. "Sit up," she said. "Have a drink of tea. There's a little more to tell and I want you to hear all of it now, while we have the opportunity for it."

With great effort, I lifted my head from the table and sat up straight in the chair, then took a sip of tea like she said. "Okay," I said weakly, and only after a second sip from the glass. "Tell me the rest."

"You remember I said the Johnsons had a big fight."

"Yes, ma'am." I nodded my head a little, but when I did the room seemed to spin around so I stopped short. "A big fight."

"Jenny and Mrs. Johnson got back from Georgia with Lucy and Dell on a Friday."

Mention of that day caught my attention. "Friday?"

"Yes." Gladys glanced at me with a knowing expression. "Friday."

"What happened?"

"They didn't have any choice but to tell Harold, which they did as soon as they got back. I think they knew already that it wasn't going to work to bring Lucy and Dell out to the Johnsons' house so they brought their stuff to Jenny's house, then went on over to find Harold and tell him that afternoon."

"And I'm guessing that didn't go over well."

"No," Gladys said. "It didn't. When they drove up and Harold saw the four of them—Lucy and Dell in the back seat, with Jenny and Mrs. Johnson up front—he flew into a rage. Started screaming and cussing. Mrs. Johnson got out of the car to calm him down only there wasn't any calming him down." Gladys looked away as if remembering the moment now brought back all of the pain from back then. "He was always like that," she added. "Even when he was a boy in school."

"You knew him?"

Gladys looked over at me. "Oh, yeah," she sighed. "I knew Harold from a long time ago."

"So what happened when Mrs. Johnson got out of the car?"

"She started toward him and he lit into her with both fits."

"He hit her?"

"Oh, yeah."

"With his fists?"

"As fast as he could go."

"Damn," I whispered.

"That's not the worst of it."

"What happened?"

"When he started hitting on Mrs. Johnson, Jenny got out of the car and stood between them to try and stop him but Harold shoved her aside and went back to beating on Mrs. Johnson. Finally, he hit her so hard she fell and banged her head against the porch steps."

"Wow," I said softly. "That is beyond words."

"It was bad," Gladys said. "Real bad."

"Did they stay together after that?"

Gladys looked over at me and I could see her eyes were full. "Mrs. Johnson was dead the minute her head hit that step."

All I could do was stare at her in disbelief and we sat there in silence, me trying to imagine what that must have been like and her trying to forget the memory of it. Finally, I said, "What happened to Mr. Johnson? What did they do to him?"

Gladys' face went cold as stone. "Nothing," she said grimly. "Not one damn thing."

"They didn't investigate?"

"Yeah. They investigated. At least, that's what they called it. Questioned everybody who was out there by the car. But the only people who were there besides Harold were women and the sheriff wasn't about to side with a woman against Harold, even if it was his wife and children."

"Why not?"

"Because they were women—and Harold was a man—and he was big in the Klan."

A puzzled look came over me. "The Klan?" We had our share of rednecks, and I knew from conversations with Daddy that Harold Johnson and my grandfather were members of a secret society, but no one ever said it was the Klan.

"Uh huh." Gladys nodded her head slowly. "I think that's what put an end to it up here."

"End to what?"

"The Klan."

"The Ku Klux Klan?"

"Up here they went by the Knights of the White Camellia. But it was the Klan just the same."

"They were here when I was a boy."

"Uh huh." Gladys nodded her head. "And a long time after that. Some say they're still here. But whatever they are now, it's not like it was before."

"And you think him killing Mrs. Johnson led to the end of the White Camellias?"

"In this part of the state." She tapped the tabletop with her index finger for emphasis. "That was the end of it."

"How?"

"For one thing, everyone figured out real quick what happened— Harold killed Mrs. Johnson and the sheriff covered it up for him. The whole county knew it and none of the decent people liked it."

"What did they do?"

"There wasn't much anyone one could, really. We could vote, but the next election was a couple of years off. And I think one or two of the men tried to talk to the sheriff about what he was doing and the way he was handling things, but nothing came of it. Harold controlled most of what went on around here." She looked me in the eye. "Harold and your grandfather."

Grandpaw and his entanglements wasn't something I wanted to discuss right then. Besides which, I didn't know much about it and had only heard stories I didn't really understand. Instead I said, "Harold got away with it?"

"Not for long." Gladys had a satisfied smile. The kind that comes from knowing what happened next and liking it. "A few months after Mrs. Johnson died, the feds came in here and a bunch of people got arrested. Had a big trial down in Birmingham." Gladys looked over at me. "You don't remember anything about that?"

"You mean, when they tried the Claxton brothers?"

"Yes," she replied. Her smile spread, turning up the corners of her mouth. "So, you do remember some things."

"I remember that, but I didn't realize it had anything to do with Harold Johnson killing his wife."

"The Claxtons were charged with extortion, I think. And maybe two or three other things. But it was the Klan, or the Camellias, or whatever they called themselves that the feds were after. That's just the way they charged them."

"Mr. Johnson is dead now."

"He died not too long after the Claxton trial. Some people said he was scheduled to be next in court but I don't know. Anyway, he died and that was the end of that."

"How'd he die?"

The smile vanished from Gladys' face and an odd look came over her. "Nobody knows much about that, either. They found him in the barn behind his house, face-down on the dirt floor. A flock of chickens were pecking at his head when they found him."

I sat there a moment, thinking about that and all the other things she'd said and trying to piece together where I came into the story, then I looked over at her and said, "So that's how Dell came to be with the Briggers."

"Yes. He was at the Smith's house for a few days, then Lucy went to the home at Bright's Mountain and Dell went to live with Alice Briggers. The next year, Dell started school in the first grade and that's how you knew him."

"But I never knew all of that about Arkansas."

"No. I don't expect you did."

"Did Dell's father ever come around?"

Gladys frowned. "Odell Horton?"

"Yes. Did he ever come around after that?"

"A few times." Gladys looked away, as if to avoid my gaze. "Which is part of the reason nobody really thinks about him being from here anymore," she continued. "He grew up here. Went to school here. Then went off to the University down at Tuscaloosa and ended up in Arkansas. By then, his parents were living up there, too. I think that's where Mrs. Horton's mother was from. He left here and never really came back."

"Except for a few visits."

"Right."

"Hot Springs, Arkansas?" I asked with a hint of expectation.

"Yes." She seemed surprised. "You knew about that?"

"It came up at the funeral."

Gladys' countenance dropped. "Frank," she said in a dour tone.

I grinned. "Why do you say his name that way?"

Gladys rolled her eyes. "He's been causing trouble since the day he was born."

"I never knew him and I don't think I ever even heard of him until that day at Dell's funeral."

"He was older than y'all." Once again Gladys avoided eye contact with me. "And he got in some trouble. They sent him off to a boarding school and after that, he wasn't around much and even when he was, he wasn't."

"I just don't remember him."

"Probably never came around y'all. And if he did, you might not have paid him much attention."

Gladys fell silent, as if she'd said what she meant to say and had talked the topic to a stopping point. I was exhausted and after a moment I looked over at her. "This is a mess." There was a hint of desperation in my voice.

"Yes," she replied. "That's exactly what it is."

"And to think I never knew any of it at the time."

Gladys' eyes opened wider. "They didn't want you to know it."

"Who didn't?"

"The Briggers. The Smiths. The Johnsons. Even your own parents."

That caught me by surprise. "My parents?"

"Yes."

"Why didn't they want me to know?"

"They thought it was better for you and Dell to just be friends and not cloud things up with all of the things that happened before he arrived. You couldn't do anything about it anyway. And with your mother the way she is, they just decided to go along with it. The whole town did, too."

"Dell must have been lonely."

"He was something alright," Gladys conceded. "But I'm not sure it was lonely."

We sat in silence again, both of us thinking about all that we'd discussed, and then Gladys slapped her hand on the table. "That's all I know about it," she said.

"Mrs. Smith said Odell Norton lived in Florida. Any idea where in Florida?"

Gladys looked down at the tabletop. "I couldn't say." There was more to it, but I could see she didn't want to talk about it. I let it pass because I knew I would have other questions to ask as I continued to unravel the story.

"I appreciate you telling me about all of this," I said. "Is Lucy Johnson still over at Bright's Mountain?"

"Yes. Are you thinking about going to see her?"

"I am. And I'm thinking about talking to Mama about this, too."

Gladys leaned back from the table. "Not today," she said. "Friday isn't a good day for your mother."

"You're right," I said. "It's not a good day for Mama. And I think it would be better for me to see Lucy Johnson first."

"When are you planning to go see her?"

All of my appointments were entered in a calendar app on my smart phone. I took the phone from my pocket and checked for an open date. We had two jobs scheduled to start the following week but one of them was running behind while we waited on delivery of a stove, which meant I would have a few hours free on Wednesday. I looked over at Gladys. "Wednesday afternoon of next week looks good. Think that will work for her?"

"Afternoons are usually good. But come get me after lunch. I'll ride over there with you."

"You want to see her, too?"

"I usually go about once a week and if I'm with you, things might go a little better for your visit."

"That would be great," I replied. And, not knowing what to expect, I really thought it would help to have her with me.

# 5

Friday evening after I got home from work and from talking to Gladys, Babs and I skipped our usual time on the back porch and went out for dinner at the All Steak restaurant in Cullman. We ran into friends from Decatur, spent the evening eating and talking, and returned home later than normal. The next day was Saturday. Having returned home later than usual we slept late and it was almost ten before I began mowing the lawn.

With my hands occupied, my mind was free to wander over the things Gladys had told me about Dell and what I had learned about him so far. As I rode back and forth across the lawn, my mind bounced from one thought to another. The horror of Mrs. Johnson's death. The fact that Mrs. Smith at the library was Dell's aunt. And so was Mrs. Briggers, even though they all referred to Mrs. Briggers as his mother and Dell always called her Mama. And for some reason that caused me a problem.

Mama was more than a term of endearment. A mother might be a parent but mama was the one who looked after you, listened to your dreams, told you it was okay when you cried. You wanted to sit on mama's lap. She was personal. Mother was more remote. Referring to Mrs. Briggers as mama went well beyond acknowledging her position as Dell's parent. And she was much closer to him than merely an aunt who took him in when he had nowhere else to go.

About that time, I came to the azaleas that grew in a flower bed along the far side of the yard and had to slow down while I ran along the edge. I depressed the clutch pedal with my foot and moved the shifter on the mower into a lower gear. It wasn't altogether necessary but by running at a slower speed I could make sure I kept the blades off the monkey grass that formed a border around the bed.

A few times before, I let the mower get away from me and cut into the border. Babs let me know she didn't like it. So, after arguing with her a time or two I finally gave up on getting the job finished quickly, resigned myself to the fact that it would take most of a Saturday morning to cut the yard, and operated the machine at a snail's pace near the flower beds. We had a lot of flower beds.

After a round or two past the flower bed with the azaleas, the mower was far enough away from the monkey grass to shift it back to a faster gear. As before, I depressed the clutch pedal to change gears. As I released the pedal and the mower lurched forward, I thought of a time when I spent the night at Dell's house. It was in the fall when we were in the seventh grade.

The Briggers lived in an old two-story house on the north side of town. It had been part of a farm once but all of the land had been conveyed away except for the house and an acre or two around it. Dell's bedroom was on the second floor but across the back of the house was a sleeping porch which we used more often than his room. The porch held several beds, one of which was made with an iron frame and had a feather mattress that was thick and soft and when you laid down on it the sides curled up around you. We slept out there one night that fall. The night air was cool but we had a couple of quilts for cover.

Dell and I lay next to each other and talked until after midnight. I loved the sound of his voice and often asked questions just to keep him talking. That night, I listened as long as I could but as the night grew later and later I couldn't stay awake any longer. I think he still was awake, though, because as I drifted off to sleep I heard angry voices coming from downstairs and then I felt Dell's hand take hold of mine. The touch of his hand against mine seemed strange at first but it made me feel good and accepted and warm deep down inside, too. Not warm with passion or embarrassment but with a sense of acceptance at a level that was deeper than anything I'd ever known before and a sense of rightness that was more right than I'd ever experienced before. And that's how we went to sleep, lying on our backs, holding hands.

When I awoke the next morning, I was lying on my side, facing away from Dell, and he was on his side facing towards me with his arm over me near the middle. I liked that, too, and didn't want to get out of bed but his mother called for us and we had to get downstairs for breakfast. Dell and I never talked about that night and, although I spent the night with him many times afterward, we never had a moment like that again. I didn't think of him as a lover. Nor did I think our friendship was strange. I just thought he liked me. And I liked him.

Just then I heard an awful clattering noise and realized I was still on the mower but off the lawn and onto the gravel driveway. The mower blades were slinging gravel halfway across the yard and I saw Babs standing on the porch staring at me, hands on her hips with a worried expression on her face. I waved to her and she went back inside but I expected to hear about the gravel later. She had definite ideas about how the place was supposed to look and gravel strewn across the lawn, glistening in the afternoon sun, wasn't the kind of look she wanted.

With the mower back on the lawn, cutting grass instead of the driveway, my thoughts turned again to how much I had learned about Dell in the short time since his funeral. His mother was his aunt; his mother, the woman who gave birth to him, was in a nursing home; and the lady at the library was his aunt who rescued him and brought him to Tenaca. His father wasn't really his father but a famous writer instead of someone who worked on nuclear submarines. And his mother wasn't an actress but a woman with a mysterious and painful past. Pain was emerging as a recurring theme. The pain of Lucy and of her mother and of her sisters. And even Harold. No one could act like they said he acted and not act out of pain. To that point, my effort to understand Dell had been tentative at best but even with that, I realized he had a lot of pain in his life of which I had been unaware. And the quest that began as an effort to understand him was rapidly becoming much bigger and going much deeper than I'd imagined when I first conceived of the idea.

When I stopped at the library that day and talked to Mrs. Smith,

I had imagined I would find the usual information one finds in records—names, birthdays, a smattering of court documents. What I'd learned was intriguing and arresting and unsettling, but it wasn't merely taking me into the life of Dell Briggers. It was taking me into my own life, testing the boundaries of what I knew about myself and what I knew about people I thought I had known all of my life. It also was testing the way I understood relationships in general. What did it mean to be a parent or to have a parent? What made a son a son? A friend a friend? More startling, who was I back then and what did it mean to be a friend? And, though I resisted delving too deeply into the topic, I could sense the subject of love and lifelong relation-ship opening to me in a new and, already at times, terrifying way. A simple question—who was Dell Briggers—was drawing me into the bigger and scarier question of who was Billy Thomas.

In spite of my mishaps with the mower that morning, I finished the yard at noon. With the mower cleaned and put away, I went inside, took a shower, and changed clothes. We ate lunch on the back porch and I was thinking about taking a nap but Babs wanted to go shopping in Birmingham. So instead of napping in comfort, we left the house and headed in the direction of the stores she wanted to visit. I let Babs drive. Things usually worked out better that way, especially if I slept or stared out the window or did anything except notice her driving, which scared me in an abnormal way. My driving did the same to her but it was easier for me to handle her driving than to deal with her comments about mine. So most of the time I just let her drive and concentrated on keeping quiet about how close we were to the car up ahead or how fast we were taking the exit from the highway.

Babs, however, liked to talk while she drove. She would talk about the weather or something she noticed along the way or things she'd heard from a friend or just about anything. That day, as we rode toward Birmingham, all I wanted to do was sleep and avoid a conversation about the gravel from the driveway that now lay in the grass.

Not too far out of town I could tell she was warming up to say something and I was mentally searching through options for dealing with the gravel issue when she said, "Vicki saw your truck parked in front of Gladys Haywood's house. You went to see her?"

"Yes," I said. If that was the topic on her mind I was glad to discuss it, rather than argue over the way I mowed the lawn that morning.

"Why were you over there?" she asked. "Are y'all doing some work for her?"

"No," I replied.

"Oh." She had that tone in her voice. "This was about Dell, wasn't it?"

"Yes," I said, not really wanting to say more. Especially not after what I'd been thinking that morning. But Babs didn't let it drop.

"Why did you go see her about him?" she asked. "I know you mentioned you wanted to find someone to talk to about him, but why her?"

"She's the oldest person I know who might have been around when Dell and I were growing up and actually remember some of what we did. I thought she might know something about him no one else knew."

"How would she know that? I mean, she's not related to him, is she?"

"No," I replied. "They're not related."

"And she doesn't have children."

"Gladys is the kind of person who knows things about people. A living catalog of the town's memories. She's the one people ask about where someone came from or who they're related to. I forgot about that until you and I were talking the other day. But that's who she is and why I went to see her."

"Okay," Babs said slowly. "I can see that."

"She's the one who told me that Uncle Johnny had been married before and that I had cousins over in Smithville by another last name, aside from the ones we already knew about who had our last name."

"Blakely?"

"Blacken," I corrected. "But yeah. Those."

"And you thought she might know things like that about Dell?"

"Yes."

"Did she?"

"Yes. I wanted to know who Dell's mother was. I thought she might know."

"Mrs. Smith could tell you? I know you said you forgot to ask her, but wouldn't she know?"

I looked over at her. "I'm not going back to see Mrs. Smith again if I can help it."

"I thought the woman who raised Dell was his mother." Babs glanced in my direction just as a log truck rounded the curve ahead of us. I tensed. Bab's kept talking. "Didn't you tell me that?"

Babs didn't always keep up with the things I told her and some-times I had to repeat myself in the same conversation. It was occa-sionally a source of aggravation but that day in the car, with Babs talking, and trucks zipping past us, and the car wandering from one side of the lane to the other, I had to work to keep from snapping at her.

"He always referred to her as Mama," I explained. "I know about her. At least a little bit. Not quite as much as I thought, but a little. The person I want to know about now is the woman who gave birth to him."

"His birth mother."

A frown wrinkled my forehead. "Do what?"

"Mrs. Briggers mothered him. She's his mama," Babs explained. "The person you want to know about is his birth mother."

"Okay." I hadn't heard that term before, but it seemed to fit the situation.

"So, what did she have to say?"

The questions and the traffic and Babs' driving were getting to me, so I chose to be difficult. "What did who say?" I said it as if she'd confused me but she saw right through that, like she always did.

"Gladys Haywood." Babs popped me on the leg with her fist. "You knew what I meant." There was a playful note in her voice but the force of her knuckles made the muscles in my thigh sting.

I rubbed the place on my leg where she hit me, but I couldn't keep from grinning. "That hurt."

"Good," she said. "Don't mess with me like that."

"It's just difficult to talk about this sometimes." I still was rubbing my leg but I turned to look out the window, hoping she would change the subject.

"Why?"

"Why what?"

"Why is it difficult to talk about?"

"I don't know." I had a faraway sound in my voice, which I hadn't expected. "It just seems like I should already know this stuff."

"But you don't," Babs replied. "So, what did Gladys Haywood have to say?"

"Quite a lot, actually."

"Well, tell me."

Delaying the topic seemed pointless so I leaned the seat back and closed my eyes. If I had to talk at least I didn't have to see what was happening on the road. "Gladys said that Dell's mother was a woman named Lucy Johnson."

"The Johnsons that live in Tenaca?"

"Yes. The parents had four or five girls. Maybe a son. I can't remember."

"That's what she told you?"

"We talked about it, some, but I remembered that after she told me about Lucy and the others."

"The others?"

"I'll get to that."

"Okay."

"Anyway," I continued, "Lucy went off to college in Arkansas and got pregnant. After that, Mr. Johnson didn't want to have anything to do with her. The man who got her pregnant was Odell Norton."

"The same Odell Norton that Mrs. Smith told you about?"

I could tell from the sound of her voice that she was looking at me while she spoke and I wondered whether she'd let the car drift into the oncoming lane, but I refused to open my eyes. "Yes," I said. "Lucy was with Odell Norton for a while, mostly while she was pregnant I think, but he left her not long after Dell was born."

"They ought to castrate men like that." Even without looking, I knew she was gripping the steering wheel with both hands and there was a glare on her face.

"There's a lot of men like that in this story," I said.

"Something you need to tell me?"

A pang of guilt shot through me but I wasn't sure why. I knew from her voice that she was looking at me again and this time I opened my eyes. "What do you mean?" I said it in a defensive tone.

"A child you never mentioned, maybe?"

"No." A sense of relief swept over me and I made sure to lean into it. "Why are you talking to me like that?"

Babs grinned in my direction. "Just checking. Keep going with the story."

"Keep your eyes on the road," I said, violating my rule of remaining quiet while she drove.

She turned away and focused on the highway. "I have things under control over here," she snipped. "You just keep talking."

"So, Lucy got a job teaching in Georgia and she moved there with Dell."

"Valdosta?"

"Yes."

She glanced at me with a knowing look. "Notice the pieces of the story? Valdosta. Arkansas."

"Yes. I did." I closed my eyes once more. "They lived in Valdosta a while and then Lucy had a nervous breakdown. Mrs. Smith at the library found out about it and—"

"Mrs. Smith?"

"Yeah."

"How did she find out?"

I opened my eyes and looked over at Babs. "She's Lucy's sister," I said dryly.

Babs' mouth fell open and she turned her head to look at me.

When she did, she turned her hands in the same direction—while holding a white-knuckle grip on the steering wheel. The car went in that direction, too, and the tires on the right side—the side where I was sitting—dropped off the edge of the pavement. The car bounced onto the shoulder of the road while I flopped around in the seat, trying to cover my head with my arms and keep my head from hitting the roof. Weeds flapped against the side of the car and mud splattered the fender wells while Babs wrestled it under control. It was a struggle, but eventually she guided the car back onto the pavement.

When I looked at her again we both burst out laughing. "Scared you, didn't I?" she said.

"Yes," I replied. "Maybe you should find a place to stop before I tell you the rest of it."

"There's more like what you just said?"

"Yes."

"Then go on." She gestured for me to continue. "I'll watch the road."

I wasn't sure she watched the road during a regular conversation, much less the one we were having right then, which wasn't much like our usual discussions, but I didn't argue with her. After a moment to gather myself, I took a deep breath and began again. "Mrs. Smith's first name is Jenny," I explained. "She was Jenny Johnson before she married."

"Wow." Babs kept both hands on the wheel and her eyes focused on the road. I was watching that time just to make sure.

"Yeah. It was a little much for me, too. But it explained a lot of what happened that day I went to the library."

"Yes," Babs agreed. "But keep going. What's the rest?"

"Mrs. Johnson—their mother—told Jenny about what had happened to Lucy. Jenny insisted on going to Georgia to see about her and Mrs. Johnson insisted on going with her."

"That was a positive move."

"Wait until you hear the rest of the story."

"Okay," Babs said slowly. "I don't have much choice about that. Keep going."

"Jenny and her mother rode over to Georgia, picked up Lucy and Dell, and brought them to Mrs. Smith's house."

"Then they put Lucy in the home at Bright's Mountain?"

"Yes," I said. "She stayed with Mrs. Smith a day or two until they got things worked out but eventually that's where they put her."

"And that's when Dell went to live with the Briggers?"

"Yes," I replied. "But there's more to that part, too."

"Okay." Once again, Babs spoke slowly as if she was unsure about whether she wanted to hear more but unwilling not to.

"After they brought Lucy back here," I said, "they couldn't really keep the situation a secret from Mr. Johnson so rather than even try to, when they got to Tenaca they went straight over to see him. Mrs. Smith, Lucy, Dell, and Mrs. Johnson."

"What happened?"

"When Mr. Johnson saw Lucy and Dell in the car, and Mrs. Johnson in there with them, he went berserk. Mrs. Johnson got out to talk to him and he went off on her."

"Verbally?"

"With his fists. Beating on her. And somewhere in the struggle he hit her and she fell. She banged her head against the steps and died, pretty much right there on the spot."

Babs' mouth fell open in a look of horror. I acknowledged her response with a nod. "That's awful," she said. "Did they arrest him?"

"There was an investigation, of sorts," I replied. "But he never was charged with anything."

"He just went free?" She pretty much screamed that at me.

"For that," I replied, as if there still was more to tell.

She had a puzzled expression. "What do you mean?"

"Not long after Mrs. Johnson died, the FBI came up here to investigate the Ku Klux Klan."

"We have the Ku Klux Klan in Tenaca?"

"They did back then. I don't know about it now. They called themselves the Knights of the White Camellia, but Gladys said they were the Ku Klux Klan, just by another name."

"I've never heard of that."

"I remember a little about it, and a little about what happened, though at the time I didn't know it had anything to do with Dell or his mother or any of that."

"The FBI arrested Mr. Johnson?"

"No. Several people were arrested, though. And they had a big trial down in Birmingham. Pretty much put an end to the Knights of the White Camellia."

"You never told me about that."

"Like I said, it was a long time ago. I was young at the time and I didn't realize that's what it meant until Gladys talked to me about it."

"So, what happened to Mr. Johnson?"

"He died before they got to him. According to Gladys, some people thought he was next on the list, but he died before they got to him."

"He got off easy," Babs snarled.

"I suppose."

"Is that all of it?"

"Almost."

"Almost?"

"Dell needed a place to live so the Briggers agreed to take him. They'd already had at least one child, though I never knew about him. And besides that, Mrs. Briggers—the woman you and I and most of Tenaca referred to as Dell's mother—is really Dell's aunt."

Once again, Babs' mouth fell open and she turned to look at me. This time, though, I grabbed the steering wheel to keep the car pointed in the right direction. "Maybe you should look at the road," I suggested.

Babs focused on the highway. "But he called her Mama," she said.

"I know. And I wonder if he ever knew she was his aunt but I'm gonna find out."

"How are you going to do that?"

"I don't know but I am."

She had to slow for a car making a turn but after it was out of the way she glanced over at me. "So how is Mrs. Briggers his aunt?"

"She is Lucy's sister."

"Mrs. Briggers was a Johnson, too?"

"Yes," I said. "Her name is Alice. Before she married, she was Alice Johnson."

"So there's Alice Briggers and Lucy?"

"And Mrs. Smith."

"At the library."

"Right. Jenny Johnson Smith."

"And Lucy lives at the home at Bright's Mountain?"

"Yes."

Babs glanced over at me again. "Have you been to see her?"

"Not yet."

"But you're going to?"

"Gladys is going with me on Wednesday."

# 6

Babs and I made it back from Birmingham that Saturday without any trouble and got up the next morning in time to go to church. After the service ended, we went over to my parents' house for lunch. Mama was in a pretty good mood and once or twice I considered asking her about Dell and the things I'd learned from Gladys, but every time I thought about it I decided against it. She was having a fun time with Babs in the kitchen and they didn't always get along that well together. I didn't want to spoil the moment. At least, that was my excuse. Thinking about asking her was one thing. Standing in the kitchen with her just a few feet away and me about to open my mouth was another. I might have just been plain scared.

Besides all of that, and in light of the surprises Gladys had given me, I thought it would be better if I talked to Mama in private, which wasn't possible right then. She always handled difficult topics better when no one else was around. I learned that lesson once when I broke her favorite vase and told her about it when Martha and Butch Lewin were there. She didn't take it well and later Daddy told me I should have made sure to tell her in private. "She'll take it better that way," he said. "Believe me. I've had a lot of experience with it." So, I didn't ask her about Dell that Sunday and just enjoyed eating lunch.

Monday and Tuesday were regular days at work for us. We had projects starting and projects ending and I was too busy to stop for lunch either day. By Wednesday things were in better shape. Around two that afternoon I went by Gladys' house to pick her up for the ride to Bright's Mountain. She was waiting for me on the front porch and came down the steps carrying half a dozen pink roses in a clear glass vase like the ones from the flower shop in the grocery store. I got out of the truck and helped held the door while she climbed in on the passenger side with the roses. She wouldn't let me hold them.

From Gladys' house, we rode to the nursing home. The afternoon was sunny and the sky was clear and blue which any other time would have made for a pleasant drive, but for us it was an odd experience—I don't think we said two words to each other the whole way. Gladys just sat there across from me with the vase resting on her lap and her head turned at an angle toward the side window. The expression on her face, as much as I could see of it, struck me as curious—like she knew something was about to happen that she wished wouldn't happen but there was no way to avoid it. Maybe I just made that up. Maybe it was obvious. Maybe I read it into my memory of the moment, after I found out what I was going to learn. I don't know. I just know that when I think of it now I can see her sitting in the cab of the truck, her head turned away from me, her eyes staring out the window, her face with an expression like her mind was far away and her thoughts were not pleasant.

When we arrived at the home—Mountain View Extended Care Facility was its official name—Gladys' mood changed and her countenance brightened, or so it seemed. She greeted the nurses with a smile and chatted with them as if they knew each other, which they did, and they seemed very glad to see her. I let her do the talking and followed a few steps behind, happy to remain in the background as a nurse led us down the hall to Lucy Johnson's room. I wasn't sure what awaited us there.

Lucy's room was near the end of the hall, one of the farthest from the nursing station. A good sign, or so my mother always said. An indication, I think, that the professional staff did not judge the patient to be in immediate physical danger.

We reached Lucy's room without incident and Gladys walked right in. "Lucy," she said, "I've brought someone to see you." The nurse lingered at the door, but after a moment she left us there to visit.

Lucy was seated in the corner opposite the door, next to a window that afforded a view of the lawn outside. She'd been looking in that direction when we arrived but as Gladys spoke, she glanced in my direction. For a moment she seemed unsure of herself, then a smile came to her and she said, "Billy Thomas." There was a friendly lilt in her voice that seemed genuine. "It's been a long time."

Gladys had told me that Lucy was able to function normally when she took her medication, but I was unprepared for her greeting and I'm sure was unable to contain the surprise I felt inside. She did, indeed, appear to be normal. Not just nearly normal, but as normal as Gladys or I or anyone else.

"Yes, ma'am," I said, doing my best to display a calm exterior. "It has been quite a while." I had no memory of ever seeing her at all, or even of knowing that she existed until Gladys told me about her, but I knew better than to tell her that. Still, I wondered how she knew my name, much less how she knew me by sight. If I had seen her, if she had seen me, it certainly wasn't since I graduated from high school. I could remember that far back in great detail and I knew I'd never seen her after that. For certain, not after college.

"Last time I saw you," Lucy continued, "was when you and Dell were graduating from the sixth grade. Do you remember that?"

"Yes, ma'am I do." That was a special day and I thought of it often, but I didn't remember seeing her there.

"Gladys took me to see y'all," Lucy explained. I glanced in Gladys' direction but she was staring out the window and the troubled look she'd had in the truck on the ride over had returned. Lucy seemed not to notice any of that and pointed to a chair in the opposite corner. "Bring that chair over here," she said. "We need to visit." She sounded like one of my aunts when I went to visit them, which wasn't very often, so I did as she said, wondering all the time what we could talk about and what I would say. As I took a seat next to her she said once more, "Last time I saw you was at the sixth grade graduation."

A sense of relief swept over me and I understood the kind of conversation we would have—the same kind I had with my aunts. Rambling and repetitious. "Yes, ma'am," I replied politely. "But I don't remember where you were sitting."

"In back. Gladys brought me." Once again, Lucy cast a glance in Gladys' direction. "Gladys is my friend. She looks after me."

Gladys turned to acknowledge her with a smile, but quickly directed her attention to the scene outside the window. "That was a hot afternoon," Gladys said. Her voice had a faraway tone and so did the look in her eyes.

"You and Dell." Lucy smiled at me and gently patted my knee. "You were his best friend."

"He was a better friend to me than I was to him."

"Ha," she laughed lightly. "He used to tell me the same thing about you."

Gladys shifted positions and let her hand brush against my shoulder. As it did, I felt her pinch me lightly. I knew she meant for me not to pry too deeply. "Did he visit you often?"

"Not when y'all were in school, but later, when y'all were in college he used to come by on Saturdays sometimes. And then after that, he came a few times each year."

Now I understood better. Gladys hadn't pinched me to warn me about questioning Lucy too closely, but to warn me that something was coming I hadn't anticipated. Indeed, the news of Dell's visits caught me off-guard. Emotion welled up inside me and I had to swallow hard to contain my response to the realization that in the years following his move to Chicago, Dell had come to Tenaca and not visited with me.

"He never brought me with him," I said, finally.

"He said you were busy with your family."

I nodded my head. "Yes. I suppose I was."

A dresser was located along the wall on the opposite side of the room and I glanced in that direction, trying to think of something else to talk about while processing the overwhelming sense of betrayal I felt inside. We were best friends. The best. More intimate with each other in many ways than I'd ever been with anyone else in my entire life. And yet, he had come all the way to Tenaca to visit his mother, a mother I never knew existed, and had not told me of his intended arrival. Had not phoned to arrange a brief meeting. Had not stopped by unannounced even for a quick word, a glass of tea, or a hug. And he had done that on multiple occasions.

As my eyes scanned across the top of the dresser, I noticed a picture in a frame. It was a photograph of me and Dell when we were about ten years old. The photo had been taken at my grandfather's house, near Whitesburg. He had a pond in the pasture and we went fishing up there a bunch of times. I remembered the day it was taken—my mother took it with her Kodak camera—but she never said anything about giving anyone a copy of it. Certainly not Lucy. And until that moment, I didn't know that Mama knew Lucy existed, either.

"That's a picture of me and Dell," I said, pointing to the photograph.

"Yes," Lucy replied. "You all were fishing at your granddaddy's farm."

At once, a thousand questions arose in my mind, but I pushed them aside, certain they would only cloud the moment for Lucy and ruin any hope of learning anything else from her. Instead I said, "Dell always caught the most fish."

Lucy smiled. "He used to say the same about you."

"Every time we went, he made us stay until he had one more fish than I had."

Lucy smiled again. "Billy, the last time I saw you was at your sixth grade graduation."

"Yes, ma'am."

"Gladys took me."

"Gladys is a good friend."

Lucy smiled at me. "She didn't want me to get out of the car but I couldn't see from where we parked. That football field was too far away." The sixth grade graduation ceremony was held outdoors on the high school football field. "I opened the car door and got out anyway. Dell was my boy. You were his best friend. I had to see you all graduate."

"He was a better friend to me than I was to him."

Lucy nodded. "He thought the same about you." Suddenly her

expression changed. She leaned toward me and lowered her voice. "Did you meet his other friend?"

A puzzled look came over me. "Who was that?" I asked.

"Steve Atterbury."

And with that, the betrayal felt complete. Dell brought Steve to meet his mother. What more needed to be said? He didn't care about me. Not then. Not after college. Steve had taken my place. Pushed me to the side. Kicked me to the curb. I was nothing. Maybe I didn't really believe that. And maybe I did. I couldn't tell right then. But I knew one thing, I was more hurt than I'd ever been in my life.

Still, sitting with Lucy in her room wasn't the time or place to vent about how I felt. Instead, I took a deep breath and forced my emotions to the side. "Oh," I replied. "You knew Steve?"

"Dell introduced me to him. Once." She held up her index finger to emphasize the point "That's the only time I ever saw him." She patted my knee again. "I'm glad Dell introduced you to him. I told him he should."

"When did you meet him?"

"Last year," she said.

"Year before last," Gladys corrected.

"Dell came to Tenaca more than once?"

"Oh, my," Lucy said. "He came several times. Brought Steve with him once, though." She leaned near me again and, as before, lowered her voice. "If Dell was going to be with someone, I would have rather it had been you."

"Yes, ma'am."

"Not that I think you're one of them." She spoke as if we understood each other. As if I knew what she meant and agreed with the implication. "I just think, it would have been better for both of you."

"Both of us?"

"Yes," she said with a nod. "For you and Dell. It would have been better if you had been with him, rather than Steve."

From the corner of my eye I could see Gladys was grinning, and I knew why, but she had no sense of the hurt and confusion that swirled around me right then. Lucy knew me and she knew

Steve. Gladys knew it, but hadn't bothered to tell me that part. Instead, she brought me out there to be blindsided by it. Not only that, Gladys knew Dell had been to Tenaca and hadn't visited me. Came to Tenaca with another man and I never knew about any of that. And now his mother is telling me she thinks I should have been Dell's partner rather than Steve. In spite of her disclaimer, the suggestion that we should have been together implied that she thought I would be comfortable in a same-sex relationship with her son. Did she think we cared for each other that way? Is that how everyone else thought of us? As a couple? Is that how they thought of me—as a gay man? This was more than I had allowed myself to consider, and I had allowed myself to consider a lot since Dell's funeral. And remember a lot. And speculate. And—

Lucy repeated her side of the conversation two more times and I dutifully played along, then Gladys turned away from the window and said it was time for us to go. We said our goodbyes, repeating ourselves two or three times for Lucy's sake, then finally started toward the door. Lucy made me promise to come see her often, then Gladys and I came from the room and started up the hall.

As we walked toward the front desk I said, "You didn't tell me all of that."

"We'll talk about it in the truck." Gladys' tone was business-like and I knew she meant it but I wasn't in the mood for avoiding the subject.

"Who else visits her?" I asked, pressing the point.

Gladys shook her head. "I said, we'll talk about it in the truck."

"To hell with the truck, Gladys." My voice was louder than I expected but I didn't care. "Who else visits her and what else is there that I don't know about?"

Gladys stopped abruptly and turned to face me. "Look," she said. "I knew you were going to hear things today that would hurt you. Okay? I knew it. I just thought it would be better coming from someone else."

"Someone else?" I was mad and the look on my face showed it. "You think it was easier for me to hear it this way than sitting at your kitchen table? You knew everything she told me today, didn't you?"

Gladys looked me in the eye. "Yes," she said. "I knew it when we were talking the other day."

"Then why didn't you tell me?"

"I didn't have the heart." Gladys turned away and continued up the hall.

I followed after her. "Where was I when Dell came to town?"

"I don't know, but I told him he should see you."

"You saw him?"

"Yes."

I was beside myself with frustration. "You talked to him?"

"Yes."

"Dell came to see Lucy. He came to see you. And he didn't come to see me?"

"He came by the house. I didn't invite him."

Against my best efforts to resist, tears formed in my eyes and trickled down both cheeks. "Why didn't he come by my house?" Gladys turned to look at me and I could see from the look in her eyes that she knew I was hurting but I pressed on. "Why didn't he come see me?" I cried.

"This is why I said we should talk in the truck."

"Why?" I insisted. "Why didn't he visit me?"

Gladys put an arm around my shoulder and led me toward the door. "He said he didn't want to hurt your feelings," she replied.

"By visiting me?"

"Steve was with him," she said, as if that explained it.

"And he thought seeing him with Steve and knowing how they were together would hurt my feelings?"

"Wouldn't it?"

"Yes," I whispered. "I guess it would. But it hurts now to know that he came to town and didn't come to see me." It hurt even more to know that he was with someone else in a way more intimate than he had been with me, but I didn't tell her that part. It was too much to explain and I wasn't even sure how to do that.

Gladys rubbed my shoulder. "I know," she said in a motherly

tone.

We walked the rest of the way to the truck in silence but as we backed from the parking space I asked again, "Who else came to see her?"

"To see Lucy?"

"Yes." There was an edge to my voice but after all that I'd heard it seemed warranted. "Who else came to see her?"

"Just me and your mama."

"I saw the picture."

"I know you did."

"How does my mother know her?"

As she had done earlier that day, Gladys turned her head slightly to the right and looked out the window of the cab. "You'll have to ask your mother for that part of the story," she said. "I've told you all I can tell you."

"Is talking to her gonna hurt like what I just heard?"

"Talk to her." Gladys still wasn't looking at me. "Talk to her," she said.

"Yeah," I sighed. "I guess I will."

"Just be kind when you talk to her," she added. I wondered why she said that, but right then I wasn't sure I wanted to know the answer. Right then, I wasn't sure I wanted to know any more about Dell, either.

# 7

As I rode home after dropping Gladys at her house, I tried to process everything I had learned during the visit with Lucy Johnson, but dealing with it seemed an impossible task. So many issues had come to light. Things I hadn't thought of. Things I hadn't wanted to think of. Things I never knew. Like not knowing who Dell's mother was, or his father, or his aunts. Not knowing he'd visited Tenaca after he moved to Chicago. Or that my mother knew Lucy. Or that Lucy knew me. Even more than that, not realizing the depth of my feelings for him years ago. And knowing that maybe I did realize it but was too afraid to talk about it.

When I began this quest, I thought that I would merely confirm all the things I already knew about him and find peace of mind in knowing that he really was the person I had known him to be, rather than the person suggested by what I'd heard at the funeral. Now, just a few weeks into that effort, I found that nothing was the way I thought it was—nothing about Dell, nothing about me, nothing about the people I'd known or the town where I had lived most of my life. And even the things I did remember of my past were understood wrongly. Things had happened around me of which I was blissfully unaware—completely unaware—primarily because I assumed a context that never existed. The real context was right in front of me the whole time, I just never paid it any attention.

By the time I arrived home that evening, I felt oddly detached from reality. Babs noticed something was wrong and when she poured a cup of coffee for our evening ritual on the back porch, she prepared mine as well, which she almost never did. We'd had several running discussions about how much sugar and cream a cup of coffee required and rather than repeating that discussion too many times she simply ended it by saying, "Fix your own." Which I had been doing every day since.

That night, though, she prepared my coffee for me—without asking first—then we went out to sit on the porch. After the first sip I understood why she'd been so gracious. "There's bourbon in this coffee," I said.

"Irish whiskey," she corrected. "Bourbon only comes from Kentucky. The whiskey in your coffee came from Dublin."

"Courtesy of your cousin?"

"Rita is a good girl."

"I don't know about that." I paused to take another sip of the coffee and let it slide slowly down my throat. "But as an Irish whiskey smuggler, she's first rate."

"So," Babs said. "What put you in a funk today?"

Sparing her the unnecessary details, I told her where I'd been and what I'd learned, beyond the things she already knew. That Lucy Johnson recognized me by sight. That she'd attended the graduation ceremony when Dell and I completed sixth grade. That she and Gladys were old friends. And, that she was acquainted with my mother.

"Gladys, I can understand," Babs said. "And coming to your graduation makes sense. But the part about your mother seems a bit of a stretch. Are you sure your mother knows her?"

"Lucy has a photograph in her room that my mother took."

"How do you know your mother took it?"

"It's a photo of me and Dell at Grandpaw's farm. I remember the day we were there. I remember my mother taking the picture with her camera. Lucy knew all of that, too."

"Your mother has been to see her?"

"Yes."

"You know what this means." It was a statement, not a question.

"What?" I asked, not really wanting to hear the answer.

"You have to talk with your mother about this."

I shook my head. "I can't right now."

"Why not?"

"We have work to take care of tomorrow and Friday is out of the question with her. Maybe I'll see her next week."

"Work or no work, you should go over there tomorrow, even if you have to go at night."

"You make it sound urgent."

Babs moved her cup toward her lips. "If you'd seen the look on your face when you came home tonight, you'd think it was urgent, too."

"That bad?"

"I wasn't sure you knew where you were."

"Me either." I took another sip of coffee. Then another. In spite of the beverages I'd consumed as a student, my tolerance for alcohol was rather low. Already I was feeling the effects of the Irish in the coffee, so I took another sip to be sure.

After talking to Babs, I began to think maybe she and Gladys were right. That I should visit with my mother and talk to her about Dell and me and the things I'd learned. It was an odd moment for me—I wanted to talk to her, but didn't want to, all at the same time.

The next day, I was busy through the morning, keeping everyone else busy on three different jobs. In the afternoon, however, a storm blew in and we had to knock off at two of the sites. The other one was a house we'd already roughed in and were working on the interior. My father was over there with the crew. He was a great finishing carpenter and he enjoyed that kind of work. It was too precise for me.

With Dad on the job to keep things going, I didn't have much to do, so around three that afternoon I slipped away to see my mother. She was in the kitchen when I arrived.

As I came in the room, she looked at me with a hint of concern. "Everything alright?" she asked.

"Yes, ma'am. Everything's fine."

"You don't come around much during the week anymore."

"No, ma'am."

"Something must be on your mind."

"Yes, ma'am."

"Is this about those questions you've been asking?"

"Questions?"

"I talk to Gladys two or three times a week."

"Yes, ma'am."

"She told me about your trip to Bright's Mountain."

"I met Lucy Johnson."

"So I heard."

"She has a picture you took in her room."

"I gave it to her."

"That's what she said."

"Something wrong with that?"

"Until a few weeks ago, I didn't know Lucy Johnson even existed. Now I've learned that she knows Gladys, she knows you, and she knows me."

Mama smiled. "That must have been a shock for you."

"A shock?!" My voice was louder and rawer than I'd intended but I didn't apologize.

Mama took me by the arm and led me to the table by the window, then pointed to a chair. "Sit down." It was an order, not a request and I did as she said. She took a seat opposite me. "What did you want to know?" she asked.

"You knew Lucy Johnson."

"Yes."

"How did you know her?"

"I've known Lucy since—I can't remember a time I didn't know her."

"So, when I was growing up, you knew she was Dell's mother?"

"Yes."

"And you knew the woman I thought was his mother was really his aunt."

"Yes. But is that really what you want to know?"

"I'm just trying to make sense of this."

"Of what?"

"Of who Dell was. Of who I am."

She had a puzzled expression. "This is hard for you?"

"How did you know Dell was Lucy's son and I didn't?"

"That's the way they wanted it."

"They?"

"The Johnsons."

"Why did they get to decide what I would know?"

"Dell was their child."

"The Briggers?"

"Yes."

"Dell was Lucy's child."

Mama let my argumentative tone pass. "You still haven't asked me what you really want to know."

"Why do you go to see her?"

"I go every Friday."

"But why?"

"Because Friday is the day everything happened."

Suddenly I realized what she meant. Friday was the day Lucy and Dell arrived from Georgia. Friday was the day Mrs. Johnson was killed. Friday was the day. "You were at the Johnson's house." I said it as a statement. Not a question.

"Yes."

"And you saw what happened to Mrs. Johnson."

"I saw a lot of things."

"Tell me."

"Tell you what?"

"Tell me everything."

"I don't think—"

"Mama," I snapped, interrupting her. "Tell me. And tell me all of it."

At first she didn't respond and I wondered if she would tell me anything at all. Then she took a deep breath. "Like I said," she began. "I've known the Johnsons all my life. Lucy and I were about the same age. We weren't great friends in school but we were friends enough. Your father knew her better."

"Daddy?"

"They dated a few times when we were younger." She sighed. "But look, you want to know what happened when Lucy and Dell came back to Tenaca. That's where the story picks up and I'm the one to tell you that part."

"You and Gladys divided this up?"

"Not exactly, but that's how it worked out."

"So?"

"So, Jenny and her mother—Gladys told you about how Jenny Smith was Jenny Johnson before she married, right?"

"Yes."

"I couldn't remember all she said she told you." Mama looked at me. I nodded for her to continue. "So," she said, "they brought Lucy and Dell back to Tenaca. They knew they couldn't bring them back here without Mr. Johnson finding out about it, so the day they came back, Jenny brought them over to the Johnson's house to tell him."

"What were you doing there?"

"Gladys worked for them some. Cleaning the house mostly. And—"

"So, Gladys' family really didn't have as much money as everyone used to think."

"No. Like I've told you before, they didn't have that much to begin with and not nearly as much as people thought after her father died. So, Gladys worked for the Johnsons sometimes."

"What does that mean, sometimes?"

"Off and on. They would call her to come over and she went. Mostly cleaning the house. On the days she cleaned house, she sometimes asked me to go with her. Your father and I were married by then. You were a little boy. Your father's business wasn't as good back then as it is now and we needed the money. The Johnsons paid Gladys. She paid me."

"And you were there that day."

"Yes. And I saw what happened."

"You saw him kill her."

"He hit her so hard." A chill ran through Mama's shoulders and I saw her shake. "Her head snapped back like a whip. I was standing at the window and I saw her eyes as she fell backward. The light was gone from them before she hit that step."

"Did anyone talk to you about it?"

"You mean like the sheriff?"

"Yes. Or the police."

She shook her head. "No one talked to me about it except Harold Johnson."

"Mr. Johnson talked to you?"

"He talked to both of us."

"Both of you? You and Gladys?"

"Yes."

"What did he say?"

"He said, 'You didn't see nothing. You were working inside. Heard a sound on the front porch. When you looked out, she'd already fallen and was lying on the ground. Looked to you like she tripped and fell.' Then he looked me in the eye and said, 'Got it?' and I nodded my head."

"And that was on a Friday?"

"Yes. And I've been visiting her ever since."

"On Friday?"

"Yes."

"And then you come home and drink yourself into oblivion."

That was something I'd wanted to say to her for a long time—the part about drinking herself to oblivion. I didn't know before about Mrs. Johnson. Only that Mama spent most of the weekend inebriated and many times was unable to go to church with us on Sundays.

She didn't argue the point. "At first, that's what it was," she said. "Then I started drinking on Thursdays because I was thinking about seeing her on Friday. And then I was drinking on Saturday to stave off a nasty headache from Friday."

"And now?"

She stared out the window. "Now, I just drink whenever I think I need some help getting through the day."

"There's more to it, though."

"More to what?"

"More to what happened at the Johnsons. I can see it in your eye. What's the rest of it?"

"Nothing."

"Did you do something besides clean the house for them?"

"No." She had an indignant tone in her voice and an offended look on her face. "How dare you talk to me that way? I'm your mother."

"Did Gladys do something else?"

"More like it was done to her."

The tone in her voice bothered me. "What do you mean?"

"I mean, she didn't have much choice."

"Mr. Johnson raped her?"

"I don't think it was rape," she replied. "I don't exactly know what happened. All I know is that sometimes when we were over there, and Mrs. Johnson wasn't at home, Mr. Johnson would call Gladys into a room and then—"

"He raped her."

"I don't know what they did. The door was closed. I never heard her scream or cry or complain."

"Did he ever come after you?"

Mama looked away. "No." Her voice trailed away and I was suspicious about whether she'd told the truth or not.

"Why not?"

"Because he knew your father and your grandfather."

"Mr. Johnson?"

"Yes."

"How did he know Daddy?"

"From those meetings they used to attend."

"Meetings?"

"Harold Johnson was a member of the White Camellias."

"And Daddy, too?"

"Yes."

"You're saying Daddy was a Klansman?"

"Your father wasn't in there long. He joined because your grand-father was a member, but then he found religion at church one Sun-day and decided he couldn't do that anymore."

The flippant way she referred to the experience bothered me. "You say that like you don't care for what happened to him at church."

"I think his faith is genuine, I just don't believe that much."

"That much?"

"Your father believes enough for the both of us."

"I don't think that's how it works."

"That's what he says, too."

We'd reached an awkward moment and I didn't want to leave it there. I still had questions to ask, so I said, "So, he got saved and they just let him go?"

"Your grandfather had more sway with the Knights of the White Camellia than even Harold Johnson so, yeah. They let him leave and left him alone."

"More sway?"

She tilted her head down and glowered up at me through the tops of her eyes. "Do I have to spell it out for you?"

"No, ma'am," I said. And she didn't. I understood more than I'd wanted to know. Grandpaw was a Klansman. They didn't call it the Klan. Their group had a less notorious name. But as I mentioned to Gladys, I had heard the familiar stories about what they did. Lynch-ings. Church burnings. House burnings. Over the last half of the nineteenth century and the first half of the twentieth century, they inflicted a lot of misery on a lot of people for the sole purpose of imposing their will on everyone else. When Gladys told me about it, I had no trouble understanding Harold Johnson might do that. But with Grandpaw, it was a bit more disturbing. Not only did the John-son sisters have a questionable legacy. I did, too. "You don't have to explain."

"Good."

"Why didn't you tell me about Dell and Lucy and how the Brig-gers weren't really his parents?"

"Now stop right there." Her voice was stern and her tone unflinching. "Charlie and Alice were his parents. They raised him. They loved him as much as anyone ever loved a child. And he loved them, too."

"So, why didn't you tell me about them, though? And about Lucy?"

"I thought it was Dell's story to tell. And so did your father. So, we just never said anything. We figured if Dell wanted you to know, he would tell you. And if he had told you, we would have filled in the details."

"But he never said anything."

"And there you go." She gestured with her hand to stress the point.

"Daddy knows about what happened at the Johnson's house that day?"

"Yes."

"And what did he say about it?"

"When I told him what Harold said, he said that I should do what Harold Johnson said and keep quiet about it."

"Did you know Lucy came to our sixth grade graduation ceremony?"

"Yes."

"She remembers being there. And she remembers me."

Mama smiled at me. "She asks about you every time I go to see her. Always has."

"Why didn't she say anything about our high school graduation?"

"Gladys wouldn't take her."

"Why not?"

"Because we knew Odell Norton would be there."

"We?"

"She and I talked about it and decided it was best if Lucy didn't attend."

"Was he there?"

"Yes."

"Nobody ever said anything about seeing him or anything."

"Nobody else knows about it."

I was a little skeptical they could pull that off. "How did he keep that a secret? He was well-known even then."

"Grew his hair and his beard longer," she explained. "The ceremony was held on the football field. He wore a hat and sat to himself. Nobody even recognized him except me, your father, Gladys, and the Johnson girls."

We talked a while longer and I had more questions to ask her, but right then my mind was tired and I could see she was getting fidgety from sitting in one place too long. So, I glanced at my watch and said, "I better get going."

She seemed relieved to hear it and stood immediately. "Tell your father not to be late for supper." As she leaned over to kiss me on the cheek I smelled alcohol on her breath and knew she'd been drinking already. I turned toward the door and she followed me across the kitchen. As I made my way in that direction, I remembered what Lucy had said to me the day before, about how she had wanted me and Dell to be together the way he was with Steve. That part had bothered me the most and I had felt uneasy about asking Mama about it, but as I reached the door to step outside I decided to ask about it anyway.

"There was one other thing," I said.

"What's that?" She had a hint of impatience in her voice.

"At Dell's funeral, I found out he was gay and had been living with a partner in Chicago for several years."

She grinned. "Son, Dell was always gay."

"You say that like it was a known fact."

"It was," she said with emphasis. "Everyone knew he was gay." She poked me on the chest with a sense of nervous playfulness. "Everyone thought you were, too."

A look of surprise was impossible to keep from my face. "Why did they think I was gay?"

"They thought Dell was. And you were always with him. And the two of you acted like you were dating. So, we just all thought of you as a couple."

"But no one ever said anything. Not a single person ever called me a name about it, like they did other people."

"They knew your father."

"But he thought I was gay?"

"Worried about it all the time."

"But he never talked to me about it."

"I know. That's just the way he is." She reached around me and opened the door. "Now don't misunderstand me. He didn't like it. And he didn't think it was right. But he wouldn't say anything because he knew about what happened at the Johnson's house. And—"

"You mean with Mrs. Johnson?"

"And with Gladys. And with the White Camellia thing. And he was afraid you'd start asking questions and get on one of those quests of yours—like you're doing now about Dell."

"And he didn't want to risk opening up all of that."

"That," she acknowledged. "And you were always a sensitive boy."

"Sensitive?"

"Your father wondered about you." Her head bobbed to one side in a way that told me she'd had more alcohol than I'd realized at first. And she was repeating herself.

"He never said anything to me about that kind at all."

"No," she said. "He wouldn't have. And then you went off to college and met Babs and, you know, things were different after that and he stopped worrying."

"So, these White Camellias—they were against gays?"

"Oh, my, yes. They didn't call them gays back then, but they certainly were against them."

"So, if he thought I was gay, did he hate me?"

"You're father never hated you for one moment. Talk to him." She patted me on the back in a way that doubled as pushing me out the door. "If you ask him, he'll tell you what you want to know."

"You also mentioned he was worried I might ask too many questions back then. I'm asking questions now and he hasn't said anything about that, either."

She gave me one of her ironic smirks. "He's said plenty to me."

"Like what?"

"Like, 'I guess he'll find out the truth now.'"

"And will I find out the truth?"

"Ask your father." She pushed me toward the door, this time omitting the pat in a move that closely resembled a shove. "Talk to him. He'll tell you what you want to know."

# *8*

When I left the house after talking to Mama, I drove back to the job site and found Daddy sitting alone on the front steps, sipping coffee from a thermos he'd been carrying all day. As I came from the truck I gestured to it. "That bottle's a little old, isn't it?"

"It keeps the coffee hot," he replied. Which was all he really cared about when it came to coffee. We were in Tuscaloosa once for a football game and on the way home stopped at a Starbucks. He said the same thing about their coffee, too. "It's hot."

I took a seat beside him on the step. "Where is everyone?"

"They finished with the kitchen cabinets. George and his crew set the tile in the bathrooms. He wanted to come back tomorrow for the backsplash in the kitchen." He smiled at me. "So it's just me and you now."

"Anything we need to do?"

"Nah." He shook his head. "We'll call it a day. Try again tomorrow." That's what he always said when he'd had enough.

We sat in silence a moment, then I propped my elbows on my knees and looked down at the ground along the bottom step. "I talked to Mama today," I said.

"Oh?" He sounded surprised. "How was she?"

"Pretty good, I think."

He looked over at me. "You think?"

"She'd been in the bottle a little, but not too much."

"Was she cooking supper?" There was a hint of expectation in his voice.

"I don't think so. But she said to tell you not to be late."

He turned back to the coffee and took a sip. "She always says that when she's been drinking, but I've learned the hard way that it don't mean nothing unless she's already got it started. I'll go by the truck stop on the way home." His voice was flat.

"Mind if I join you?"

He looked over at me again. "Something wrong with Babs?" A note of interest returned to his voice.

"No," I replied. "Just thought I'd join you."

"If you got something on your mind, maybe we should talk about it here, where there ain't nobody around. Too many ears out there at the café."

"Okay," I sighed.

He took a sip of coffee. "So, what is it?"

"When I talked to Mama today, I asked her about Dell Briggers."

"Yeah." He said it the way he often did when he dreaded the topic that was about to follow. Like the time I had to tell him about dinging the door of his truck against a telephone pole in the parking lot at school. And the time Mama told him she'd slept all day instead of going to the grocery store—that happened often when I was kid.

"At the funeral, I heard things about him that I didn't know."

"I heard something about that."

Now it was my turn to sound surprised. "How did you hear about that?"

"You've been talking to everybody." His voice had a business-like tone. "Word gets around."

"Yeah." I sounded just like him. "I suppose so."

"So, what did you want to ask me?"

"I found out about Lucy Johnson and how Mrs. Smith at the library is really Jenny Johnson Smith. And Dell's mama was his aunt before she was his mama. And his mother, Lucy, is in the home over at Bright's Mountain."

"Uh huh."

"Mama said she was at the Johnson's when Mrs. Johnson hit her head on the step."

"Yeah."

"And something was going on between Gladys and Mr. Johnson."

75

"Better leave them out of it." His spoke in a matter-of-fact tone but his voice had an edge on it that let me know he wasn't offering a mere suggestion. I'd heard the tone before, usually when he was correcting me about something.

"What do you mean?"

"I mean, Gladys is a good woman." He gestured with his hand as he spoke. "Whatever happened between her and Harold ain't got nothing to do with you and Dell and all of that. So, just leave it alone." That right there, at the end, was the sound of a father telling his son there'd be consequences if he ignored what was said. I wasn't worried about a spanking or him taking away the keys to the car. We were decades past that. But he was making his point, just the same.

"What about the White Camellias?" I was genuinely interested in knowing what happened with them, but I said it as a way of telling him two could play the hardball game.

"What about them?" The hardness in his voice said he wasn't interested in discussing that topic, either.

"They were a white supremacy group."

"Yeah."

"Mama said you were a member."

Daddy sighed. "That was a long time ago, son."

"Why'd you join?"

"My daddy was a member. He brought me in."

"You make it sound like when you got me in the hunting club up at Flint Ridge."

"That's how he made it sound."

"The Camellias did some pretty bad stuff." I did nothing to hide the disdain in my voice. "Did you ever participate in any of those things?"

"You're meddling pretty far from anything that's your business."

"I don't think so."

"Yeah?" Which was his way of saying the same thing all over again—it's none of your business, leave it alone.

"People say the Knights of the White Camellia torched that church on the road to Jasper."

"That's what people say."

"You deny they did it?"

"Get to your point."

"Were you there when they did it?"

"What's that got to do with you and Dell?"

"That was a black church."

"What of it?"

"The Camellias didn't like blacks, did they?"

"They didn't like a lot of people."

"I bet they didn't care much for gays either, did they?"

"Not really." His eyes stared straight ahead.

"Is that why you joined?"

"No."

"Is that why you got out?"

He turned his head slowly to look at me. "You think I'm gay?"

"I think you think I am."

He looked away. "I got out of the Camellias because I came to know Jesus during a revival meeting at the Baptist Church. Okay? I started reading the Bible every night and I realized Jesus didn't say any of the things Harold Johnson or your Grandpaw said He did. I figured I shouldn't be doing what they were doing, either."

"What did Grandpaw say about it, when you told him you wanted out?"

"He didn't like it that I was wanting out, but when I explained it to him, he understood."

"And the Camellias just let you go?"

"Your grandfather had a way of getting his way when he wanted it."

"What about him?"

"Who?"

"Grandpaw."

"What about him?"

"Did he stay in?"

"I guess. I don't really know."

"Was he arrested when the others got indicted?"

"No." Daddy shook his head. "No one ever said anything about him in all of that."

"Hmm."

He looked over at me again. "That strikes you as strange?"

"Well, it was the FBI," I said. "They tend to track a thing all the way to the bottom."

He set the thermos aside, leaned back against the step behind us, and propped against his elbows. "Like I said, you ought to leave some of this alone."

"When I talked to Lucy Johnson, she said something that caught me by surprise."

"I expect so."

"I told her about seeing Steve at the funeral."

"Steve?"

"Steve Atterbury. Dell's partner."

"Oh." He glanced to the left. "Him."

"I told her about seeing him and she said she had met him. That Dell had come to Tenaca to see her and he brought Steve with him."

"Lucy was his mother. Why wouldn't he come to see her?"

"I didn't know Dell knew her. All that time, I thought Mrs. Briggers was his mother. I didn't know Lucy existed and I didn't know Dell knew it, either."

"I know."

"Mama said you didn't want me to know about Lucy."

"Some things are best left unsaid." He emphasized his point with a shrug. "That's all I meant."

In spite of having broached the topic of me being gay earlier in the conversation, my heart skipped a beat when I thought about bringing it up again. Still, there was no way to avoid it, so I pressed on. "Well," I said slowly. "When I talked to Lucy and the topic of Steve came up, she said she'd always wished that Dell and I would be together like that."

"Yeah."

"Which was the same as saying she thought we were gay. That she thought I was gay. And when I asked Mama about it, she said everyone thought we were."

"Yeah."

"Did they really?"

"That's about the size of it."

"And she said you thought I was gay, too." My voice cracked when I said it, which I hadn't expected, but talking about it openly seemed to set me free inside. As if a thought unexpressed for a long time—a thought repressed for a long time—had suddenly been released and let loose.

He had a nervous smile. "I guess you proved me wrong there."

My forehead wrinkled in a frown and I sensed something inside trying to tamp down my newfound sense of liberation, but I pushed through it and said, "You mean, because I married Babs?"

"You married Babs. You have children." He seemed to tick those off as indications I was something different from what he earlier thought. As if they proved I wasn't gay after all. "You live a normal life," he added.

"Dell lived a normal life."

"Dell's life was anything but normal." There was a hint of disgust in his voice. "I mean, I liked the guy alright. And he was a good friend to you. And he was Lucy's kid. But his life wasn't normal."

"Just because he was gay doesn't mean he wasn't normal."

"Being gay ain't half the story of Dell Briggers' life."

That was truer than Daddy knew. Dell being gay was only an issue because it was an issue for us. For me. He never talked to me about it, one way or the other.

"Regardless of how someone might describe us," I replied, "I liked Dell. We got along well together. I didn't do things with other people because I didn't want to do things with other people. I wanted to do them with Dell." A sense of indignation rose up inside me. "If that's being gay then that's what was. And what it is."

"Is that why you never went out with girls in high school?"

"Yes. It wasn't because I wanted to go out with boys. It was because I wanted to go out with Dell. If there was a movie to see, I didn't think about asking Donna Wells, or Katy Lindner, or any of the other girls in my class to see it with me. I thought about Dell."

"Did you all ever do anything?" He seemed awkward in asking the question and I didn't really know what he meant. A frown formed on my forehead. "Do anything?" I asked.

"You know. Did you ever do anything?" He looked over at me. "Did you kiss him?"

"No." I turned my head away. "I don't think so."

He nudged me with his shoulder. "You don't think so?"

"Daddy, I've found out so much I didn't know that I should have known that I can't say for sure about a lot of things anymore."

"I think you would know if you'd kissed him."

There were many times when I had kissed Dell on the cheek. And he kissed me on my cheek, too. And once, when we were alone behind Grandpaw's barn, he was telling me something that happened at home—the Briggers had a fight and there was shouting and yelling like I heard that night when I slept over at their house—and it had upset him. While he was telling me about it he took hold of my hand and we were standing close and he was about to cry and I felt so warm and comfortable inside—like the night when he took my hand in bed—and I leaned forward and kissed him lightly on the lips. It was a thing that startled us both and we recoiled immediately. He let go of my hand and wiped his eyes and we went back to what we'd been doing. But I wasn't about to tell Daddy that.

"Well," he said, after a moment. "Whatever happened back then—the part you remember and the part you don't—happened in the past. I think you'd be better off leaving most of it right where it is and moving on."

That was good enough for Daddy. But not for me.

When I got home, I parked the truck near the side door and went inside through the mud room. In the kitchen I noticed the pots and pans on the stove where Babs cooked dinner, but she wasn't there. I found her sitting in the den and when I leaned over to kiss her she said, "Where have you been?"

"Talking to Daddy."

"You didn't check your cell phone?" From the tone of her voice I knew she wasn't in a great mood.

"No." I patted my pockets, but didn't feel it. "I must have left it in the truck."

I went out to the truck and found the phone. A glance at the screen showed three missed calls from Babs and a text that read, "Where are you????"

When I came back inside, Babs was putting food on the plates for our supper. "Sorry. I didn't hear the phone and didn't see your text." I kissed her on the cheek. "You must be hungry."

"Hangry," she replied.

She handed me a plate and set it on the table at her place, then returned to the stove for the other one. "I'm sorry I was late. I should have paid more attention."

"What were y'all talking about?"

"I went to see Mama today."

"Oh?" She prepared glasses of tea for us and we took them to the table. I waited while she sat down, then joined her.

"You said I should see her sooner rather than later. So I took your advice."

"How was she?"

"Okay."

We said the blessing, then began to eat. Babs looked in my direction. "She'd been drinking?"

"A little," I replied.

"I thought so."

"Why?"

"After you left her house, she called me. I could tell she was eating from the crunching sound. Figured it was an onion sandwich."

"Yeah." Mama always had an onion sandwich when she was drinking. I don't know why, but she did.

"Have you ever had one?"

"One what?"

"Onion sandwich."

"No."

"Me either." Babs looked across the table at me again, this time with a playful grin. "Want to try one for lunch sometime?"

"No," I said sharply. "And I don't want to get drunk enough to like it, either."

She laughed. "Maybe that's what you have to do. Get drunk first."

"I'm not trying it." Onions tasted great on a hamburger, but the thought of a slice of onion between two pieces of bread slathered with mayonnaise and mustard was unappealing.

"So," she said, returning to the topic at hand. "What did your father have to say?"

"Not much."

"What did he tell you?"

"Not much I hadn't already heard from Mama."

"You always give me answers like that when there's something you don't want to discuss. So out with it. Tell me what he said and get it over with."

"When I visited with Lucy the subject of Steve came up."

"She knew about Steve?"

"She knew Steve."

"How did she know him?"

"Dell brought him to see her."

"Dell knew about Lucy?"

"Yes."

"When did he find out?"

"I think he always knew. I guess he was old enough to remember her. Maybe they never tried to make him forget. I don't know. Maybe I'm the only person in the world who thought of Mrs. Briggers as his mother."

"I don't think so. But what's this have to do with your Daddy?"

"I'm getting to it." Eating was impossible now so I laid aside my fork. "After Dell moved to Chicago, he came back to Tenaca to visit Lucy."

"And you didn't know about it?"

"No. Not until she told me. And, he came to see her with Steve."

"Oh."

"Yeah."

She looked at me. "That hurt, didn't it?"

"Yes. And it happened on more than one occasion."

"Did she say why he didn't tell you he was in town?"

"She told him he needed to see me, but Dell thought it would hurt my feelings if I saw him with Steve."

"Hurt your feelings?"

"Yes."

"Why?"

We'd come to the moment and I sighed to relieve the tension I felt inside. "Because, they all thought Dell and I were a thing."

"A thing?"

"An item.

"A couple."

"Yes."

"Did you think you and Dell were a couple?"

"I didn't think of us as a romantic couple. I just liked being with him, so I tried to be with him as much as possible."

"She told you she thought y'all were a couple?"

"She told me she wished Dell and I had been with each other the way he was with Steve. She never used the word gay to describe us but from the look in her eye and tone of her voice, that's what she meant. Mama was the one who told me they all thought we were gay. Which means she thought we were gay. And Daddy thought it, too. And I guess if Dell thought it would hurt my feelings for me to see him with someone else, he must have thought we were in a relationship, too—a romantic relationship, not just friendship." A lump caught in my throat and tears came to my eyes. "I'm the only one who didn't think of it that way."

Babs took a sip of tea, then continued. "You asked your father about all of this?"

"Yes."

"And he told you he thought you were gay?"

"Yes. He thought Dell and I were both gay right up to the time I started dating you. And then we got married. And had children. And he breathed a big sigh of relief." Babs laughed in response. I glared at her. "Something about all of this seems funny to you?"

"The way you said it."

"What about the way I said it?"

"Like you were taking medicine. Gulp it all down fast. Say it quick and get it over with."

"That's what you told me to do. Say it quick and get it over with."

She could see I was upset and reached across the table to touch my hand. "I'm sorry." She smiled when she said it and I knew nothing I'd said so far changed the way she felt about me, which was a relief.

I pushed my plate away. "I'm so confused, Babs. I don't know what to think."

"Look," she responded. "You and Dell were friends. Maybe more than friends. But you dated other people besides me in college. And he dated women back then, too."

"Right."

"So maybe being gay or not being gay isn't such a fixed thing."

"A fixed thing?"

She took a bite and swallowed. "You talk about it like it's a disease." She paused to wipe the corners of her mouth on a napkin. "Or like it's a suit of clothes. Something you catch. Something you put on. You get rid of it. You take it off. You are or you aren't. Maybe it's not quite like that."

"Then what's it like?"

"Maybe it's a response to a person you meet."

"If that's true, there would be a gay guy who met a straight woman and fell in love."

She gestured to me with one hand. "And there you are."

My eyes opened wide and I blurted out, "Me?"

"Yes. You."

"You think I'm that guy?"

She pushed back her chair and came around the table toward me. "Scoot back and give me some room." I pushed my chair away from the table and she took seat on my lap, straddling my legs. Her breasts were in my face and I could smell the scent of her perfume, all of which caused a predictable physical reaction. "I love you with all my heart," she said as she leaned down and pressed her lips against mine in a long, wet kiss. "And I know what happens to you when you're with me." She kissed me again, long and slow. "And I know what you want right now." All I could do was grin at her as I slid my hands over her hips. "I'm not worried about whatever happened in the past. I'm not worried about you and Dell and your sexuality." She kissed me again. "So stop talking." She moved around to my neck, then let her lips brush lightly against my ear. "Stop worrying." A tingle ran down my back. "And follow me to the bedroom."

# 9

In spite of what Daddy told me about leaving the past in the past, I still had questions and I knew they were never going away until I found answers. So later that week I went to see Gladys one more time. As we had done before, we sat across the kitchen table from each other and talked. This time, however, there was no iced tea to sip.

"I've learned a lot since the last time I was here," I said.

"Yes." Gladys nodded her head. "You have."

"But I still have more questions."

She gave me an indulgent smile. "I know. So why don't you ask me those questions and let's see what it is that's still bothering you."

"From what I've learned so far, I would say that Dell always knew Lucy was his mother."

"That's correct," she replied.

"And I would say that he always knew Mrs. Briggers was his aunt and not is mother."

Gladys nodded her head once more. "You're correct again."

"And, I would say that he had a relationship with Lucy the whole time I knew him."

Gladys nodded. "That's correct, too."

My eyes bore in on her. "Then why didn't I know those things back then?"

"He never mentioned Lucy to you?"

"No."

"And your mother and father never mentioned anything about her?"

"No."

"And the Briggers never said anything, either?"

"No."

Gladys rested her arms on the table and hunched forward in a contemplative pose. "Then I would say this about that, people who have secrets they really don't want other people to know, don't often talk about them."

It was a smart-ass way of stating the obvious—they didn't tell me because they didn't want me to know. I understood what she was saying, but her response didn't address the point that bothered me, so I pressed the point. "Why wouldn't Dell want me to know? Why didn't he want to talk about her to me?"

"If he told you about Lucy, he'd have to tell you the whole story. About how his father got her pregnant but never was around. Back then, I don't think he'd ever even met Odell Norton. And if he told you that, he'd have to tell you that Alice Briggers was his aunt. And he would have to tell you why his mother Lucy was in the nursing home and that would lead to all that went on with his grandfather."

"What's wrong with me knowing that?"

"At first, I don't think it was anything that he thought about. I mean, telling you or not telling you wasn't something that came to him. He was a child. You were a child. The two of you enjoyed each other. He just took it as it came."

"And later?"

"Later, when y'all were teenagers and maybe he knew more details about the situation, I think he was worried that all of that would come out and it would change the way you knew him. The way you thought of him. He didn't want to take the risk that you might not like him anymore if you knew the truth."

A lump formed in my throat. "There is nothing Dell Briggers could have told me that would have made me stop liking him."

"I know. And he knew that too, at one level. But on another level, he knew his father wouldn't have anything to do with him. He knew that when his mother needed to come back home, her own father— his grandfather—turned her away. And he knew it was because of him." Gladys held up her hand and ticked her fingers against her thumb as if counting. "His father didn't want him—at least not at first. His grandfather didn't want him. His mother couldn't be a mother to him. His grandmother had been murdered because of him."

I raised an eyebrow. "Dell knew about her, too?"

"Yes."

"Wow," I whispered. "He carried a lot of pain."

Gladys reached across the table and touched my hand. "But you eased his pain."

Once again, a lump formed in my throat. "I did?"

"Your friendship was the light of his life."

The tears I'd been holding back now came freely. "That would be a great blessing, to know that I helped him."

"You know you did."

"No." I shook my head. "We never talked about it like that."

"But think about all the things y'all did talk about, and all the things you did together. Think about the smile on his face. The way he laughed when you were together. The way both of you would drop everything at a moment's notice to go off and do something together."

I wiped my eyes with my backs of my hands and smiled. "We did that."

"I know you did."

"Daddy used to get so mad at me. Dell would call and say, 'Let's go over to Pete's house.' Or, 'Let's go over to Cullman or Jasper and do this or that.' And I would run off to my room to get ready and Daddy would say, 'If that boy said, "Let's jump off the ledge," you would do it.'"

"And he was right."

"Yes." I chuckled. "He was."

"See. That's what I'm talking about."

"I don't think Dell and I ever had an argument about anything."

"And if you did, it didn't matter, did it?"

"No."

"Okay then." Gladys let go of my hand and leaned away from the table. "You did him the biggest favor of his life by not prying."

Suddenly, an awful thought struck me and my eyes opened wide with worry. "Am I taking it all back by asking questions now? Am I prying now?"

"No." Gladys wagged her finger to emphasize the point. "You're just filling in the blanks now." She looked away. "The truth is a good thing. The truth sets you free."

We sat there a moment in silence, neither of us saying anything, both of us staring blankly into the middle distance, lost in thought. Finally, I picked up the conversation again. "You said Dell didn't know his father back then."

"Right."

"Did he know him later?"

"Yes."

"When did they meet? When did Dell meet Odell?"

"Odell came to town when y'all graduated from high school. He and Dell met that weekend. Right here, at my house. They talked right here." She tapped the tabletop for emphasis. "Dell was sitting where you're sitting. Odell was sitting here." She pointed to the place where she sat. "Right here in this very chair."

"I never knew that."

"I know," she acknowledged. "But like we've discussed, it was a complicated situation."

"Did they see each other after that?"

"I think they saw each other once or twice a year after that. They had a lot to work through and I don't know if they ever got through it all. But they tried."

"Did Odell meet Steve?"

"Yes."

"What did he think of him?"

"He liked him." She looked over at me. "You met Steve at the funeral, right?"

"Yes," I replied.

"So you know what he's like."

"He's a good guy." Steve was a good guy. Even though, as Babs pointed out, I was jealous of his relationship with Dell, he was a good man and I'm certain he treated Dell as well as anyone could have treated him, except maybe for the way I would have treated him.

"Right." She nodded her head quickly. "I liked him. Odell seemed to, also."

"You met Steve?" I asked.

"Yes," she said. "Once when they came to town."

"Dell brought him by here?"

"They stayed a night or two with me."

"And I never knew it."

"It's okay." Gladys gestured with her hand for me to be calm. "People don't get to participate in every part of each other's lives. You did things that Dell didn't know about, too."

"Like?"

"Like marrying Babs, for instance. He wasn't at your wedding because you didn't invite him."

A pang of guilt stabbed me in the stomach. "I tried to, but the invitation came back."

"He was in France or somewhere at the time."

"That's what he told me later." Dell and I talked by phone a few weeks after the wedding. He knew that Babs and I were dating but I don't think he realized the relationship was that serious. And then I realized something. "He lived alone to that point."

Gladys had a puzzled expression. "Do what?"

"Until Babs and I married, Dell lived alone."

She thought for a moment. "I think you're right."

"I am." My voice had a confident tone. "Steve didn't come along until after we were married."

"So you see," Gladys said. "It wasn't just about him finding someone else. You found someone else, too. And you found that person first. Your lives turned in different directions. Diverging. Separate paths opening up to you."

"Yes," I replied. "I suppose so."

It was a moment of realization for me and a sense of peace came over me, but I still wanted to know the complete story so I turned the conversation back to where we'd been before. "So, Odell came to see Dell and he stayed here at your house."

"Yes."

"And he came to our high school graduation."

"Yeah." Gladys' response was short and clipped. She looked uncomfortable, too, and turned her head to one side, as if to avoid me, but I kept going anyway.

"When we talked to Lucy that day at the home, she said she wanted to come to our high school graduation, too. But you talked her out of it."

Gladys' eyes focused on the tabletop. "I see you finally talked about this with your mother."

"Yes, ma'am."

"Did she tell you the whole story?" She looked across the table at me. "Did she tell you all of it?"

From the tone in her voice, I knew she was asking about the things that happened between her and Mr. Johnson but I wasn't ready to talk about that just yet. "They were all in town that weekend. Odell and Dell and Lucy, but you steered Lucy away from them."

"What's your point?"

"You did that because he was with you. Not just staying at your house, but with you. You and Odell Norton were—"

"Lovers," she said, cutting me off.

"And that's the part you thought might cause a problem. For Lucy and for you."

She looked me in the eye. "How much longer is this going to last?"

"Is what going to last?"

"This fascination you have with everything about Dell Briggers."

I didn't blink. "You were seeing Odell Norton. Romantically."

"Suppose I was?" There was a defiance in her voice I'd never heard before. "I already told you we were lovers. At least for a while."

"And you didn't want risk interrupting what you had with him. Or having that relationship cause a problem between you and Lucy."

"He was special. She was special."

"And you were in a difficult position."

Tears filled her eyes. "I'd never had a man before. Not like that. Not like him. Just—"

"Just Harold Johnson."

We had arrived at that topic and it was unavoidable now, but I wasn't sure what to say next so I sat quietly for a moment while tears trickled down her cheeks. "Yeah," she sighed. "Just Harold Johnson." Her lips quivered and she covered them with her hand. "That man was so—"

Instinctively, I did for her as she had done for me earlier and I reached across the table to lay my hand gently on top of hers. "Mama told me what happened," I said softly.

"That's why I told you to see her," Gladys whispered. "I knew you needed to know what happened with him to understand all of what went on, but I didn't want to say."

"Yes, ma'am."

"But what happened between me and Harold Johnson wasn't anything romantic. Just him relieving himself into my body. That's all it was. It wasn't sex for me. It was for him, I guess, but not for me. For me it was more like me giving him a place to masturbate." I winced at the description but not at the truth of what she said. She looked over at me. "I know that's a bad way to express it but that's what it was like." She slipped her hand free from mine and wiped her eyes.

"Do you still see Odell?" I asked, moving with the conversation.

"Nah." She shook her head. "I wrote to him after Dell passed, but I haven't seen him or heard from him in two or three years."

"He's been here that recently?"

"Yeah," she replied. "He used to come through here rather frequently. Nobody knew about it except me. Maybe your mother."

"My mother?"

"Uh huh."

"Why would she know about him?"

"She and I talk two or three times a week. I told her about him. That's how she knew. No one else in town even recognized him. Or if they did, they didn't say anything."

"What happened?"

"That weekend?"

"No. Between you and Odell. What happened that he stopped coming around?"

Gladys had an indulgent smile. "He was just like that. Took an interest in someone for a while, then moved on. That's what happened to him and Lucy. It happened with others. It happened with me."

"That must have been painful."

"Not really. By the time he'd had enough of me, I'd had enough of him. It all worked out."

Gladys' response seemed rather evasive, but I wasn't in a position to delve much deeper into the issue. Besides, her relationship with Odell Norton wasn't the part of the story that bothered me, so I let the matter drop and stayed on topic. "The last time I was here I asked if you knew where he lived and you dodged the question. Where does he live?"

"Apalachicola." She looked up at me. "Are you thinking about going to see him?"

"I might. But don't tell him I'm coming. I don't want him to hide from me."

She shook her head. "He won't hide. I won't tell him, but he won't hide."

Our conversation had clarified several issues for me and there wasn't much left for us to discuss except the question that was foremost on my mind. The one that bothered me the most. The one that was both liberating and confining at the same time. The one that made me nervous at the thought of it. The issue.

Even then, after all I'd learned about myself, it still was difficult for me to form that question into a complete thought. Not because I couldn't identify it, but rather precisely because I could identify it. And sitting there with Gladys, thinking about raising the issue with her, I wasn't sure whether to ask her about it—or even if it would help to hear her response.

To buy myself some time, I leaned back from the table and stared past Gladys to the cabinets that lined the wall. Finally, though, I could wait no longer and opened my mouth to speak. The words came easier than I'd imagined. "When I talked to Lucy about Steve she said she always wished Dell would be with me like that, instead of with Steve or someone else."

Gladys had a knowing look. "Lucy knew Dell was gay."

A sense of relief swept over me. The topic was open for discussion. A weight was lifted from my shoulders. "How did she know that?" I asked.

"She was his mother," Gladys replied. "She just knew it."

"For how long?"

Gladys had a puzzled frown. "How long had she known he was gay?"

"Yes."

"A long time. Always, maybe."

"Always?"

"Look, some people are just that way. They're gay. They don't know a time when they weren't like that. It's like with the folks at church. You ask them how long they've been a Christian and some of them will tell you they don't know a time when they weren't. I think it was like that for Dell. He always was. And I think Lucy knew it that same way. I don't think there ever was a time when either of them didn't know it."

"Did they talk about it?"

"Nah." She shook her head. "I don't think so. She mentioned it to me one time when y'all were still in school, but I don't think it was a topic she and Dell ever discussed."

"Lucy mentioned it to you when we were in high school?"

"Yes."

A nervous smile turned up the corners of my mouth. "She thought I was gay, too."

Gladys seemed amused. "That bothers you?"

"I don't know," I shrugged.

"It bothers you," she said. Her voice had a matter-of-fact tone.

"You don't want it to, but it does."

"I never thought of myself that way—as being gay."

"That's what I mean. It's a topic Dell didn't think of, either."

"But his mother did."

"Yes. I suppose she did."

"I never thought of Dell that way. Never thought of us that way. He was Dell and I was me. I just didn't want to be with anyone else. I don't think he did, either. But I never saw it as an issue about sexuality or preference. He was Dell. That's all."

"And that's the way it's supposed to be between people."

That was a thought that had never occurred to me. A relationship-driven view of sexuality. No one ever talked about it that way. They didn't talk about it that way at school. And they certainly didn't talk about it that way at church. Or anywhere else I'd ever been, for that matter, except maybe with Babs. One of the things I'd learned since delving into all of this was how broad her views were on the topic. "You think that's how it's supposed to be?"

"Yes," Gladys said. "Instead of people going around announcing they are this way or that. Or condemning each other and making the issue into an us-against-them argument. I mean, there are people who consider sex of any kind as evil. Others see it as entertainment." She had a dissatisfied look and she gestured with both hands. "None of that is right. The only way it makes sense is to see it from a relationship point of view."

Gladys was surprising me.

"But to answer your question," Gladys continued. "I don't know whether Lucy thought you were gay. Or if she simply thought you and Dell would have been comfortable together on a permanent basis. I don't know."

"We would have," I said.

She frowned. "Would have?"

"Been comfortable together," I explained. "We could have lived together and got along just fine. I don't know what it would have been like. I mean, the other part. You know." It was easier to talk to Gladys about this than anyone else, but it still wasn't easy for me.

"You mean, the sexual part?"

"Yes."

"Everyone has to work that part out. Gay or straight. You had to work things out with Babs, right? I mean, just because you're a man and she's a woman, getting that part right wasn't an automatic thing."

"No." I chuckled at the memory of our wedding night. "It wasn't automatic. But is that how Dell and I were perceived around Tenaca? As the gay couple?"

"I don't know." A frown winkled her brow. "What does it matter?"

"It matters to me what people think about me."

"Why?"

"Well, I don't know. It just does."

"Did anyone ever say anything to you about it?"

"No," I replied.

"Did a teacher ever cut your grade in school because of your relationship with Dell?"

"No."

"Or because of his relationship with you?"

"Not as far as I know."

"Did the other students harass you at school over it?"

"No."

"I don't think they treated Dell that way, either."

A wry expression came to me. "But was that because of us, or was it because of my grandfather?"

She looked puzzled. "Your grandfather? Roy Thomas?"

"Yes."

"What's he got to do with it?"

"I've heard stories about him."

She propped her elbows on the table and leaned forward. "Listen." Her voice was hushed. "Most people don't know nothing about him now. And not very many knew anything about him when you were in high school. And you need to draw a line right there and not dig any deeper. Whatever he was, whatever he did, it was long before you were born and has nothing to do with you and Dell."

"But he was one of the bad guys, right?"

"I wouldn't describe Mr. Roy that way."

"Then how would you describe him?"

Gladys thought for a moment, then gave me an interesting look. "Does the term hard ass mean anything to you?"

"Yes."

"Well that's what your grandfather was. A hard ass. Especially to people outside of his family. Now, to your daddy, he was the gentlest person I ever knew. But to the rest of the world, he was tough as an oak timber."

"He didn't put up with much?"

"There's an expression some people use. They say, 'He doesn't suffer fools gladly.' In this part of the world that gets translated into, 'He don't take shit off of nobody.' And that was your grandfather." Gladys had never spoken like that around me, but I knew what she was trying to say. Grandpaw had a hard edge. Not to me, but to just about everyone else. He kept his thoughts and emotions to himself and never let anyone inside.

"I saw a tough side to him," I said. "But I never knew it personally."

"I don't expect so. Mr. Roy was kind to me, too."

We sat there a moment, neither of us saying a word. There was one more question I wanted to ask her, only this time I wasn't worried about it. I smiled at her and said, "Did you think I was gay?"

"Does it matter what I think?"

"Since Dell died, I've been finding out things about myself, about my family, about this town, that I never knew. And it seems like I lived a life that only existed in my mind. As if I lived in one context, while everyone else lived in another. And now, after all that I've learned, I'm wondering if the people around me thought I was gay. If they think I'm gay now. Is that how people saw me? Is that how they see me now?"

"As to now, I don't think anyone has a thought at all about what your sexual preference might be. As to back then, I never thought about it. I know your daddy used to worry about it, but I don't think anyone else did. Your mother didn't. I guess Lucy must have thought about it from what she said the other day. But other than those two—Lucy and your daddy—I don't know anyone who ever mentioned it to me. But I'll ask you again, does it matter what they think?"

"What do you mean?"

"Did you love Dell?"

If my question about Harold Johnson went deep into her soul, her question to me about Dell went to the bottom of mine. For me, this was the crux of the matter. Not whether I loved him or not. Because I loved him and I knew I did. The point of the thing, though, was whether I could say it out loud. As was typical for me with difficult issues, I hedged. "I don't know if it was love like a man for a woman, but yes. I did love him."

Gladys smiled as if she knew the struggle going on inside me. "And I think he loved you," she said. "You loved each other."

"Yes, ma'am."

"Okay." She gestured with both hands again. "Now let that be the end of it. Let it rest with that." She leaned away from the table. "You loved him. He loved you. And that should be enough."

But it wasn't enough for me. Whatever there was about me and Dell that had been stirred at his funeral needed more of a resolution than merely to know that we loved each other. I already knew that much before I knew he was dead. And it wasn't just that we loved each other. When we were younger, we were in love with each other and the thing that had been awakened in me at his death was the question of what that love meant about me now. I'd come to a place where I could say to myself that I loved Dell. And loved him with the affection most of my classmates had for a steady girlfriend. But that was then. This was now. And the question of what my love for him then meant about me now was still not answered. More of the story remained to be heard. I might have reached the bottom of my soul with it—to finally acknowledge that I loved Dell with a love of any kind or type one might care to describe—but I hadn't reached all the way to the bottom of the story, and I knew it.

# 10

With the help of the internet, Babs and I confirmed that Odell Norton did, indeed, live at Apalachicola, Florida. A week later, she and I rode down there. It was a long way and took from early in the morning until after dark. As usual, she did the driving. Thankfully, this time, even though she talked all the way, she kept her eyes on the road.

We arrived there on Thursday night and checked into a room at the Gibson Hotel, an historic hotel near the mouth of the Apalachicola River. After breakfast the next morning, we went over to the library to see if we could find an address for Odell. Babs parked the car out front in the shade of a live oak while I went inside.

When I asked the woman at the circulation desk about Odell Norton, she gave me a curious look. "Are you a friend of his?"

"Not exactly," I replied. "I went to school with his son."

"His son?" She had a heavy frown and a perturbed expression on her face. "Odell Norton has a son?"

"Yes, ma'am."

"He never told me about a son."

"You know him?"

"Yes," she replied. "I know him. We used to go out when he first came down here."

"So you know where he lives?"

"Yeah. I know where he lives. And I've a mind to go over there with you and beat some sense into him."

"Maybe you could do that later," I suggested. "After I talk to him first." She didn't seem to understand what I meant but she gave me directions to his house and I went back to the car. Babs noticed I was smiling as I opened the passenger door and said, "What happened?"

Her voice dropped off at the end of the sentence like it does when she's expecting that something really did happen.

"I asked the lady at the desk for Odell's address thinking this might be an ordeal just finding him. But—"

"An ordeal?" she asked, interrupting me.

"Yeah. Like, you know, the people in Tenaca who know about him think of him as someone famous. Which is fine for home. But sometimes the person someone thinks of that way in one place turns out to be no one of note to the people who live in the place where they later reside." I glanced at her. "Know what I mean?"

"Sort of."

"And," I continued, "if they really are famous, not everybody likes giving out personal information like that. They know people enjoy their privacy. And in a small town like this, people don't generally welcome prying strangers. So I thought maybe it—"

"Okay," she said, cutting me off with a wave of her hand. "You thought it might be an ordeal to get his address. What happened in there that you were smiling about?"

"It turns out, the lady at the desk is one of Odell Norton's former girlfriends."

Babs raised an eyebrow. "He's pretty old, isn't he?"

"Yes. But he hasn't always been old. And even old guys like the company of a woman."

She hit me across the chest with a backhand. "Watch out for the old comments."

"You referred to old men," I countered.

"That's different." She put the car in gear and started up the street from the library. I gave her directions as we went. At the corner by the Piggly Wiggly grocery store, we turned left onto Tenth Street and rode down it all the way down to the water where the street ends at Bay Avenue. "That's the house," I said, pointing to a white two-story on the right.

The house was old and rambling, but well kept, and afforded an unobstructed view of Apalachicola Bay. We sat there a moment, watching as the waves lapped against the shore. A flock of seagulls circled overhead, then dropped onto the water right in front of us. And just as they collected themselves, a pelican glided past.

"I could get used to this view," Babs said finally.

"It's a lot different from what we see at home."

She looked over at me. "You wouldn't like seeing this every day?"

"Yes," I said. "I would like it. I do like it. But they have hurricanes down here, too."

She shoved against my shoulder in a way that pushed me sideways against the door. "You always see the downside."

"Daddy says, the upside is never a problem. The key to earning a living is in limiting the downside."

"Well that just spoils the view." She gave me a whack across the chest but it wasn't an angry one. I've had those before. This one was playful.

A paved driveway ran from the street to a garage in back of Odell's house. There was no one behind us so we backed up to the drive, turned in from the street, and parked behind a red pickup truck.

"You go inside," Babs said. "I'll wait for you out here."

"This might take a while."

"Do you have your phone?"

"Yes."

"When you go inside," she said, "I'll go back to the street where the hotel is. I saw a shop or two I wanted to visit. You can call me when you're done."

"Okay. But wait here until I get inside."

"Okay."

The sun was bright and warm as I came from the car and made my way up the steps. A screened door opened onto a screened porch that ran along the back of the house. I banged on the door, hoping someone in the house might hear me, and in a moment a woman appeared. She wore a white dress and white apron and at first I thought she was a nurse, but then I noticed splotches of tomato on her apron and realized she was the housekeeper.

"May I help you?" she asked.

"I was hoping to see Odell Norton."

"Is he expecting you?"

"No ma'am," I replied. "Tell him it's Billy Thomas. A friend of Gladys Haywood. From Tenaca. He'll know Gladys."

The woman disappeared inside the house and a minute or two later, an old man appeared as he stepped through a doorway onto the porch. "You're a friend of Gladys?" he asked.

"Yes, sir," I replied.

"What did you say your name was?"

"Billy Thomas. From Tenaca, Alabama. I was a friend of Dell."

"Theron and Elizabeth's boy."

"Yes, sir." I was surprised he knew my parents' names. And surprised to hear them used, too. No one ever called them by their actual names. To just about everyone in town, he was Spider and she was Libby.

Odell came over to the door and unhooked the latch. "Well, come on inside," he said. "No point in standing out there in the sun all day." He held the door while I entered and as I did, I glanced back in Babs' direction and tossed her a wave. He looked over my shoulder toward the car. "Is she with you?" he asked.

"Yes," I replied. "She's my wife."

"Does she want to come inside, too?"

"No, sir. She's going up to a shop in town."

"Spending money," he said. His voice had a dry tone, as if sometime in the past he'd been disgruntled with a woman for spending what he thought was too much money.

"Probably so," I said, but I didn't mean it. Babs didn't spend frivolously and even if she did, I wouldn't have said anything. Not on a trip.

Odell led the way across the porch to a doorway that opened into the kitchen where the woman I'd seen earlier was busy at the sink. Steam rose from three large pots that sat on the stove and wonderful smells filled the air. He gestured in an offhand manner as we walked through. "Dean is getting ready for a dinner party tonight," he said. "A dozen people from Tallahassee. Supporters of the library at the university. I told them last year I would host a dinner for them. Wish now I had said no."

From the kitchen we stepped into a hallway and made our way toward the front of the house. A stairwell rose to the left and past it we came to a doorway that opened to the right. Through it was a library, the walls of which were lined from floor to ceiling with book-shelves crammed full of books and papers and bits of ephemera. A desk sat at the opposite end of the room and beside it were two overstuffed, well-worn leather chairs. Odell gestured to one of them. "Have a seat," he said. He dropped onto the one nearest the desk so I took the one beside it.

"I think you and Dell were more than just friends," he said. "Weren't you?"

"Yes, sir. We were."

"So, I suppose you were at the funeral in Chicago."

"Yes, sir. Babs and I went."

"Babs is your wife?"

"Yes."

"Well," he sighed. "I hear it was a nice send-off."

"I'm sure Gladys told you the details."

"No," he replied. "She sent me a letter sometime around then, but only to mention that Dell had died. I heard about the funeral from Lucy."

A puzzled look wrinkled my forehead. "Lucy?"

"Yeah. Didn't you see her up there in Chicago?"

"No."

"She said she was there."

Dell's funeral was scheduled for Saturday. A wake was held the night before at a funeral home near his house. Hundreds of people passed through that night. I didn't know many of them, but Babs and I were there for several hours and I didn't see anyone who resem-bled Lucy. The funeral service was conducted the next day from St. Clement Catholic Church, an old church located a little north of the downtown district and not far from the lake. Two hundred people attended. Babs and I arrived early and sat near the back. We saw every person who entered the sanctuary and talked among ourselves about most of them, providing a running critique of the clothes they wore, the look they'd created, the way they'd fixed their hair. And again, no one who was there that day looked anything like Lucy and if she had been there, Gladys would have been with her and I'm certain Gladys wasn't at the church. That led me to wonder about the accuracy of what Odell had said but I let it go.

"You're still in touch with Lucy?" I asked.

"I've always been in touch with her," he replied. "I liked Lucy, I just didn't want to be married to her. But enough about all of that." He slouched to one side in the chair. "What brings you all the way down here to find me?"

"When I attended the funeral, I learned some things about Dell that I hadn't known. And I've been trying to find out—"

"What kind of things?" he interrupted.

"For one, I always thought Mrs. Briggers was Dell's mother. And that—"

"She was his aunt."

"Mrs. Smith at the library told me. I was—"

"Jenny Smith," he said with a mocking tone, interrupting me again. "There's a real piece of work for you. I bet she showed you those newspaper articles, too, didn't she?"

"Yes. She did. You know her?"

"Yeah." He smiled. "I know her. And I know she hates me. They all hate me."

"Well." I gave him the obvious look. "You left their sister with a child to raise."

"I suppose," he conceded. "But Lucy and I hadn't been seeing each other very long. Only one or two dates when she got pregnant. They all thought I had taken advantage of her, but they didn't really know her. I felt bad about her getting pregnant and tried to help, but she wasn't interested in marrying me, so I thought it would be better for both of us if I just moved on."

"You went to prison—"

"Ha," he laughed. "Jenny showed you that article and you read it."

"Yes. And—"

"That article was a lie."

"A lie?"

"Yeah. Charlie Briggers had a brother. A younger brother. His name was Eddie, I think. It was the sixties and Eddie was into all that went on back then. Pot. LSD. Vietnam War protest."

"I don't remember hearing about any of that in Tenaca."

"Because there wasn't any of it there," Odell said. "Protests against the war had been happening everywhere, but not much of it happened in the South. Not much protest against anything there, except for civil rights marches, of course. But Eddie wasn't interested in civil rights. He was worried about Vietnam, mostly because he didn't want to go in the draft. So he and a bunch of his friends went over to Atlanta and organized a march. The city refused to give them a permit so rather than challenging it in court, they challenged it on the street."

"Protested without a permit."

"Right." Odell nodded his head. "They did the protest march. Got arrested. The whole nine yards. Somewhere along the way, chicken shit Eddie gave them my name. I'm not sure why he did that. I was living in Arkansas at the time but my first three novels were already out. I suppose he knew about me from those books and the Tenaca connection—people there were supportive of me at first."

I was skeptical. "Eddie really thought he could get away with that?"

"Eddie didn't think very much about anything or anyone except Eddie."

"What happened after that? He got arrested, used your name, then what?"

"When they booked him at the jail in Atlanta they took his fingerprints. There was no way for him to fake that part. He'd been arrested in Birmingham for fighting and his fingerprints were in the system. So eventually the fake name was discovered. I never went to court. Never went to prison. Never went anywhere near the Atlanta city jail. But it caused me a lot of grief. Had to hire a lawyer in Atlanta to straighten it all out, which I did. But before the confusion was rectified, the Tenaca News—that beacon of truth and bastion of honest journalism—published a story about the arrest and included my name."

"They didn't publish a retraction?"

"I never asked for one."

My forehead wrinkled in a frown. "Why not?"

"By the time I had the situation straightened out, the moment had passed. That whole arrest thing was history. So I just left it at that."

"Folded it into the legend," I said with a smile.

"Yeah." He smiled back. "Didn't hurt my image as a vagabond writer."

"Gladys said you came back to Tenaca from time to time to visit Dell."

"Not at first. After he was born I left Arkansas and took a teaching job in Tennessee. Not long after that, things with Lucy fell totally apart. Later, after she and Dell ended up in Tenaca, I realized I actually had a son and I felt bad about him growing up without a father so I started writing to Alice and asked about seeing him. But she and Charlie didn't want me there. Said Dell had a life of his own and it would just be a big disruption for him if I showed up. So, I stayed away."

"Until we graduated from high school."

"Yeah." He nodded again. "A little before that, I think. But about that time."

"A little before?"

"I came back the year before that. When Dell was in the eleventh grade. I heard about a high school play he was in and I just wanted to see him." He gave me a questioning look. "Wasn't that the year before you and he graduated?"

"Yes." I grinned. "I didn't know you were there."

For me and Dell and most of our class, that school play was one of the highlights of our high school years—probably the biggest. Our English teacher, Mrs. Miller, got the idea from an article she read in Dramatics magazine, a publication for high school drama teachers. Her idea was that students should write a play and perform it. And that's what we did. We wrote it, Mrs. Miller and two other teachers cast the parts, then we performed it on stage at the school auditorium. It was an incredible experience. Especially for Dell. He kept going on and on about it and for the rest of that year all he talked about was leaving Tenaca, going to New York, and making it big in the theater. But I never knew Odell Norton came to one of our performances.

"Did Dell know you were there?" I asked.

"Nah." He shook his head. "I got there right as the show started. Sat in the back. Left as soon as it ended. I didn't want to cause any problems."

"Did you stay with Gladys?"

"Yes."

"She didn't mention that."

"Well," he said with a knowing smile. "Maybe she didn't tell you everything."

The tone of his voice was a little too much but I let his response slide and moved on. "What about after that?" I asked. "Did you see him after we grew up and he moved away?"

"Once or twice."

"In Tenaca?"

"No. Over at Panama City."

"He came down here?"

"Yeah. Him and his partner." He looked away as if trying to remember the name. "Steve something or other."

"Steve Atterbury."

"Yeah. Atterbury." He looked over at me. "You know, Dell wanted you to go to Chicago with him."

That conversation with Dell had been lost to me for a long time but I had remembered it when we were in Chicago for the funeral. Right before we graduated from college, Dell got this great offer from an advertising firm but it meant he had to move up there. He asked me if I wanted to go with him and from the way he said it, I assumed he was just uneasy about leaving home, friends, the things he knew. I didn't realize the thing that actually bothered him was leaving me. Or that he wanted us to be together—as in, together-to-gether.

"We talked about it," I said, trying to sluff off his question. "But I just thought he was scared about going up there alone."

"Well, he probably was scared," Odell said. "But he asked you because he wanted you to go with him."

"He told you this?"

"Yes," Odell replied. "He told me how he felt about you and asked me if he should approach you about it. I said—"

"How he felt about me?"

"He loved you." Odell's voice was solemn and serious. "Not like the general wishing your fellow man well that sometimes gets expressed as love. He loved you."

"Romantically?"

"He described his feelings about you to me as most men would describe their love for a woman." Odell frowned at me. "You didn't know this?"

"I knew how I felt about him, but I think he was ahead of me in articulating it."

Odell grinned. "I would say so."

"And you told him he should tell me how he felt?"

"Yes. He asked me what he should do and I said, 'If that's what you want, you should tell him.'"

"And he did," I said. Emotions welled up inside me. "But I didn't understand the depth of what he was talking about."

"Well, that's what it was. He only met that Steve guy after he got up there to Chicago and you got married. Before that, though, he wanted you. I think Steve was always his second choice. He liked Steve alright, but I think the whole time he would have rather been with you."

Wow. That left me feeling flattered and sad, all at the same time.

Flattered to know Dell really loved me then the way I knew now that I had loved him. And sad to realize that I had missed something life-changing that I could have had with him.

Immediately, however, the implications of that came crashing in on me with guilt and condemnation for even the idea of a relationship—a serious relationship, a romantic relationship—with another man. Sexual practices aside, I had been told all of my adult life that men were not supposed to relate to each other that way. Not romantically to any degree.

"You know." My voice sounded tentative because my heart was reluctant to speak. "We were never together that way. Not physically." As soon as the words escaped my lips I wanted them back. They were treacherous. Dell had expressed his love for me. Odell had delivered the message, albeit after the fact, and rather than simply stating my love for him in response, I offered a qualifier. We didn't really sleep together. He never entered me. I never entered him. We didn't have sex, you know. What an asshole I was. While he was alive. And now after he was gone.

Odell seemed unfazed. "I know." He nodded. "And I'm not sure he was that way with Steve, either."

Hearing that surprised me. "Really?"

"Yeah."

"That's difficult to believe."

"As difficult as all the other stuff you've probably heard by now?"

A smile came to me. "I've heard a lot."

"Well, if you can handle that, you can handle the truth about your relationship with Dell."

"Yes," I said bravely. "I can." I'd already handled it. I knew the kind of relationship Dell and I had back then. But I still didn't know what it meant now and how it fit into the person I had become. A gay man living in a straight marriage. Or a straight man who had a relationship in the past that was pure, and good, and right, and chaste—but with a man.

"Gladys said you'd been asking questions," Odell continued. "And if you've been asking questions around Tenaca, I'm sure you got an earful."

"I have."

He had a knowing grin, like he'd thought of something uncomfortable and whether I wanted to hear it or not, he was about to say it. "Did they tell you about Charlie and Alice's son? The other boy they raised?"

"Frank?"

"Yeah." Odell seemed to take great delight in nodding his head. "Frank. I'd forgotten his name. Did they tell you about him?"

"Not much." Gladys and I had discussed him but not to any length.

"I don't doubt it," he said. "I'm surprised they mentioned him at all."

"Why?"

"Because that's where the real story lies." There was an energy in his voice that had been missing before.

"The real story?"

Again, Odell had a look people get when they know they shouldn't say something but they're going to say it anyway. A cross between embarrassment and glee. "Charlie and Alice like to talk about Frank as their child, but he really was Alice and Harold's son."

My eyes opened wide. "Harold?"

"Yes."

"Harold Johnson?"

"Yes."

My jaw dropped. "But I thought Alice was his daughter."

"She is."

"She had a son who was fathered by her own father?"

Odell nodded his head even more vigorously than before. "That's what you're dealing with. That right there." He jabbed the air with his finger. "That's where it all got started. It all goes back to the old man."

Right then, I wanted to puke. Not vomit. Not throw up. Puke. I wanted to puke my guts out all over the floor in Odell Norton's library. To cover the hardwood and the throw rugs with everything

I'd had to eat that day.

That's also when the pieces clicked into place for me and I finally understood I had been living in a world that was insulated from almost everything and everyone around me. A world created for me by my mother and father, by Dell's family, by Gladys, and by just about everyone else I ever knew or cared about. They had kept the truth from me and me from it. And this was the reason—Harold Johnson having sex with his own daughter, an act that produced a son. That was the reason I didn't know about Frank until the funeral. The reason I didn't know about Lucy until I talked to Gladys and later met Lucy at the home at Bright's Mountain. The reason I didn't know about Gladys and Harold until a few days ago. The reason I didn't know about Grandpaw and the Knights of the White Camellias. No one wanted me to know the truth—the real truth—because the real truth was a sordid mess that oozed from Harold Johnson and from my own grandfather and seeped its way into the life of every person who ever resided in Tenaca.

"Harold Johnson was a sick man," I groaned.

"No," Odell retorted. "He wasn't sick. He was evil."

"Yeah," I sighed. "He was."

"And that's what you're dealing with. When you're out there asking questions about the past, that's the thing they don't want to talk about. They've been living under a cloud of shame and secrecy since a long time before you were born and it's had an effect on all of them. Including your mother."

The mention of Mama seemed out of place. "You know my mother?" I asked.

"I met her once or twice when I came to see Lucy."

A puzzled look wrinkled my forehead. "Why did you mention her just now?"

"Because the secrets we've been talking about are the reason she drinks."

"If you only met her at the home, how do you know she drinks?"

He reached into his pocket and produced a red chip the size of a quarter. "You know what this is?" He held the chip for me to see.

"Not really," I replied.

"It's a sobriety chip. They give them at AA meetings when you reach various milestones. Our group gives this kind when you've been sober a year. I have a drawer full of them."

"You're an alcoholic."

"A recovering alcoholic."

"And you spotted my mother as a fellow addict?"

"Yes. And I know the context." He returned the chip to his pocket. "Which, as you have learned, is rather bad."

Having learned already that Harold was having his way with Gladys, and now that he did the same with Alice, I wondered who else he was abusing in a similar fashion. Odell's mention of Mama made me wonder about her. She was a young woman. She was at the house working with Gladys. I knew she had already denied that anything happened between them, but in light of the things Odell had to say, I wondered if she told me the truth.

Conversation between us lagged and my mind wandered across the rows of books on the shelfs that surrounded us. Thousands of titles stood with their spines facing us, like sentries waiting to be called into battle. Then I wondered how many of them Odell had read and whether he ever used them at all, or merely had them as decoration—a writer's library that looked the part. A backdrop for an image he had spent decades cultivating.

After a moment Odell pushed himself up from the chair where he'd been sitting. "I'm not sure if that was what you came to hear," he said, "but that's what I know about the situation." Realizing our visit had reached an end, I stood and we shook hands, then he ushered me back through the house. "I would invite you to stay for dinner," he said, "but they have a program they want to present to this group tonight. A fundraiser of some kind. I doubt you'd be interested in donating to the library fund at Florida State."

"No," I said. "Not really."

"Me either." He glanced at me with a grin. "But they've been good to me over the years and I feel obligated to return the favor."

By then we were in the kitchen. I paused near the counter that ran along the back wall, took the cell phone from my pocket, and called Babs to tell her I was ready. Odell realized what I was doing. "Oh," he said. "Your wife." He gestured to a chair in the corner near the pantry door. "I have a few things to do now or I would wait with you. But you can sit over there if you like until your wife returns. No point in you standing outside in the sunshine."

"Thanks," I said. "And thank you for talking to me."

"You were a good friend to Dell." He patted me on the shoulder, then turned away and disappeared up the hall.

When he was gone, I took a seat on the chair in the corner and Dean brought me a glass of tea. "Have a drink," she said. "I made it just a little while ago. It's pretty good." She smiled at me. "I tried it myself."

"Thank you," I said as I put the glass to my lips and took a sip. It was sweet and sharp and cold and nearly perfect. After that first sip I took another.

# 11

Babs picked me up at Odell Norton's house and we rode back to the hotel. Later that evening, we went to dinner at The Hut, a café on the highway west of Apalachicola. The following day we rested on the sand at St. George Island, then headed back to Tenaca the day after that.

The trip was enjoyable, in general, and the time alone with Babs was great, but the things I learned from Odell Norton were more than a little disturbing—perhaps the most unsettling of all the things I'd learned since we returned from Dell's funeral in Chicago. I say perhaps because after talking to him I had the nagging suspicion that Mama hadn't told me all there was to tell about what happened between her and Harold Johnson, and the thought of what that might be was very unsettling. Almost as unsettling as the thought of having to go back to see her about it one more time.

The day after we returned to Tenaca, I worked with Daddy to catch up on a few things that fell behind while I was gone. Doing that took longer than expected and by the time we had everything straightened out, Friday had arrived and you know about Mama and Fridays.

Saturday was devoted to yard work, and on Sunday Babs and I went to church. As we sat in the pew and the choir came out to start the service, Daddy leaned over and let me know Mama was having one of her days. "Friday has held over a little longer than usual," he whispered. Instead of going to their house for lunch, Babs and I rode over to Top Hat Barbecue in Blount Springs. Fluffy and Scott Mathers were there and we ate with them. It was good to catch up on recent events in their lives and even better to spend time thinking about not much at all for a change.

Monday was work as usual, but by Tuesday afternoon I couldn't put it off any longer. When the crews were busy again after lunch, I went over to the house and sat at the kitchen table with Mama. "I knew you'd be back," she said.

"You did?" I said it as a conversation prompt. I knew she knew I would return because I knew she knew she hadn't told me every-thing.

Mama had that look she gets when something isn't going exactly like she wants it to but there's no way for her to avoid it. "Your father said he told you to leave this business with Dell alone. And Gladys told you pretty much the same thing. But when I heard you and Babs had gone off to Apalachicola to see Odell Norton, I knew I'd be hearing from you."

"Yeah."

"You've been like this all your life. Even when you were a little boy." There was a tone in her voice that always irritated me. It came with a knowing look that bordered on a smirk and was usually fol-lowed by a condescending comment she masked as motherly insight. Doing me that way put me on edge back then, and it still did. "You never could let a thing rest," she continued. "Always had to run it down to the bitter end. Said you had to take it to a spot where you got comfortable with it." That right there—the way she said the word comfortable—that's the part that grated against me.

"And that's what I'm doing now." My voice had a strident edge but I wanted her to know I meant to find whatever it was I was look-ing for.

"I know." She stood and crossed the room to the refrigerator. "You want a Coca-Cola?"

"Sure," I replied.

Mama liked Coca-Cola almost as much as she liked gin, though for different reasons. She took two bottles from the refrigerator, popped off the caps with a bottle opener from the drawer, and brought them to the table. She never poured it into a glass. "Fizzes it too much," she always said. She handed one of the bottles to me and I took a sip.

"So," she said as she returned to her chair. "Ask me whatever it is you want to ask me and let's get on with it."

"Okay," I replied. "Tell me about Frank Briggers."

From the look on her face I could see she wasn't ready for that question and focused her eyes on the drink bottle to cover for it. "What about him?" She had a surly tone.

"Is he Charlie Briggers' son?"

She looked up at me. "What difference does it make?"

"Apparently a lot," I replied, "since no one wants to talk about it."

Mama took a drink of Coca-Cola. "Frank Briggers," she sighed, "was conceived by Alice Johnson after one of the many times when her father forced her to have sex with him." Her eyes bore in on me with a "go to hell" look. "There. I said it. You satisfied now?"

"Is that the truth, or are you just telling me that to be difficult?"

"It's the truth. And I'm not telling it to you to be difficult. I'm telling it to you because you asked and so you won't ask Alice about it."

"I hadn't planned to."

"Good. Because Alice is a lot like her father. She might be a petite woman, but if you go around there asking questions like this, she'll knock you through the wall. Understand?"

"Yes, ma'am." I took a sip of Coca-Cola to collect my thoughts. "This was an ongoing thing between Harold and Alice?"

Mama gave me that look again. "He started having sex with her when she was about fifteen."

"Did Mrs. Johnson know about it?"

"I expect so."

"Did she ever try to stop him?"

Mama blinked her eyes nervously as she looked over at me. "Son, you didn't know Harold Johnson. Not really. Not like the rest of us did. If he wanted to do something, there wasn't anyone who could stop him." Her eyes darted away and her voice dropped. "Certainly not Verlene Johnson."

"When did it stop?"

"With Alice?"

"Yes."

"When she got pregnant."

"Is that when Gladys started working at their house?"

"I suppose." A cloud seemed to come over her, as if she was remembering something deep and dark. Her voice took a faraway tone. "I'm not sure."

"Were you working there before Gladys?"

"No." She shook her head. "Gladys started working for them. And then she got me to help her. We needed the money, so I went."

"Were Charlie and Alice already married when she got pregnant with Frank?"

"No. Charlie had been coming around, but they weren't married."

"Did Charlie know she was pregnant?"

Mama cut her eyes at me. "You sure are asking a lot of questions. Even for you."

"Well, I started out with Mrs. Smith at the library, just trying to find out where Dell was born and if he really came from Valdosta, like he said, or Arkansas, like Frank said. And I've gone from one person to another, and back again. And every time I talk to someone, I learn a little piece of the story I didn't know before. And I finally ran into a piece of the story no one wants to talk about and you were there so that's why I'm here. To find out about Harold and Alice and Frank."

"That's how it is when people have something they don't want to talk about. They don't talk about it."

"Well, I'm tired of chasing myself around town, around the county, around the country, trying to find out what people in Tenaca and people in my own family know that I don't. So, yeah. I'm asking a lot of questions because it seems like that's the only way to get the whole story." I paused to take a breath, then started again. "When Charlie married Alice, did he know she was pregnant?"

"Yes."

"Did he know the child Alice was carrying had been sired by her father?"

"No."

"He thought Frank was his child?"

"Yes."

"Did he ever find out the truth?"

Mama leaned away from the table. "You remember telling me once—maybe more than once—that you'd been over at Dell's house and you heard people yelling and screaming at each other?"

"Yes, ma'am."

"You were about twelve or fourteen, right?"

"Yes, ma'am."

"That's what they were arguing about."

My forehead wrinkled in a frown. "You know that for a fact?" After all of the back and forth I'd already encountered, I wanted to make sure.

"Yes." She nodded. "I don't remember the exact time you told me that. Not the date or whatever. But I remember you telling me about hearing an argument and I remember that when you told me about it, I knew what they were fighting about."

"How did you know?"

"Because Gladys knew what happened and she told me."

"What happened?"

"As Frank got older, he started getting into trouble. They tried several approaches with him and finally sent him to a military school in Sulligent. Someone at the school discovered that Frank had difficulty reading and suggested that was the source of his trouble."

"Reading?"

"Yes. Couldn't read well. Became frustrated. Didn't know what to do. Acted out."

"How does that relate to Charlie and Alice and what I heard at their house?"

"They had Frank tested for reading. The person who administered the tests said they needed to screen him for physical problems. A doctor in Tuscaloosa examined him and sent him to Birmingham. That led to a diagnosis."

"Which was?"

"Klinefelter syndrome."

"Never heard of it."

"Most people haven't."

By then, I realized where the discussion was going. "And Klinefelter syndrome is genetic."

Mama nodded her head. "And because it's a genetic condition, the people in Birmingham wanted to screen Charlie and Alice to see if they carried it. That's when Alice told Charlie the truth."

"And that's what I heard."

"Some of it."

"It was worse than what I heard?"

"Charlie felt manipulated—which he was. And deceived—which he had been. And horrified by what had happened to her. So, it was a difficult situation all the way around."

"Is that why I never saw Frank?"

"Yes. Once the truth came out, Frank wasn't around at all."

"Did he know about Harold?"

"Yes. And it was terrible for him at first. Knowing his mother was his half-sister and his grandfather was his father."

"I can imagine."

"No, you can't." That was true. I couldn't really imagine it. And I didn't want to imagine it, either.

"I told Gladys I'd never seen him, but she said that was because we just didn't see him enough to remember him."

"No." Mama shook her head. "You didn't know him because he wasn't around."

"Where was he?"

"When he turned seventeen, he dropped out of school and went to live with his uncle." She gave a heavy sigh at the end of that sentence.

"His uncle—Charlie's brother?"

Mama shook her head again. "Alice's."

My mouth fell open in a look of shock. "Alice has a brother?"

"Yes."

"Harold Johnson had a son?"

Mama held up two fingers. "He had two of them."

That took a moment to settle in. "I never knew that," I finally said.

"I know."

"Where are they?"

"One of them is dead. The other one lives in New Orleans."

"What were their names?"

"The dead one was Albert. The one in New Orleans is Travis."

"What happened to Albert?"

Mama got up from her chair again and walked across the kitchen to a bread box that sat beside the stove. "The Johnsons owned a saw mill." She opened the bread box and took out a box of Krispy Kreme doughnuts, then started back to the table. "Albert was working over there. One day a board flew off the saw." She set the box in front of me and took a doughnut from it for herself. "Have one," she said, gesturing to the box. "They aren't too stale yet." She took a bite from the doughnut as she settled onto her chair. "The board hit him in the head. Killed him right there on the spot."

"How old was he?"

"Sixteen."

The fact that Albert died was tragic, but in the context of the Johnson family it seemed oddly fitting. I felt guilty for thinking that, but that's the thought that came to my mind. "That's sad," I said.

"Yes. It was." She took a sip of Coca-Cola.

I took a bite of doughnut to let a moment pass. Mama was right, they were stale, but not too much. "And the other one," I said. "Travis?"

"Yes."

"I've never heard of him, either."

"After high school, he went off to Tulane. I don't think he's ever been back here since."

"What does he do in New Orleans?"

"Retired now, I imagine. I think before that, he owned a bar or a restaurant. Some kind of business."

"He didn't want to take over the farm up here?"

"I doubt it," Mama replied. "But he didn't really have a chance to."

"Why not?"

"Travis found a boyfriend down there and—"

A startled look came over me. "A boyfriend?"

"Yeah," she sighed. "I thought that would be of interest to you."

"I bet that went over big with Harold."

Mama looked away again. "When Harold heard about it he cut Travis off from everything."

"Disinherited him?"

"Disinherited. Disowned. Dismissed. All of the above. Travis didn't even attend his father's funeral."

"That's as sad as the other one getting killed at the saw mill."

"Yes." Mama nodded her head slowly. "Sadder, maybe." She glanced in my direction. "It really is."

"Do the sisters have anything to do with him?"

"I don't know." Mama shrugged. "I don't think so. I've never heard them talk about him." She took another sip and held the bottle at an angle to see how much was left. "Is that about it for you or do I need to a get another bottle?"

A frown wrinkled my forehead. "About it?"

She looked at me with a disgruntled expression. "Does that cover everything you wanted to know?"

We were only a third of the way through, but I didn't tell her that. Instead, I ignored her question and said, "When I talked to Odell Norton, he told me he learned the details about Dell's funeral from Lucy. How did Lucy know about it?"

"You'd have to ask Lucy. But I suspect Alice told her."

"Alice?" My eyes opened wide as a sense of realization swept over me. "That must be it." Alice attended the funeral. She came with Frank. Charlie wasn't there. Alice was Lucy's sister. Surely she visited Lucy regularly.

Mama had a curious expression. "Why are you asking about that?"

"Odell knew some of the details about the funeral, but he wasn't there and when I asked how he knew about what went on, he said he learned about it from Lucy. But I saw everyone who was at the wake, the funeral service, the gathering afterward, and I'm positive Lucy wasn't there."

"No," Mama agreed. "She wasn't there. She was at the home. I went to see her that Friday. Gladys was with me. Neither of them went to Chicago that weekend." She took another sip from the bottle. "What else you got?"

My eyes darted away and I focused on the calendar that hung on the wall beside the refrigerator. "This is the worst part," I said.

When I looked back at her, the expression on Mama's face seemed cold and her eyes had that steely tension that meant trouble was coming. I knew right then that she knew what I was going to ask. "You've gone pretty deep into this already," she said. There was a hint of anger in her voice. "Aren't you comfortable yet?"

"Harold got Lucy pregnant," I said. "And he had his way with Gladys, too."

"And?"

"You were at the house when he was doing those things with Gladys."

"And?"

My eyes focused on hers. "Did Harold Johnson do anything like that with you?"

Mama took a gulp from the bottle and set it on the table. "I told you before, nothing ever happened with that."

"That's what you said, but—"

"He cornered me one day in the pantry," she said, interrupting. "Blocked my way to the door so I couldn't get out. I could tell by the look on his face what he was interested in and I was scared. But there was no way I was giving him what he wanted without a fight. I grabbed a bottle of syrup from the shelf—one of those tall ones made of glass. I held it by the neck to use it as a club and I meant to hit him upside the head as hard as I could. He started toward me and just as I was about to hit him, Gladys appeared in the doorway behind him. She grabbed him by the belt and pulled him into the hall. Said, 'Come with me, old man,' and took him to a bedroom that was down by the kitchen. While she had him occupied, I ran out the front door and I never went back over there again."

"Did you tell Daddy?"

"No." She shook her head from side to side, her eyes looking at the tabletop the whole time. Then she paused and looked up at me. "I didn't tell your father. But your grandfather found out."

I raised an eyebrow in response. "How did he find out about that?"

"He was in the driveway when I ran out of the house."

"At the Johnson's?"

"Yes."

"Why was he there?"

"I don't know. He was friends with Harold. All of that Knights of the White Camellia crap. And they did business with each other, buying and selling and trading."

"What did you tell him?"

"Nothing right then. I went right past him, got in the car, and headed to the house." Once again her gaze fell to the tabletop. "But a few days later he came over to see me and said Harold was asking about me. Your grandfather wanted to know what happened. So, I told him."

"What did he say after that?"

"Nothing." She looked up at me. "Not a word. Just walked out to his pickup and drove away."

"Did he say something later?"

"No. Not a word that day. Not a word the next. Not a word ever. Never brought it up again."

"That's strange."

"Yeah." She nodded. "I thought so, too."

She didn't look at me and once again I had the feeling she wasn't telling me everything. "You look like there's more to it than that. What else is there?" I had an insistent tone.

"When Harold Johnson died, some folks around here thought

your grandfather killed him."

"That was several years later, though. Right? He died sometime after Lucy came back."

"Yes. But when I heard Harold was dead, that was the first thing I thought about, too."

"Because of what he did to you?"

"And Gladys."

A puzzled look came over me. "Grandpaw knew about Gladys?"

"After he talked to me that day, he went to see Gladys. I didn't find out about that until after Harold died. She and I were talking and she told me your grandfather came to see her and he asked about the things Harold was doing to her. I didn't tell him about Gladys and Harold and don't know how he knew there was anything between her and him."

"You didn't tell him about Harold and Gladys?"

"No."

"Why not?"

"He didn't ask and I didn't think about it. But when he talked to Gladys, she told him what Harold had been doing to her."

"He must have thought something was happening."

"I think he already suspected what happened with Alice. But he might have gone to see Gladys because he knew she was there that day when Harold tried something with me. Maybe he just wanted to verify what I had said."

"Why would Grandpaw kill Harold over that? I mean, these guys killed people because of the color of their skin. Would they kill a man because he had sex with a woman other than his wife?"

"She was his own daughter," Mama blurted.

"I know."

Mama changed positions and leaned against the table. "Your grandfather believed things like that weren't natural. There was a line and that kind of thing was over it."

"Rather strange mixture of morality."

"He believed in the old way."

Once again, I was puzzled. "The old way?"

"Self-help justice," she said.

"Vigilante."

"It was more than that," she explained. "Back then, your grandfather and Harold Johnson had the county divided between them. They thought of themselves as lords of the manor. A position they inherited from their fathers. This kind of thing had been going on for a long time between the Johnsons and the Thomases."

"Plantation owners."

She nodded. "Something like that. To them, people like the sheriff and the courts were for everyone else. For the weak. He used to say, 'Strong men take care of themselves. And they look after their own.'"

"That doesn't sound like any old way I ever heard of."

"You'd have to go back pretty far."

"But Harold didn't die until sometime after I was in school."

"Yeah."

"Seems like a long time for Grandpaw to wait to do something about the things you told him."

"It was a few years," she acknowledged. "Something else might have happened and all of it just built up. And they might have killed him because they thought he was going to cooperate with the FBI."

"In their investigation of the Camellias?"

"Yes. People said Harold was supposed to be the next one to get arrested and one or two said they thought he was thinking about talking." She looked me in the eye. "Your grandfather would have never allowed Harold to talk to the FBI. He knew way too much."

We had talked about most of the things that were on my mind but I sat there a moment taking inventory just to make sure. However, when I didn't speak right up with another question, Mama took the opportunity to stand. "I think that's about enough for today," she said. "You can think about what I told you and if you come up with something else to ask me about, I might give you an answer." She could be ornery when she'd had enough so I stood, too, and leaned over the table to give her a peck on the cheek, then started toward the door. She followed after me and as I opened it she said, "I think you should get happy right where you are now and stop bothering yourself with all of this."

"Everyone keeps telling me that," I said.

"Maybe you should listen to them." She meant well but hearing that from her only made me wonder what else there was that I didn't know about my past.

# 12

After talking to Mama, I had almost reached a comfortable place with Dell. Most of what I knew about him, either from experience or from talking with others, had found a place in my understanding of him and of myself. Only one or two things remained unresolved.

Dell came from a rough start and lived his childhood among rough people, which made the person he'd become all the more remarkable. That much of what I'd learned had found a place in my understanding of him and of us. The part that was unresolved lay on the other side of the relationship—my side. That was the part I still struggled with. Not about what my relationship with Dell meant to me or said about me when we were young and in school, but what it meant and what it said about me now.

Most of what there was to know about Dell's life was known to my mother and father and to the people of Tenaca of their generation—people whom I was with every day, yet who kept the truth from me. To be fair, people of my parent's generation—and especially the generation of my grandparents—came of age at a difficult time in the South. A horrible time, actually. For my grandfather and Harold Johnson, powerful institutions of the Old South had been outlawed, but only just. Barely one generation removed from the plantation era, they remained trapped by its remnants and devoted to its mores. Attempting to impose the views of that bygone society on an unfolding age bent toward change made Grandpaw and Harold hard, harsh, and blind to the immorality they embraced.

With my father and mother's generation, the institutions of the past were gone as was much of the overt dedication to its values, but the influences of the past remained noticeably present. A dark past, indelibly ingrained in the hearts and minds of people who physically experienced nothing of what the past had been like and who had found a way, whether comfortable or not, to live in what the South was becoming.

Yet in spite of all that had happened—Harold and Alice, Harold and Gladys, Harold and his wife, Lucy and Odell, Travis and his life in New Orleans. Regardless of the fact that they sat every Sunday in a church that taught a sexually based morality—that sex of any kind was bad and that anyone engaged in a same-sex relationship was bound for hell straight away. Even with all of that, no one ever told me to stay away from Dell. As far as I know, they never told him to stay away from me, either. And although the bullies in our high school harassed many of our classmates, they never said a word to us. Nor did I ever notice a derisive look from a teacher, store clerk, or gas station attendant when Dell and I were together.

When I visited with Dell at his parents' house, Alice Briggers was as nice to me as anyone could have been. Likewise, Dell often came to our house and my mother went out of her way to dote on him. I now knew my father worried that we were gay, but in all that time he never mentioned those concerns to me or told me to stop seeing him. More than that, Lucy—Dell's mother and as much a product of Tenaca as the rest of us—hoped we would be together.

For the remainder of the week, those thoughts wallowed around in my mind and by Friday I had decided there was one more person I needed to talk to. It would be difficult, but I felt I had to do it. Mama was right—I couldn't talk to Alice, though I wondered every day what she would have to say. And I didn't want to talk to Charlie. In spite of having lived in Tenaca my entire life and being friends with Dell and spending the night at their house on numerous occasions, I hadn't said more than five words to Charlie Briggers and I wasn't interested in changing that now.

The one last person I decided to talk to, the person whom I thought might help me close this up, was the person I saw first—Jenny Johnson Smith—Mrs. Smith at the library. She'd been curt and rude to me the first time around, which made it difficult to go back to her one more time, but I was certain she could bring my search for an understanding about Dell to a conclusion and decided the risk of being humiliated again was a risk I would have to take.

When Lucy and Dell got into trouble in Valdosta, Jenny was the one who went to get them. Harold was still alive then and she knew how he felt about Lucy. She knew what had happened with her father and Alice. Probably knew what was happening at the time with Gladys. Yet knowing all of that, and knowing how her father would likely react, she did what needed to be done. She did the right thing. That suggested to me that she had a bigger view of things than I had experienced or understood before and although things hadn't ended well between us with our first encounter, I thought she might be the one to get me to where I wanted to go on the topic.

On Friday afternoon, I stopped at the library on my way home. As before, Mrs. Smith was at the circulation desk when I entered. "Never thought I would see you in here again," she said.

"Yes, ma'am."

"You didn't like the way I talked to you before."

"No, ma'am. I didn't."

"Is that why you came back?"

"No."

"Still more questions?"

"Yes."

A stool stood behind her and she backed up to prop against it. "What is it this time?"

"When I came home from Dell's funeral I came home with some questions about him. To find answers to those questions, I started with you. Then talked to Gladys Haywood. I talked to your sister Lucy Johnson. My mother. My father. And Odell Norton."

Her eyes brightened at the mention of Odell's name. "You found him?" she asked.

"Yes, ma'am."

"In Florida?"

"Apalachicola," I said.

"Someone said he was down there. I wasn't sure he was still

alive."

"He's alive."

A wisp of a smile came to her. "Think he would talk to me?"

I smiled back at her. "He thinks you hate him."

She frowned. "I don't hate him."

"He thinks you all hate him."

She looked puzzled. "All?"

"You and your sisters."

"Lucy doesn't hate him."

"No," I admitted. "She doesn't."

"The only one still aggravated at him is Alice, but that's her own fault."

"Her own fault?"

"She thought Odell had taken advantage of Lucy and refused to accept that Lucy made her own choices about Odell."

"To get away from your father?"

Her eyes darted away. "That was part of it."

"Part of it?"

"She was Lucy. Doing things like that was just who she was. She'd been hurt by the things our father did to her, but no one else ever took advantage of her. That wasn't what she was like."

We were talking about a sensitive subject and I hesitated a moment, unsure how far to take the conversation, but this had been a difficult question for me, too, and I wanted answers, so I pressed on. "I know about Alice and Frank." My voice was softer and I tried to say the words with kindness.

Mrs. Smith moved from the stool and stepped up to the desk. "I'm sure you do," she said. As she spoke, her fingers were busy rearranging the pencils in a pencil holder that sat nearby.

"Did your father have his way with Lucy?"

She glared at me. "This is none of your business, young man." A smile tried to form on my face but I forced it back. No one had referred to me as a young man in a long time.

"Did he do that with you?"

"You can stop right there," she snapped. "This is—"

"No." I snapped back so sharply it startled her. "It is my business."

"What makes you think our lives are yours to plunder?"

Anger rose inside me—anger that I had suppressed since the funeral, since hearing about Harold and Grandpaw and Steve and all that I had missed, since realizing what I could have had with Dell. Standing there at the circulation desk, with her talking down to me again, it suddenly came pouring out. "I began this quest to find out about Dell because I realized that in spite of all I had experienced with him, things happened around me when I was a boy that I was completely unaware of."

My voice was too loud for a library but I didn't care and I kept going. "As I dug deeper, I realized that the reason I didn't know about many of those things was because the people around me intentionally kept them from me. You, Alice, Charlie, Gladys, my mother, my father, your father, my grandfather."

The words came rapidly and I jabbed at the air with my finger while I spoke. "All of you kept the truth from me. All of you intentionally let me live in a world that did not exist. That never existed. And now I want to know about it. I realize some of this is painful to talk about but much of it is pain that has built up through decades of hiding. Hiding the things that really happened and hiding the truth about the people who were involved. So I'm asking again, did your father have his way with Lucy?"

Tears filled her eyes and she glanced down at the desktop. "Yes," she whispered.

"And that's the reason she went all the way to Arkansas to go to school?"

"Yes."

"And Albert?"

She sagged back onto the stool and folded her arms across her midriff. "Albert died trying to save her," she sobbed.

As it had happened so many times before, a frown wrinkled my forehead. "Trying to save Lucy?"

Tears rolled down Mrs. Smith's cheeks and her lips trembled.

She put her hand to her mouth and nodded. It was an awkward moment and for once I kept quiet and waited. I wanted to hear what happened and I didn't want to let her escape from telling it. Finally, she moved her hand away. "Daddy had Lucy out in the workshop," she said. "Albert walked in on them and realized what Daddy was trying to do. He forced his way between them and Daddy hit him. Hit him so hard he knocked Albert to the floor. When Albert tried to get up, Daddy hit him in the head with a length of two-by-four."

"And that's what killed him?"

"Yes," she sobbed.

"My mother told me—"

She cleared her throat and wiped her eyes with her fingers. "Your mother told you Albert died at the saw mill," she said, cutting me off. "Which is the story we told everyone. But that was a lie, too. Just like all the rest of it. The stories we told about Alice, Lucy, Mama, Albert. All of it was a lie."

"Did your father ever try that with you?"

She shook her head. "He never got to me."

"Why not?"

"Because I married and moved out of the house."

"When did it start with your father?"

"The things he did with my sisters didn't start until he and Mother found out about Travis."

"Your brother in New Orleans."

She nodded. "Something in Daddy snapped when he found out about that. He was always harsh and more than a little cruel, but after he found out about Travis' first boyfriend, he was different. Terribly different." She wiped her eyes and looked at me. "I'm sorry. Sorry for the way things turned out. Sorry you felt deceived. I think people acted that way because they thought they were being kind."

"Kind?"

"Everyone knew about Dell's past. All of the adults did. They all knew about your grandfather and my father. And all of them— except for Lucy, maybe—thought that two boys being together as a couple wasn't right. But you both were so devoted to each other. So kind. So loyal. So trusting with each other. And after all that Dell had been through." She smiled at me with a kindness I had never seen before. "And besides that, you were ours."

"Ours?"

"You grew up here. You were a product of this town and the people who live here. You were one of us. And yes, most people around here have ideas about how life should be lived, but most of them realize that those are ideas in the abstract. They wouldn't say it that way but that's what they mean. Should two men be together as a couple? No. Then what about Dell and Billy? Oh, that's just Dell and Billy. We know them. They aren't a problem."

"You really think that's what it was?"

"Yes. At its best. At our best. That's what it was."

The way she described my past made it seem as though the entire town knew me far better than I had ever known myself and that they cared for me with a collective benevolence that bordered on myth, but I didn't want to argue with her. Instead, I focused on the things I'd come there to talk about. "Why doesn't Travis come around?" I asked.

"Travis' experience with Tenaca and Daddy and all of that was different from ours."

"Different?"

"Yes. He was the oldest of us and the one closest in time to the way things were when Daddy was a boy. He was supposed to take over after Daddy, but he was never like Daddy or your grandfather or any of those men. I don't think he ever saw himself living as they lived, even when he was a little boy."

"Why?"

"He grew up and was gone from the house by the time we entered high school, so I didn't know him that well, but I think he always struggled with who he was and what this place was like back then and just never saw himself finding a place here."

"I never knew him."

"Most people around here don't know anything about him now. But when you and Dell were young, they did. And in some ways, I think what happened with Daddy and Travis—and everything that followed after that—showed people just how wrong the old way was. And helped them realize they didn't want to repeat it with you and Dell."

Maybe she was right. Maybe that's why people treated us the way they did. It was a little hard for me to believe, but it made for a nice ending, even if it was a glorified version of what really happened. Even if it was merely one more Johnson story meant to obfuscate the truth. Regardless, there was no point in trying to disabuse her of it and after a moment to think, I responded. "Somewhere along the way, Dell must have come to the realization that he was gay—a realization I never considered, but he must have."

She smiled again. "Yes. He did."

"Gladys Haywood says he always knew he was gay and that Lucy did, too. Was there ever a time when Dell said to you and your sisters, 'Hey folks, I'm gay?'"

"You mean like coming out, the way people talk about it now?"

"Yes."

"Not like you read in the magazines or on the internet."

"Then what was it?" I wanted to ask if he ever referred to us as a couple. As lovers. But I still couldn't bring myself to talk about our relationship that way, which once again left me feeling like I had betrayed him.

"We had one conversation on the topic," she said. "That's all. But it was just me and Dell. It wasn't like a big announcement or anything."

"What did he say?"

"Dell found out about Travis and he came to see me about him. I think he'd come to the conclusion by then that he was gay and talking about Travis was a convenient excuse to talk about the subject. But it wasn't an announcement or anything. And he never admitted anything to me directly about his own life."

"When was that?"

"About that time y'all did that play with Mrs. Miller."

"The play." A smile pushed up my cheeks. "That was fun."

"People still talk about that sometimes."

"Yes," I said. "They do."

"Dell was really excited about acting in that play and in talking about it with him, Lucy mentioned that Travis had appeared in a Tennessee Williams play in New Orleans. He wanted to talk about that, but I think he wanted to know about Travis' lifestyle, too."

"He knew that about Travis?"

"When Travis was mentioned there was an exchange of knowing looks," She explained. "He wouldn't let the matter drop until we told him. We talked about that and what it meant and somewhere in our discussion he mentioned that you were his friend and he could never imagine being without you, but that's as close as he came to saying he was gay."

A lump formed in my throat and I had to swallow hard to keep from crying. "We never talked about that, either. We just enjoyed each other."

"That's the way it's supposed to be." She glanced at her watch. "It's time for me to close up." She pointed down the aisle past a stack of books. "Walk down to the wall and flip that light switch for me." The tone in her voice indicated we'd reached the end of our conversation, so I turned in the direction she pointed and made my way past the stacks of books, feeling all the while like a high school volunteer.

The switch for the lights in that section of the building was located next to a window and as I reached for it my eyes fell on a sidewalk that ran along that end of the building below the window. As I mentioned before, when I was in the seventh grade Daddy won the contract to renovate the library. Pouring the sidewalk that ran past the window was one of the last things he and his crew did on the project. Dell and I came by after school to watch and Daddy let us create and imprint of our hands in the wet concrete. As I glanced out the window I saw our prints still in the concrete and the tears I'd choked back earlier returned only this time, instead of holding them back, I let them tumble down my cheeks.

Dell was gone and he wasn't coming back and there wasn't anything I could do about that. The things I had learned about him and about us had taken me to a place that was as comfortable as I could get. We could have been together once, if I had paid attention. If I had understood the seriousness of his offer and moved to Chicago with him. But that moment had passed. And while the nature of our relationship might have defined us if I had gone with him, it no longer did. I loved Babs with all my heart—not the way I loved Dell, but then, I didn't love him the way I loved her, either. Whatever I might have been in the past, and whatever I might have become if I had made different choices, I was no longer that person. I wasn't with Dell now and I never would be again, not like that, not physically. Which meant there was nothing left to do except say goodbye and I had an idea of how to do that.

# *13*

Saturday mornings were normally reserved for yard work but that Saturday I made an excuse for going to the service station to fill one of the gas cans we used for the lawnmower. With the gas already in the tank on the mower and the little bit that remained in the can, I could have mowed the yard but I had someplace else I wanted to go. Filling the gas can offered a convenient way of getting there without having to tell Babs the rest of it. I put the can in the back of the truck and drove over to the Texaco station near the high school.

Filling the gas can didn't take long but as I was moving it from the ground to the bed of the truck, a car pulled up beside me. It came to a stop and the passenger door opened, then a young girl stepped out. "Excuse me," she called from the far side of the car.

At first I didn't recognize her but then I realized she was Jenny Smith's granddaughter. "Yes, ma'am," I replied. "What could I do for you?"

"Aunt Alice was wondering if you could come by the house this morning."

I glanced inside the car and saw Alice Briggers sitting in the backseat. She gave me a wave and I waved back, then looked over at the girl. "Sure," I said. "Are you going home now?"

"Yes, sir."

"Okay," I replied. "I'll be over there in a few minutes."

The girl returned to the car and they drove off and as I reached for the door handle to open the door to the truck I wondered why Alice Briggers would want to talk to me, but it seemed like a good thing. If she invited me to her house, I might have an opportunity to ask her a few questions and even though I had learned all I needed to learn, one more round of conversation about Dell couldn't hurt.

And besides, going to her house was on the way to where I'd wanted to go that morning when I made up that excuse about filling the gas can.

The Briggers lived on Jasper Road. From the Texaco station it took all of five minutes to drive over there. Alice was seated in a rocking chair on the side porch when I turned into the driveway. I parked the truck near the steps and got out.

"Haven't seen you since the funeral." She was a little older than my mother but not as old as Gladys and when she spoke she had that aged tone in her voice that people get when they know they're old but they like it.

"No, ma'am," I replied. "We've been busy."

"Yeah," she said with a chuckle. "That's what I hear. At least that you've been busy."

I smiled up at her. "You've been talking to your sisters about me."

"Among others," she said. "Come up here and have a seat." She gestured with her hand. "No point in you standing down there in the yard."

The steps were four treads high with a handrail on each side. I grasped the rail on the right, made my way up to the porch, and dropped onto a rocker next to her. That's when I noticed the padded envelope resting on her lap.

"This came from Steve." She handed the envelope to me and I took it. "There was a note inside that said it was for you," she continued. "He asked me to see that you got it."

The envelope had been opened on one end and I could see it held a framed photograph. I slid the picture carefully from the envelope, but even before I had it all the way out I knew it was the photograph of Dell and me behind Grandpaw's barn. A lump formed in my throat but I swallowed hard and did my best to keep from crying.

A note taped to the front of the picture read, "Billy. This was the picture from Dell's desk at his office. I'm sure he would want you to have it." Tears I'd tried to contain filled my eyes.

Alice rocked her chair gently. "Dell always said you were his best friend in the whole world."

I cleared my throat and responded. "That's what I said about him."

"You gave him a wonderful gift."

"What was that?"

She looked over at me. "The gift of never asking a single question about his life."

"I didn't realize until his funeral how little I knew of him, or that the stories he used to tell me about his childhood weren't actually true."

She smiled. "The one about the birds waking him up in the morning?"

"Yes. And his father worked on nuclear submarines for the navy."

"And his mother was a friend of Tallulah Bankhead."

"That one about the birds. I wanted that one to be true."

She chuckled. "He made up those stories before he knew you would accept him just the way he was."

"Did he know about all the things that happened to you and your sisters and his grandmother?"

"And him," she added. "Yes. And he knew Daddy and Odell didn't want to have anything to do with him."

A sense of sadness came over me. "That must have been difficult for him."

"He had an awful time with it at first. For a long time he wanted to live with Lucy at the home and he tried to. Ran away two or three times before I took him to your birthday party."

"I remember that day. And the cowboy outfit he wore."

"And the one he gave to you."

"Those hats were so big. I think we looked like mushrooms walking around in the yard."

"Y'all wore them all day that day, then you came over here the next day and y'all played together and he wanted to go live with you."

"I didn't know that."

"Begged me several times to let him."

"I still have the pistols from that cowboy outfit. They're in a trunk in the bedroom."

Alice reached over and patted my leg. "You were the best thing that ever happened to him."

Tears filled my eyes and this time I couldn't stop them. "No," I sobbed. "He was the best thing that happened to me." I stared out at the yard and the pickup truck parked on the driveway and let the tears come. Alice didn't say anything and we just sat there, both of us rocking and thinking and not talking for a good long while.

Finally, I wiped my face with my hands and took a deep breath to calm myself. "So, where did Mr. Briggers work if it wasn't on a nuclear submarine?"

"Construction," she replied.

"Construction," I repeated. It made sense. Most people who worked that way worked on jobs that kept them away from home for extended periods of time.

"He was a welder for a construction company," Alice continued. "Worked all over. Was gone most of the time."

That brought a smile to my face. "And the part about Tallulah Bankhead?"

"She and I were acquainted, though not very well. She was born in Huntsville but grew up over at Jasper and I knew her back then, before Hollywood and all the rest. Daddy had dealings with the Bankhead brothers. Your grandfather, too."

"That Dell," I said with a shake of my head. "He had an imagination."

"Yes, he did."

"Why didn't he just tell us the truth? That his father was a famous novelist?"

"Not enough flair, I suppose. And if he told you the truth about Odell Norton, he'd have to tell you the rest of it, too. And that was too much."

"So he remade the world into something he could handle."

"Yes. Particularly before you all became good friends. But after that, you transformed the real world in such a way that he didn't need all of that. He kept telling tales for entertainment, but he didn't need the tales to survive after you came along. You saved him."

Tears wanted to come again but I choked them back. "I've been thinking all of my life that he saved me."

She patted my leg again. "That's the way it's supposed to be. Friends rescue each other."

Alice and I talked a while longer, but I didn't ask her any more of the questions I'd asked everyone else. There wasn't any reason to. All of the angst I'd felt at the funeral and on the way home from Chicago—and as the discoveries unfolded in the days that followed—melted away right there on the side porch. A sense of peace swept over me and I knew I could say goodbye to Dell without any regret that I had missed an opportunity or let something pass by that I should have held onto. Only one regret remained and that was simply the regret that he wasn't alive anymore. Not the regret of blame that I had felt before.

An hour later, I stepped from Alice's porch, returned to the pickup truck, and headed down the driveway to the road. Instead of turning east toward home, though, I turned west and rode out to the farm that once had belong to my grandfather's, which was the place I wanted to go to when I left the house with the gas can. Grandpaw's farm. The same place where Mama took the picture of Dell and me—the same photo that was on the desk at his house, on the dresser in Lucy's room, and now lay beside me on the seat of the truck.

Grandpaw's house was still there. Daddy owned it now and he kept it painted and clean and from time to time rented it out but right then no one lived there. It looked just as it always had when I was a boy—the same as it had looked on the day that picture was taken—with white clapboard siding, a swing on the porch, and two huge flowerpots at the base of the steps. The pots came from a store in Collinsville. Grandmaw bought them when she was a young newlywed.

The driveway at Grandpaw's was paved with gravel and ended near the side door to the house where the gravel ran out into the grass and disappeared. I stopped the truck there, got out, and made my way across the yard to a gate that opened into the pasture. The barn was fifty yards beyond. When Grandpaw was alive, the driveway went all the way to the barn but when Daddy started renting the house he replanted the yard as a way of eliminating the temptation for tenants to use the barn. "They're renting the house," he said. "They don't get the barn with it."

Weeds around the barn were knee high and as I tromped through them I realized we needed to bring a tractor over there to mow it. With a little effort, though, I made my way toward the back and as I came around the corner, I saw the spot in front of the barn's rear doors. The place where the picture had been taken when we went fishing in the pond. The place where we later had a moment and I gave Dell a kiss. The place where we... My thoughts faded away as I began to cry, just as I had the day before when I saw our handprints on the sidewalk and as I had earlier while sitting on Alice Briggers' side porch.

After a moment, though, the thoughts of Dell and me together returned and a warm sensation came over me. Not the warmth of passion but the warmth of acceptance, of belonging, of being me that I'd experienced when I was with Dell and like I had experienced that Saturday when I was mowing the lawn and didn't realize I was slinging gravel everywhere.

I stood there basking in that moment, letting it wash over me and fill me, then I shoved my hands in the pockets of my jeans and said, "Dell, I love you. I have always loved you. From the day we met until now, there never was a time I didn't love you. And if you were here right now I would kiss you again and tell you the same thing in person."

All at once I was transported in my mind to the day Dell told me he was leaving for Chicago. We were having lunch at a small café near the college campus and he told me about the offer. "The money is good enough," he said, "that I can rent a place without any help." He smiled at me. "You want to come up there with me?"

If I had known how Dell felt, I would have gone off with him to

Chicago. I would have said yes that afternoon and we would have been together all this time. But I didn't realize it was a proposal. I thought it was a friend asking another friend to join him because he was afraid of leaving his life behind. Dell wasn't scared of leaving Tenaca behind. He was afraid of leaving me behind. But in that same instance I realized that if I had done that, I wouldn't have Babs or our children. I wouldn't have the life I had or the friends or any of it and just as suddenly as I had been overwhelmed with sadness before when I thought of Dell, I was overwhelmed with joy and gladness at the thought of Babs. My life, I realized, had turned out well. Not the way it would have been if I had made a different decision that day in the café when he told me about Chicago, but equally as rich and wonderful as the life I thought I had missed.

Sometime later I checked my watch and realized I'd been gone from the house quite a long time. Babs would be wondering where I was and I didn't have my cell phone with me to call her. So I glanced around one last time, smiled again at the thought of Dell and me running across the pasture, then turned away and started back to the truck.

On the way home from the farm I continued to think about Dell and Babs and all that had happened in my life. The quest I'd been on since the funeral was helpful to me. Learning all that I had not known about my past helped me understand myself. Thinking about what might have been if I'd made different choices in the past was instructive for me, too. All of it helped me understand things better, but it didn't really change much. Not really.

Sexuality, I'd learned, isn't as fixed and set as some people like to think. Being gay isn't always a choice and, as Gladys pointed out, it's certainly not something you catch or put on. Who we are in every respect is malleable and subject to an array of influences, not the least of which is the other people involved. I found myself in Babs. I could have just as easily found myself in Dell, and did for a long time. But when I let him go to Chicago without me, I made a choice that turned my life in a different direction. I didn't realize it at the time, but it did.

Babs was in the college bookstore the first time I saw her. The term was over and students were arriving for summer school. Dell and I had graduated and Babs had just arrived on campus as an incoming freshman. My heart skipped a beat when I saw her. It still does every day. And as I thought about that moment I remembered she was waiting for me at the house so I pressed the gas pedal a little firmer.

When I arrived at home, Babs was in the kitchen preparing lunch. She glanced at me as I entered the room. "Did you get lost?"

"No," I replied as I moved to the sink to wash my hands.

"Took a long time just to get gas for the mower."

"Yeah."

"You gonna tell me where you went?"

"I went to see Alice Briggers," I replied.

"What for?" She gave me a frown. "I thought you weren't going to talk to her."

"She asked me to stop by."

"Oh?"

"She gave me this." I had the picture tucked under my arm and I handed it to her.

A grin broke over her face. "This is you and Dell," she said.

"At the farm. We'd been fishing that day."

"You were so young," she said, still staring at photograph.

"I went out there after I talked to Alice."

"To the farm?"

"Yeah."

"What for?"

"To think."

"About what?"

"About how glad I am to be with you." I leaned close and kissed her. She kissed me back and then pushed me gently away. "Come on." She picked up two plates from the counter and started toward the kitchen table. "I made those sandwiches you like."

"Turkey with Swiss and whatever that sauce was?"

"With lettuce and tomato and bread from the bakery on Morris Street."

"You know what I like."

She smiled at me. "Time for that later, dear. Let's eat and then you can mow the lawn."

By then we were seated at the table and I looked over at her. "Rather late to do that now, isn't it?"

"It's only noon." Her foot rubbed against my ankle. "You can get out there by three and still be finished before dark." She had a knowing smile and we both giggled.

Trying to think about a physical relationship with Dell was more than I could do. At that point in my life, the imagery just didn't work for me, so while we ate I changed that fantasy to a different one and began to think what it might have been like if I met Babs, dated her a while, and sixth months or so into our relationship, I found out she really was a man. It was a strange fantasy, but I wanted to know if my relationship with her would have changed. Six months into our relationship was about the time she and I were close enough, under the right circumstances, to know the answer to that part of the gender question without asking. What if I—

Babs kicked me under the table. "What are you doing?" she asked.

I glanced up at her and did my best to appear nonchalant. "What do you mean?"

"You have that look on your face."

"What look?"

She had a strange smile. "That look."

"Oh."

"Yeah," she said with a nod. "So what were you thinking?"

There was no way I was going to tell her what I was thinking. "I was just remembering the first time I kissed you," I replied. She knew from the tone of my voice that I was making up an answer and I expected her to give me a sassy comeback, but instead she scooted her chair away from the table and stood, then offered me her hand. "To hell with lunch," she said. "Come on."

"What for?"

She grabbed my hand and gave it a tug. "Come with me to the bedroom and find out."

And that's when I knew for certain the answer to the questions I'd been asking myself since the funeral. Yes, I could have loved Dell with all that might imply, but that moment was gone. Now there was only Babs. And whatever and whoever she was, she was more than enough for me.

# Hornwallace Korlinheiser

## *A Short Story*

Sunlight shining through the window of the day room felt warm against my skin and I sat there, basking in its rays, all the while staring at my hand and wondering when I would move it again. Not that I couldn't move it—I possessed all the physical capacity necessary to lift my hand from the table and do with it as I pleased. I wondered not if I could but rather when I would. Would it be now? Or now? Or would it be later?

And if I lifted my hand, what might prompt me to do so? Perhaps I might get hungry and decide to have a snack. Then I would lift it. Or, I might cease thinking of the topic altogether and simply stand to stretch. But as I stared at my hand, my thoughts moved beyond the obvious and beneath the external to focus on the unstated and understated internal. Perhaps I might, by some random act of my mind set in motion by causes and effects from long ago and imperceptible to me now, decide that a particular moment was the right one. Almost as a matter of happenstance. Perhaps. Or perhaps I might not. Perhaps I might—

"Mr. Dornblat." A familiar voice interrupted my thoughts.

Having heard that voice many times, I recognized it immediately, but it always accompanied an unwelcome intrusion, as it did right then, so I ignored it and continued to focus on my hand and the question I posed to myself of when I might lift it from the tabletop. The proposition was an odd one, for certain. Intriguingly circular in nature, though—me forming the question for myself and waiting to be surprised by the answer I might provide. Only now, with the familiar voice calling to me, I found the suggestion of a new option to consider. Perhaps I might lift my hand from the table to slap the person who spoke, particularly one who referred to me by that infernal name.

"Mr. Dornblat," the voice repeated, in spite of my choice to ignore it. "Time to return to your room."

Mr. Dornblat…

For as long as I can remember, people have called me Mr. Dornblat, or some version of it—often simply Mister. When I was a boy, even my father's friends called me Mr. Dornblat. Never Steven, which was the name my parents gave me when I was born. Just, Mr. Dornblat. And they looked intimidated when they said it, as if they knew something disturbing about me and approached me with suspicion. One or two of them even looked afraid. Especially Mr. Daniels … and that guy from the cabinet shop whom I could never stand to be around and whose name, consequently, I chose never to remember.

The reaction of my father's friends was a curious thing for me. At once both troubling and mysterious, which only served to encourage my imagination and at a very young age I began fabricating stories in my mind to account for their awkwardness. Rather quickly, I convinced myself that I had been an axe-wielding toddler and had hacked my father to pieces—my biological father—and that the man they all knew as my father was merely a stand-in. A look-alike appointed by the authorities to cover for my missing father in order to preserve the illusion to society and themselves that my family and I were normal. That the situation was normal. That nothing untoward ever happened. Especially not with me. So as to preserve the even greater illusion that nothing awful ever involved children. Or the more preposterous myth that they—the adults—were normal, too. It was, after all, the 1950s. A time when everyone and everything was perfectly perfect.

Throughout my childhood, as I continued to fantasize about the nature of the responses I received from my father's friends, my thoughts turned in a different direction and I came to imagine that Father—not being my actual father but the appointed stand-in who looked after me—must have done something terribly wrong and was being punished by being forced to live in close proximity to me, the axe-wielding toddler. And of course, I began to imagine what his transgressions might have been, which took my mind deeper and deeper into the convoluted morass that even then I knew lay at the bottom of my soul.

Imagining all of that was a sordid affair that took place solely within the confines of my mind and an endeavor to which I devoted enormous amounts of time and energy, but it could have been easily avoided if they had merely called me by my name. My proper name. The name my parents had given me at birth. But none of them did. Even my father called me Mister—Little Mister, he used to say when I was a child. Not Steven, or Steve, or even, "Hey, you." I never understood why he and Mother went to the trouble of naming me, then never bothered to use the name.

After enduring the names everyone else gave me, and after noticing that my parents failed to use the name they had officially bestowed upon me, I decided to choose a name for myself, one that I liked, and after some thought settled upon the name Hornwallace Korlinheiser. By then I was in second grade and my classmates thought it was a stupid name. Several of them showed no hesitancy in telling me so to my face, but it was the name I liked and when they persisted in refusing to call me Steve, I became equally obstinate in demanding they call me Hornwallace.

For almost three weeks, I refused to answer the teacher when she addressed me as Steven—it was too late for that name. I had moved on. As a result of my obstinate attitude, I was sent to the principal's office. An event that occurred every day. But I refused to address the principal, too, which he found amusing.

I refused to talk to my friends for the same reason and was the object of their ridicule, especially in the cafeteria where they threw things at me and called me all manner of names, many of them I could not even repeat to Mother, the one person to whom I could tell everything. And then, Benny Smith tried to eat carrots from my plate. Just once, though, because I doused him with a carton of milk. His parents were at work, which meant they couldn't bring him fresh clothes and he was forced to wear a soured shirt the remainder of the day. I, on the other hand, received an afternoon at home with the housekeeper, free to do as I pleased.

The following day, Father accompanied me to the principal's office and at last I explained the issue about my name, thinking he would help me rectify the situation. Still, it made no difference. No one ever called me Hornwallace and finally I relented and went in the opposite direction, responding to whatever name anyone used. To my surprise, they began calling me Mister, just like my father, which even now is the way I am known by those from earlier in my life who think they are my friends. In truth, I have very few friends. Only acquaintances. A long list of acquaintances. And all of them call me Mister. Everyone except the nurses and orderlies here at Broadmoor where I reside.

The man who spoke to me that day as I sat by the window staring at the back of my hand—the orderly behind the voice—thinks he is my friend, though he persists in calling me Mr. Dornblat, even after a thousand corrections. That's why I call him Homer, though he tells me his name is something else. He doesn't like Homer any more than I like Mr. Dornblat, which makes us even I suppose.

One thing about Homer that I do like is the pants he wears. They're white, like all the other orderlies, but his are tailored nicely with the hem of the legs just touching the tops of his shoes and the seat of his pants fitting snugly across the cheeks of his butt. Not too tight but not baggy like all the other orderlies. He has a nicely rounded butt, too, and evenly proportioned on each side, though you can't really say that to anyone. At least not from one man to another. Start talking to a straight man about a man's butt and he'll categorize you as gay, then he'll never take you seriously about anything else you have to say. Ever. Which is interesting because that kind of prejudice contradicts many of the things they claim to believe. Like, when I was a child and my parents occasionally took me to church, I heard the preacher talk about how God made all things that exist and that all things God created are beautiful. But no one back then would have allowed us to say that a man's butt was beautiful, though not all are, really.

Homer is handsome enough. And the preacher who occasionally visits me is handsome, too, but I can't tell him that. Homer might not mind, but the preacher would think I'm gay. Not that it matters to me what the preacher thinks, or whether I really am gay, but with some people if they think you think you're gay they'll ignore everything else you say, same as if you'd said you were gay. So I don't tell the preacher he has a handsome face, and I certainly don't tell him he has a cute butt. Which makes sense because his butt is flat and not cute at all.

Most of the time when Homer returns me to my room, it's for meals. When I first arrived at Broadmoor I ate meals with the others in the dining room but Morgan Jackson, an idiot who lived on the next hall, kept eating food from my plate. That, of course, brought back memories from my childhood and the anger that went with it. I did my best to remember that he wasn't Benny Smith but finally I could stand it no more. When he reached for my plate the third time, I dumped his plate in his lap. He howled and cried and made a scene until the orderlies escorted him from the room.

That should have been the end of the matter but others who were seated at our table seized the moment as an opportunity to start a food fight, which they very much enjoyed until orderlies attempted to determine blame for the incident. They all pointed to me and said I started whole thing, which wasn't true. I dumped Morgan's plate in his lap, true enough, but did nothing more. The others, however, availed themselves of an opportunity for the kind of pleasure the idiots at Broadmoor enjoy.

After I explained the situation to Homer, he began to watch and soon after they allowed Morgan back in the dining room, Homer caught him in the act of eating my food but did nothing to stop him.

A few days later, when Morgan began eating the carrots from my plate for the third time, I stabbed the back of his hand with my fork. Not a light poke either but a genuine stab that inserted the tines all the way in. Someone in the infirmary had to remove the fork with one of their instruments, which I understand required a great deal of effort. Thereafter, I received meals in my room, an arrangement I very much enjoyed. Eating alone was something I'd done since childhood and I found it to be a peaceful experience.

At other times, Homer took me to my room because it was time to take The Pill. I did not like The Pill at all and soon noticed it came in the afternoon, midway between lunch and dinner. When I remembered to remember that fact, I did my best to be somewhere else. They usually found me and made me take it, but I always tried to avoid it—if I remembered. That day, as I sat at the table with the sunlight coming through the window, wondering when I would lift my hand from the tabletop, I had forgotten about The Pill until Homer called for me.

My sister says The Pill makes me more like myself. I say it makes me more like the self she and others wish I would be. The Hornwallace that I am without The Pill is someone they can't manage, manipulate, or understand. Hornwallace without The Pill sees too much, knows too much, understands too much, and that makes everyone uncomfortable—like the way I made my father's friends nervous when I was a boy. People hide things about themselves all the time and they think they're clever, that no one will ever notice, but most aren't that clever and when someone notices the things they've tried to hide, it makes them angry. And when they notice that someone has the capacity for noticing, it makes them nervous. People have been nervous around me all my life.

In truth, no one really minded the way I was without The Pill, except my sister. She's the one who put me in here. Not because the doctors found anything wrong with me, but because she wanted to control the money. All of it. Her part and mine. She couldn't do that without having them put me in here and getting me on The Pill. That's the only way she could manage the money. She had to manage me first. Otherwise, I saw things no one else saw and knew things no one else wanted me to know. It's like what I said earlier about being gay or talking about gay topics. Tell them you saw something that no one can confirm and they'll think you're crazy. Talk to the people that only you see and they'll say you've lost touch with reality.

At first, no one seemed to notice that I saw people no one else saw. When they finally realized it, most were amused by it and when I failed to mention the people I saw, they asked about them. Had I seen the man with the little girl who walked through the woods behind my house every day at noon? Or, did the woman who went for a walk with her dog at two in the morning really wear nothing but a T-shirt and underwear? Everyone tolerated me and some were even amused by the things I said, but then I started talking about the man who came to visit Gemma Mayfield after her husband left for work in the morning and not long after that, the trouble began.

Gemma was in her mid-fifties. Not bad looking but not a young girl either. She was from a little town near Round Rock, and attended St. Edwards University, where she met Tony Mayfield. Tony was a nice guy, though I did not see him often. He came from a family of successful lawyers and by the time I met him he was already a partner in the family firm, a position that seemed to take most of his time. He left the house early in the morning every day except Saturday and didn't get back until after six in the evening, which meant Gemma was at home alone all day. They had no children.

Gemma used to come to my house after Tony went to the office and we had coffee together several mornings each week. I always thought she was interested in more than coffee. I wasn't even interested in having coffee with her, much less anything else, but when someone knocks on your side door in the morning and you're holding a coffee cup when you answer, it's rather difficult not to offer them a cup, too, which I did and then it became a tradition—knock at the door, it's Gemma, cup's on the counter waiting for you. I suppose I could have avoided the whole thing by not answering the door in the first place but she knew I was at home. I was always at home—everyone knew that—so avoiding her by ignoring her knock would have been rude. We were not allowed to be rude.

Coffee in the morning with Gemma went on for a year or two but then one morning she didn't come over and she didn't the next morning, either. So I started watching and that's when I noticed the blue pickup. It was parked on the driveway near the street at first, like a repairman or something, then I saw it around back and that's where it was parked all the time after that. Showed up about nine each morning and stayed until one in the afternoon. The driver was a young guy and by young I mean a lot younger than Gemma, though by no means a minor. He was tall and muscular but in a rawboned way. Angular, not buff. After he started parking his truck behind the house, Gemma didn't come over for coffee anymore.

Nothing much happened about it until one day Mrs. Washington, who lived across the street, saw me when I went out to get the mail and asked me if I had noticed the blue pickup truck at Gemma's house. I didn't want to talk about Gemma or anyone else and certainly not to Mrs. Washington, and for good reason. She repeated everything she ever heard about anyone or anything she'd ever known. I was certain that whatever she knew about me she repeated, too, so I didn't want to tell her anything about anything because I didn't want her mentioning me in connection with whatever she told to whoever she told it. They could think she was a gadfly if that's what she wanted, but not me.

That morning when I went out to get the mail, Mrs. Washington saw me and before I could retreat to the house she was standing right there beside the mailbox. "Mister," she whispered—even she refused to call me by my proper name. "Have you seen that blue pickup next door?"

"Good morning, Mrs. Washington." I spoke as politely as possible. In addition to all the other things that have been said about me, people have often told me I am too abrupt. At times I do not care what others think of me and at times I do. I was in one of the periods of caring and was making a concerted effort to do better with personal interaction, though I had very little of it as a matter of routine, which suited me just fine, but right then I was caring about not being so abrupt. In retrospect, I should have ignored her.

"That truck is over there every day," she said. "The blue one. It's always on the driveway. Have you seen it?"

It wasn't always there—not every day—and the dissonance created by the inaccuracy of her remark compelled me to correct her. "Actually," I said. "It's only there Monday through Friday and only from nine in the morning until one in the afternoon."

"So, you have seen it."

In spite of my attempts at not being abrupt, I did not wish to continue the conversation so I smiled at her and said, "Have a good day, Mrs. Washington." Then I turned away and started back to the house. And that's all there was to it, but, as things turned out, it was too much.

A week or two later I received a phone call from my sister. My sister hardly ever contacted me unless there was trouble and I should have known her call that morning meant nothing but trouble. She wanted to know why I was spreading malicious gossip about Gemma. I had forgotten that they were friends.

"I've never spread gossip about anyone," I retorted. "Mother did not allow it."

"Mother was the biggest gossip in town."

The arrogance in her voice set me on edge. "Was there a point to this phone call?"

"You should stop talking about Gemma."

"I'm not talking about Gemma."

"You've been spreading stories about her to Mrs. Washington."

"I didn't spread stories to anyone. Mrs. Washington saw me at the mailbox and asked if I had seen the blue pickup truck in Gemma's driveway. I tried to deflect her question but she kept talking and somewhere in the stream of self-important gibberish she said the truck was always there. That wasn't true. It's not always there. And I felt compelled to correct her. So I told her the truck wasn't always there. That it was only there Monday through Friday from nine in the morning until one in the afternoon. And that is absolutely the truth." Then I hung up the phone.

Not long after that, Gemma came to see me and I told her the same thing all over again. She seemed to believe me, but a few days later I noticed my sister's car was parked in her driveway and I remembered they had been roommates at St. Edwards. At first I thought nothing of it, except to note that my sister's car appeared in the driveway shortly after our telephone conversation. Then I noticed that the blue pickup truck stopped coming to the house and instead, my sister's car was parked there every day, Monday through Friday, from about nine in the morning until one in the afternoon. You can draw your own conclusions about what they were doing. I drew mine, but I've never told anyone what I was thinking. My thoughts were unsubstantiated by any facts other than where and when my sister parked her car at Gemma's house, which meant any discussion of it would have been gossip. Our mother didn't allow us to gossip.

For a month or so, nothing else happened. My sister came and went from Gemma's house with great regularity, but never stopped by for a visit with me or even tossed so much as a wave in my direction, though I was never outside during the day, but she knew I often stood near the window when the sunlight was soft enough not to bother me.

Then one day in the spring, Tony came home at noon, which was really early for him and highly unusual. So unusual that I thought something grave must have occurred as he'd never done that before. Turned out, he had planned a round of golf for after lunch that day and had forgotten to take his clubs with him when he left for work that the morning. He came home at noon to get them and that's when things fell apart.

The first indication I had that something was amiss came from the sound of angry voices inside Gemma and Tony's house. Voices so loud and intense that I heard them even with the radio playing in my kitchen.

Shortly thereafter, the voices were followed by the sound of breaking glass and not merely the tinkle of an accidental goblet bursting against the tile floor—Tony and Gemma had terrazzo tile floors in their kitchen. This was the sound of someone repeatedly smashing glass objects with great force deliberately against a hard surface.

The commotion from next door was so alarming that I went to the dining room window to see what might be happening. That's when I saw my sister rushing across the back deck, clothes in hand with only a shirt wrapped around her waist, a scared look on her face. She hurried to her car and dressed from inside but she only got the top on all the way before Tony came down the back steps after her. She locked the doors as he approached and I heard him shouting angrily while she pulled on her skirt.

A landscaping block lay nearby—part of the border of the kitchen garden that no one ever tended. While my sister tried to dress herself, Tony wallowed the block from its place and lifted it above his head as if to smash it against the hood of her car. Before he could do that, though, I heard the car start and my sister backed it to the street with a speed faster than was safe for such a narrow space.

The car bounced over the curb and Tony tossed the landscape block aside, but he stood in the driveway glaring at her as she drove away. As my sister's car topped the hill near the Johnson house and disappeared from sight, Tony turned to go back inside. That's when he looked over at me and flipped me off with a raised middle finger. I did not respond.

Mrs. Washington from across the street later told me that Gemma had been having an affair. "With a woman." The tone of her voice dripped with disapproval. "Ever since the man with the blue pickup stopped coming over," she explained. "His truck left one day and the next day that lady's car appeared." That lady to whom she referred—the object of Gemma's affection—was my sister. Mrs. Washington didn't live across the street from us when we were growing up. She only moved there a few years ago, after our parents were dead and I had the house to myself. That was all she'd ever known. Just me and the house and Gemma next door. She knew nothing of my sister and I did not bother to inform her.

The day Tony came home and found them, Mrs. Washington had been in the yard working in her flowerbed. She heard their angry voices more clearly than did I and thought once about calling the police, but just as she gathered the courage to do so my sister appeared in the driveway. Mrs. Washington was so startled—my sister was, for all intents and purposes, nude and apparently running for her life—that she could only stare, her mouth agape in a slack-jawed expression. When she told me that, I at once regretted looking out the dining room window. The view from the living room, which faced Mrs. Washington's direction, would have allowed me to watch her reaction, which I am certain would have been far more entertaining than what I actually saw.

Two weeks later, the moving vans arrived and then Gemma's house sat empty. No realtor's sign. No tenants. Just empty. The yardman still came to mow the lawn every Tuesday morning. And the tree service kept the trees pruned and the limbs removed. And someone swept off the porch every few months. Otherwise, it was completely unoccupied.

About a month after all of that, my sister started coming around to see me. She showed up unannounced one morning as I was having coffee. By then I'd heard about her taking Gemma as a roommate. My sister lived in a house twice the size of anything she actually needed and had more than ample space to accommodate two or three roommates, though I couldn't imagine anyone actually wanting to live with her, much less share her bed, as apparently Gemma did.

My sister's troubles—being caught up in litigation over Gemma's divorce, as she apparently was—did not surprise me. Her sexual proclivities were well known to most of us from an early age, though not to our parents at first. Then Father discovered her in the attic naked with a classmate during her senior year in high school and there was no denying it after that. She was gay. Not that it mattered to me, then or now.

Father reacted in his predictable manner—he ranted and fumed for a week or two, then let it drop. Mother simply ignored the matter altogether. And ignored my sister, too.

From my perspective, Gemma and my sister got whatever they wanted and whatever they deserved. I felt bad for Tony, though. He was a nice guy and not bad looking, either. When he and Gemma first moved in next door he used to lay by the pool in the back yard on Saturdays and enjoy the sun. A few times, when he thought no one was watching, he slipped off his swim trunks. I watched him for as long as I could, taking care not to reveal my position by the upstairs window, but could have watched much longer had my eyes tolerated the glare from the sunlight. He really was quite nice to look at. But the light bothered me and so I couldn't stand at the window for long. Which is why I stayed inside and mostly kept the house dark all the time.

When Father was alive, he wanted me outside and, if not, he wanted the draperies open and the house filled with sunlight. He talked all the time, too, and the noise grated against the surface of my brain. Noise bothered me, except for the radio which I kept tuned to public radio broadcasts. I had a radio in every room of the house, all tuned to the same station. The sound of their voices soothed my mind. Father's voice did not sound like that.

After Father died, the house grew quiet and still and I could set the drapes anyway I liked, which was darker than most would have preferred. I could function that way, though not so much when Mother turned on all of the lights. Those days, when she fluttered about the house in a frenzy, doing this and that and then another, I retreated to my room with the lights off and the curtains drawn, which is how I came to be standing at the window when Tony was sunbathing next door on a Saturday morning, back when he and Gemma were much younger.

So, after Gemma and Tony divorced and Gemma moved in with my sister, my sister started showing up at my house with uncharacteristic regularity. She was never regular. Never on time. Never on schedule. As a child she was always late to dinner and when she was in school she was never on time for class. Father left her at the store more than once because she wasn't at the car when he was ready to leave, which necessitated a trip by Mother to retrieve her, which meant I had to go along, too. Mother was never allowed to go anywhere alone because Father was afraid that she might not remember to return. Not that he was obsessive. Mother's disappearance was a problem that had been made evident more than once, usually following a period of regular medication after which she convinced herself that she was well and no longer needed the pills from the bottle in the cabinet beside the refrigerator.

With my sister's newfound interest in me, she began arriving for a visit in the morning, about the time I was having coffee. Of course, I answered her knock on the side door with a cup in my hand and felt compelled to offer her one, too. After the second time, I just opened the door and gestured toward the kitchen. "Cup's on the counter. Coffee's in the urn." I think she mistook my response—an acknowledgment of the inevitable more than anything else—as a gesture of warmth and a hint that I was pleased to see her. Nothing could have been farther from the truth. I didn't want to see her or have her as a guest in my house and, indeed, felt not the slightest hint of warmth for her. It's just, when someone shows up at your door in the morning and you answer their knock with a cup of coffee in your hand, it's rude not to offer them one, too. Mother never allowed us to be rude. And she didn't allow us to gossip, either, despite what my sister might say about her.

Every visit was the same. She asked how I was doing. Then about some memory of what it was like in the house when we were children. And then she got to the point.

"Did you really see the blue truck on the driveway?"

"Yes," I replied. As I did every time she asked. "Why?"

"Because Gemma isn't sure that ever happened."

"Isn't sure it was there. Or isn't sure I saw it?

"Isn't sure."

"It was there. I saw it. On multiple occasions."

"How do you know?"

"I have eyes that see."

"And Mrs. Washington saw it?"

"You can ask her."

"I did."

"Then you have your answer."

Every day it was the same and I began to think she was crazy, then I realized she wasn't crazy but she wanted me to think I was. That much seemed certain to me. But the thing I was unsure about was why she wanted me to say the truck wasn't there, because that's the direction she was trying to take the conversation. I knew because I had known her all of my life and I had seen this before from her. First, if she could, she would get me to say the truck might not have been there. Then she'd get me to say it wasn't there at all. But why did she want it not to be there?

If the truck wasn't there, the man who drove it wasn't there. And if the man who drove it wasn't there, then whatever happened when he was there didn't happen. I was never in Gemma's house when he was there so I had no idea what actually occurred when he was present. Fantasies about it, but no actual knowledge. But I did know that the truck was parked on the driveway every morning, Monday through Friday, from nine in the morning until one in the afternoon. That was certain. I never budged on knowing it. I never budged on it having happened. I never said the things my sister wanted me to say. She wasn't the first person who tried to gaslight me in some form or another. And I assume from the way things turned out, Mrs. Washington didn't change her story, either.

Then one day, she stopped coming around. The neighbor still walked her dog at night in her underwear with just a t-shirt to cover it. And the man still walked through the woods behind the house with a little girl at his side. But no sister. No Gemma. No blue pickup parked on the driveway.

Eventually, Tony filed for divorce. Rather than settling quickly, Gemma claimed she was entitled to half of everything so they went to court and litigated. Father said lawsuits made everyone miserable and lawsuits taken to trial made all of their friends miserable, too. I was forced to give a deposition in Tony and Gemma's case. But at least I didn't have to appear in court. Things were bad enough without that. Father, by the way, was correct. We all were made miserable by their dispute.

When the subpoena arrived to compel me to testify at a deposition, I was perplexed as to why they wanted me to say anything to anyone about their situation. Most of what I knew I learned from Mrs. Washington across the street. Of a firsthand nature, I only knew what I had seen from the dining room window—the blue pickup truck parked on the driveway and a description of the driver, along with my sister's car parked in the same place and a few details about the day Tony chased her naked from the house. But when I arrived at the appointed time to give my testimony, things became much clearer.

For one, my sister was present and Gemma was not. I knew at once what was happening and what they were trying to do. They were going to attempt in a formal manner what my sister had attempted when she visited me at my house for coffee—to convince me to say the things they wanted me to say, the things they needed me to say, rather than to speak the truth. Father demanded that we always tell the truth. I always complied. My sister did not. She cared little for the truth except for those few occasions when it served her own purposes. Gemma's divorce case was not one of those occasions where the truth could help anyone except Tony.

I also knew that Gemma was not interested in what I had to say. I think she already knew what I would say. She'd had coffee with me, too. And at a time when there were no expectations on her part or mine. She knew from that experience that I would speak plainly and that I would not care what the people in the room thought of me. On that much, she was absolutely correct. One must always speak the truth and speak it plainly. Father demanded it. I was not about to risk the belt over Gemma's situation, even if Father was long since dead. His belt was wide and he swung it hard. Once had been enough for me. And besides, Gemma had no one to blame for her situation except herself, though for certain she was urged along by my sister.

The deposition began innocently enough. Tony's attorney conducted it and he began by asking the usual perfunctory questions about name, address, and the like. Then he moved on to the salient details rather quickly—the blue pickup truck parked on the driveway and the man who drove it; Gemma's car in its place and details I knew about the day Tony chased her from the house. It made me nervous to have my words recorded by a court reporter but Tony's attorney did not challenge my integrity.

When Tony's attorney finished, Gemma's lawyer took his turn. As I said, Gemma was not present for the deposition but my sister was and as soon as the lawyer got hold of me, she started passing him notes and whispering in his ear. As a result, he asked the same sort of questions she had asked me when she came over for coffee. Did I really see the truck? The driver? Was I certain it was my sister's car on the driveway? Or had Mrs. Washington from across the street suggested it to me? Over and over. Trying to get me to say what they wanted me to say to help their case.

After a while everyone in the room except my sister seemed to understand that I was telling the truth and that I was not going to change my version of it to suit her. Even if I had wanted to I couldn't, and I assure you I had not the least desire to do it. But I couldn't change my story, not for her or anyone else, because I had told the truth the first time and the hundredth time and I wasn't about to risk a belting from Father just to say what my sister wanted me to say. As I have noted several times already, I did that once and I wanted nothing to do with it again, even if Father was dead and gone and not coming back. Father required us to always tell the truth. Which I did that day. Many times over.

Tony's lawyer finished with me by mid-morning. Gemma's lawyer droned on and on into the afternoon, asking the same questions over and over. Asking the same thing but in a different way. I answered the same every time, repeating what I'd said earlier and held it together to the end, which I am certain surprised my sister and frustrated her no end. She wanted me to crack. To change my story so they could discredit everything I and all the others had said. To scream and yell and cause a scene. Anything to help their cause. But finally the futility of the effort taxed the patience of even Gemma's lawyer and when we reached three in the afternoon and my sister handed him yet one more note, he brushed her off with a shake of his head, glanced at the court reporter, and said, "We're done with this witness."

My sister slumped in her chair, a sense of defeat evident on her face, but I rose at once and started toward the door, not giving them a chance at even one more go at me. By then, my clothes were too tight and I felt them rubbing against my skin. The light was too bright, too, and I was getting a headache. And it was hot in there.

As I reached the door to the outside my skin began to crawl and I could stand it no more. I ripped off my shirt and walked to my car, naked from the waist up. When I was behind the steering wheel with the door locked and the windows up, I unfastened my belt and unbutton the top of my pants to let the fabric loosen from against me. I hated it when my clothes touched my skin and they had been touching me all day.

At home, I went straight to my room, turned off the lights and drew the drapes, then stripped naked and lay on my bed. Almost immediately I fell into a deep sleep and remained there until sometime later when I awakened to find myself wrapped in the comforter. It was dark outside and I checked my phone to find three days had passed since the day of the deposition. The inbox for my voicemail was full of messages.

After a moment to gather myself, I put on a pair of soft house shorts and the most worn and ragged t-shirt in my drawer, then went downstairs and made a full pot of coffee. It was three in the morning but after all of that sleep I was wide awake. I sat at the kitchen table until the pot was empty, then went to the bathroom.

Later that morning, after the sun was up, I lay on my bed and listened to the voicemails from my phone. All of them were from my sister. In the first one she screamed at me. I deleted it before she finished and went to the next. She screamed at me some more. I deleted that one, also. In the next, she was calm and spoke in clear, cogent sentences. That's when I knew she was drunk.

A month after the deposition, Gemma and Tony's divorce case came to trial. The man in the blue truck was forced to appear before the judge and Tony's lawyer showed him to be Gemma's paramour. Then my sister took the stand and Tony's lawyer proved her to be Gemma's paramour, too. And Gemma lost a fortune. I wasn't there to see it. They didn't call me as a witness and I didn't go anywhere near the courthouse while they were holding the trial.

Mrs. Washington told me about it, though, and from the result I knew they all had one thing in common—they hated me. Gemma, my sister, and the man with the blue pickup truck because I told what they had been up to, which forced them to admit what they had been doing and prevented them from lying, even without me actually appearing in court. They knew what I had said and what I would say if asked again and had no choice but to own up to what they'd done and who they were. And even though things worked out in his favor, Tony hated me, too, because I didn't say something to him about all that happened when it actually occurred.

Late one night, about two weeks after Tony and Gemma's divorce trial, Julia Bristow, the woman who walked her dog at night wearing nothing but underwear and a t-shirt, came by for a visit. She was a kind woman with a good heart and, in spite of the way she dressed when she walked the dog, was really quite modest. Like me, she did not care to have her clothes touch her skin, which was the reason she dressed the way she did. I only knew what she wore when she walked the dog because city ordinances required pet owners to pick up after their dogs and one night when the dog relieved himself on my lawn, she bent over to gather the droppings in a plastic bag she carried for that purpose. Rather than stoop or squat she leaned down and as her head went lower than her waist the t-shirt she was wearing slid over her torso and gathered against her armpits. That's when I saw what she wore. Or, rather, what she did not.

The night that Julia came for a visit, she had on shorts and the familiar t-shirt with a man's shirt layered over the top, for which I was quite thankful. Talking to her in the attire she normally wore at night would have been a challenge. She was beautiful and comely and my eyes would have wandered to the enticing parts much too easily for polite conversation. I didn't ask how she acquired the shirt.

It was late, perhaps midnight, when I went out to check the mail that night and Julia was coming along the street, but without the dog. I was suspicious of her presence—it was early for her to be out and she was clothed in a presentable fashion—and without the dog—all of which gave me the sense that the moment was less than spontaneous.

Nevertheless, when an attractive woman chats one up on the street at night and you want to go inside—the mosquitoes were terrible just then—one has no choice but to invite her to continue the conversation elsewhere. When I suggested we do that, she readily agreed.

Because of the lateness of the hour, and owing to the similar nature of our schedules, I offered her a cup of coffee which she accepted without hesitation. None had been made since the middle of the afternoon so I put on a fresh pot. We sat at the kitchen table and talked while it brewed. Julia sat with her back to the window.

"I heard from Margaret that Mrs. Washington's family is putting her in a retirement home."

This surprised me. "Really? She was in the yard a few days ago, digging in a flowerbed. She looked fine to me."

"They say she hasn't been the same since she testified at Gemma's trial."

"It affected her that much?"

Julia shrugged. "That's what they say."

"Her family says that?"

"Yes."

"Where do they live?"

"Her daughter lives in Colorado. I think her son is in Brenham."
My eyebrow arched involuntarily. "I didn't know she had a son."

"Neither did I," Julia replied. "But that's what Margaret said."

Margaret was a friend of Julia's who lived on the next street over, behind Mrs. Washington. I knew her only by name, but had never seen her in person, though Julia referred to her every time we spoke.

The coffee was ready and I poured a cup for us, then returned to my seat across the table and took a sip. As I placed the cup on its saucer I said, "I don't think I've ever seen anyone at Mrs. Washington's house other than her."

Julia nodded. "Neither have I."

"I should go see her," I remarked. "Where did they put her?"

"Somewhere in Colorado." Julia had a sorrowful expression. "Margaret said she's already gone."

That troubled me and I made a pouty face to show my displeasure. "When did they do that?"

"A few days ago."

Then I began to wonder again about Julia's unexpected appearance that night near my mailbox. Was she in league with my sister? Attempting to sway me to a perspective that benefited her? Surely not Julia. She was always so nice to me. And she seemed attentive to detail, too much so to fall victim to my sister.

Julia seemed to notice my apprehension. "That's the reason I came to see you," she said.

A frown wrinkled my forehead. "You intentionally came to see me?"

"I knew you checked your mail at night sometimes and was watching to see when you came out."

"You were waiting for me."

"Yes."

I was both flattered and concerned. Normally, I checked the mail much earlier in the day—Mother insisted we check it as soon as it arrived, which I always did while she was alive. After she died, I began checking it at night because I didn't like going outside during the day, though I did not often wait as late as midnight to get it. That afternoon had been different for me. I started watching a television show through a streaming service, which turned into a binge, and by the time I had caught up with the latest episode for the current season, the hour was quite late. While I was watching the show, Julia was watching for me. I liked that.

At the same time, however, it occurred to me that she had been watching and waiting for me. An intentional act. The act of someone with a purpose. That part left me concerned. She had a purpose. What was it?

"And why were you waiting for me?" I asked.

Julia took a sip of coffee and swallowed it slowly. "Margaret's daughter works in the Wilson Building, downtown. Her office is on the same floor as Wright Martin Wendell. The investment firm."

The financial firm of Wright Martin Wendell was well known to me. After Father died, Mother inherited everything that had been theirs. When Mother died, her estate was divided evenly between me and my sister. Most of it was held in the form of financial assets. A broker at Wright Martin Wendell looked after it for us.

Julia took another sip of coffee before continuing. "Margaret's daughter saw Mrs. Washington's daughter coming from that office the other day."

"The daughters know each other?"

"Yes."

"We live in a small world."

"It gets smaller," Julia said.

"How so?"

"The next day, Mrs. Washington's daughter was up there again."

"Two days in a row?"

"Yes." Julia looked over at me. "This time, she was with Gemma and your sister."

My mouth fell open in a look of surprise, but it was nothing like what I felt inside. "My sister?"

"Yes," Julia said. "Your sister, Gemma, and Mrs. Washington's daughter."

"That makes no sense, unless they're up to something."

"I know."

"And if it involves my sister, that most assuredly is the case."

"I knew you would see it that way."

"Mrs. Washington just testified against Gemma in a case that undoubtedly affects my sister."

"And might affect you."

"You think what they've done to Mrs. Washington portends something dreadful for me?"

"I don't know your sister, except for seeing her once when she came from the car at Gemma's. But from the way you describe her, I thought you ought to know."

I thought for a moment. "If Mrs. Washington's daughter lives in Colorado. And her son lives in Brenham. How did they know her condition had changed after the trial?"

"Someone had to tell them."

"They weren't here for trial, were they?"

"No," Julia answered.

"And I haven't seen anyone at Mrs. Washington's house since the trial. Have you?"

"No."

"And Mrs. Washington wasn't living here when my sister was still at home."

Julia nodded. "Right."

"So, how does my sister know Mrs. Washington's daughter?"

"Through Gemma?"

"Okay," I conceded. "But why would Gemma and my sister be involved with Mrs. Washington's situation?"

"Aren't they together now? Gemma and your sister."

I nodded my head slowly. "You think Gemma merely invited my sister along because she is now her companion?"

"Could have."

"Perhaps she did."

"But you don't think so."

"I think there's more to it than we know."

Julia took another sip of coffee. "It could be that they were simply going and coming from that office at the same time."

"But they were together the second day. Daughter alone on the first day. Daughter with Gemma and my sister on the second."

"Yeah." Julia sighed. "Not much chance that was coincidence."

"My sister doesn't deal in coincidence," I offered. "She has concocted some intrigue."

"But not Gemma?" Julia asked. "She's not part of it?"

"Gemma doesn't think that way," I replied. "You know her at least as well as I do and I think we both know that if she was a person given to subtlety and intrigue, Tony never would have caught her in bed with a lover."

Julia grinned. "You're right about that. She is fully capable of having sex with just about anyone, but not of doing so without getting caught."

When we'd finished the pot of coffee, Julia excused herself and returned home. After she was gone, I went upstairs to the second floor and sat in a straight-backed chair by the window in the front bedroom, from which I could view almost the entire neighborhood. As I sat there for the remainder of the night, I thought about what Julia had said.

Gemma, Mrs. Washington's daughter, and my sister. All of them together, at the office of the financial advisor who administered our parents' estate. It was strange, but it was also clumsy, open, and obvious. Which was the way my sister operated. She and everyone who knew her thought of her as clever. I knew her as obvious, a point that had been proven to me many times in the past and would be again in the days that followed.

Attending to my half of our parents' estate required periodic trips to the office of our financial advisor at Wright Martin Wendell. In spite of my relationship with my sister and the separate nature of our affairs, she and I still used the same person to manage our business. Louis O'Neill. A broker who happened to be the same person

Father and Mother used during the final years of their lives.

A week or two after Julia visited me and we drank coffee at midnight in the kitchen, I paid O'Neill a visit. It was a regularly scheduled appointment to discuss ongoing matters pertaining to my investment accounts, but that day my sister was in O'Neill's office when I arrived. From the way he acted and from the positioning of the chairs near his desk, I was certain he knew in advance that she was going to be there. Which meant regardless of whatever was about to happen, he had already taken her side in the matter.

They began by mentioning that they had heard how I reacted following the deposition I gave in Tony and Gemma's divorce case. "What about it?" I responded.

"You took off your shirt before you even left the building," my sister said. She had an indignant tone in her voice that made it seem as though this was a great surprise to her. Which, of course, it was not. She'd known this was sometimes my reaction to stress since…a long time ago and she had seen it many times before.

I gave her a smart-ass look. "And you know why, too."

"You don't like to feel your clothes touching you." She said it in a mocking tone that belied the ongoing nature of our relationship.

I responded with a condescending tone. "That's nothing new to you, is it?"

"And then you went home and slept for three days straight," she continued.

A frown wrinkled my forehead. "Who told you that?"

"What does it matter?"

"You weren't there," I countered. "You didn't see me. You don't know what I did."

"You were seen arriving at the house that afternoon. After the deposition." She was using her best know-it-all voice. "And then you weren't seen again until three days later."

"Which means?"

"I know you." Her voice was more strident that before. As if I had offended her by challenging her view of the situation. "I know what you were doing. You were doing what you always do."

Clearly, this was no mere meeting, but an intervention. I should have known right then that she was watching the house, but I was angry over being blindsided by her and O'Neill—the one person in the room who was supposed to be on my side, which undoubtedly he was not. "Then if you know me so well, you wouldn't be surprised if I had slept for three days," I snapped. "Would you?"

O'Neill spoke up. "I understand you sometimes see a woman walking past your house at night."

I glared at him. "What of it?"

He had a pained expression. "You've said she walks her dog in her underwear?"

"With a t-shirt over it," I added. "She doesn't care to have her clothes touch her body and there's no one else out at that time of night." As if that explained the situation.

My sister spoke up. "Do you know that no one else on the street has ever seen her?"

"They've never seen her?"

"At night, I mean." She was aggravated at having to correct herself. "And dressed like that."

"I don't doubt it."

"Why is that?" O'Neill asked.

"None of them stays up that late at night."

"And how late is that?"

"Two or three in the morning."

"What about the man who walks through the woods in the afternoon with the little girl," my sister chided. "Tell him about that." She nodded toward O'Neill when she spoke.

"There's not much to tell," I said. "He walks with her through the woods. They come from up by Mrs. Montgomery's house and go down past the Edleberry's."

"Never in the opposite direction?"

"No." I looked over at her. "Why do you ask me these questions? These matters are well known by many. And especially by you."

"That you have talked about them is well known," she snarked. "But would it surprise you to know that none of your neighbors can verify the man and girl even exist? They've never see the man and the girl. They've never seen the woman walking the dog at night in her underwear. They've never seen either of them."

My sister's motives were easily deduced. She only wanted money, power, and sex. Appetites which had driven her every action and thought all of her life. Obviously, she had lived through her share of the money and was now after mine. The only way she could accomplish that goal was to remove me from control of my own affairs, which I was certain she was now orchestrating events to accomplish. But the great unanswered question for me remained, as it had earlier, with O'Neill and his interest in the matter. So I ignored my sister's question and turned to him. "I am well aware of my sister's intentions here." My eyes bore in on him. "But what are yours?"

O'Neill fidgeted nervously in his chair before saying, "I assure you, my only desire is to preserve your well-being." He looked down as he spoke, with his eyes focused on the desktop, and then I knew why he was there.

"And…?"

He looked over at me. "And what?"

"You've not mentioned the real reason you took this meeting."

"Which is?"

"To protect the firm."

He frowned. "What do you mean?"

"I mean, the real reason you're here is to protect Wright Martin Wendell."

"Well." He glanced away. "We do have liabilities in this regard."

"My sister has asserted that I am no longer competent and you take that as notice of a risk to you."

"Perhaps. But I'm not—"

Anger rose inside me but I kept it bottled up. "I am certain that I need not remind you that, in regard to my investments, you have a fiduciary duty to me. Not to her."

O'Neill leaned back in his chair. "I fully understand my fiduciary responsibilities, which is why I agreed to meet with you on this."

"No," I said, wagging my finger for emphasis. "It is why you agreed to join her in this charade. Why you agreed to blindside me."

Again O'Neill looked away. "I was only interested in your well-being."

"Then tell me something," I responded. "In all of your dealings with me, have I shown the slightest indication that I am not in full control of my faculties?"

"N...no." He spoke in a tentative voice. "None that I have noticed."

"Have I suggested we invest in tulip bulb futures or some equally ludicrous venture?"

"No. Not really."

"In fact," I continued. "All of the investments in my accounts have been made as a choice between options you provided."

"Well...I've done my..."

"When we met, you offered an array of three or four possibilities. Never one. Never a dozen. But always enough so that I didn't have to choose between only two."

"That's—"

"You arranged it that way so that no one could say that I was guided toward any particular investment option by you. And then I made the choice. I determined which among your suggested alternatives I would choose. Isn't that how it worked?"

"Yes." He was sweating. "I believe so."

"Then I must ask, how is it that you think your firm has any exposure to any risk at all in dealing with me? If there is any risk to the firm, it's in the array of choices you presented to me. Is that not true?"

"Well, I don't—"

"Which means the risk to this firm comes from you. Not me." Then I leaned closer to his desk and with my eyes focused on him, but my finger pointed in my sister's direction, I said firmly, "If she touches so much as one cent of my money, I will sue this firm for fraud. And you will be subject to criminal prosecution."

And with that, I left the building. Only this time, I did not take off my shirt or go home and sleep for three days. This time, I went home and prepared myself for what lay ahead because by then I knew what was coming. My sister intended to file a petition with the court to have me declared mentally incapable of managing my own affairs. If successful, I would be placed in an institution and she would be the obvious choice to control my half of the estate.

As I expected, less than a week after the meeting with O'Neill, a soft, round-bellied sheriff's deputy was at my door with papers requiring me to appear in court on a petition filed by my sister to have me declared incompetent. A notice with the papers indicated that because I was not deemed a threat to my own safety, I was allowed to remain free pending the hearing that had been scheduled on the matter. That fact alone seemed to settle the issue there and then—if I was competent to care for myself in the meantime, as the court assumed by allowing me to remain free, I should be held competent in every respect—but the deputy insisted I had to appear in court.

Later that day, I hired an attorney, Porter Fulbright, to represent me. He was tall and young, with short hair and a muscular build that radiated a certain level of physical prowess—a heady, musky blend of desire and desirableness—evident even from beneath the cover of his dark gray business suit. Though, as with Homer and all the others, one cannot say those things aloud. But best of all, Fulbright was not the lawyer who guided us through the settling of Mother's estate. That one led us on a needless journey through the wilderness. Fulbright, I knew, would be fully capable of dealing with the likes of my sister. I could tell it from the look in his clear blue eyes.

From the things discussed during the meeting at O'Neill's office, I knew how the hearing would go. My sister would testify about the things I said about the people I saw. People that she would contend no one had ever been able to verify—the woman who walked her dog at night in her underwear with only a t-shirt to cover it, the man and the little girl who walked through the woods together, and perhaps the presence of the blue truck at Gemma's house. I wasn't sure whether she would raise the issue of the truck, but something Julia said when she visited me that night made me think the topic might come up.

When I explained this to Fulbright, he said, "We'll need to locate those people and get them to testify."

"The woman who walks her dog at night is easy to find. She is my neighbor."

"What about the man who walks through the woods with the little girl?"

"I haven't seen him in a few days and I'm not sure where to find him."

The lawyer looked determined. "We need him."

"Okay," I replied. "I'll see what I can do."

"Did anyone else see the pickup truck at the house next door?"

"Yes," I said. "Mrs. Washington, who lives across the—" And that's when I realized just how serious this situation really was. My sister had maneuvered Mrs. Washington's daughter into placing Mrs. Washington in a retirement home so she would be out of the way when this hearing came up.

Fulbright gave me a nudge. "Is everything all right?"

"Yes." I cleared my throat. "Mrs. Washington is in a retirement home. Her daughter placed her there a week or two ago. I believe the facility is located in Colorado. Margaret, who lives on the next street behind her, can tell you about it. She is friends with the woman who walks her dog at night. You should speak to both of them." Then I gave him Julia's name and address.

Because of his relationship with the court, Fulbright had the hearing on my sister's petition delayed for a week. I used the time to sit at the window in the back bedroom, watching the woods for the man and the little girl. When, after two days, that proved fruitless, I went into the woods myself, hoping to locate them and convince them to come to court and testify on my behalf. As an added measure, I took my cell phone with me to record our conversation and capture an image of them, thinking that if all else failed the images and recording might somehow help my case.

For three days I sat in the woods, night and day, enduring mosquitoes, wildlife, and rain, but caught not a single glimpse of the man or the girl. As a consequence, I arrived at the courthouse for the hearing freshly cleaned but dotted with welts from mosquito bites and really quite famished. Fulbright, it seemed, had no better success with Julia or Margaret.

"I have been unable to locate either of them," he reported.

As I suspected, my sister took the witness stand and testified about all of things I had said that I saw—the man with the little girl, the woman who walked her dog at night in her underwear, and the blue pickup I reported seeing on Gemma's driveway. She was especially distraught over the matter about the blue pickup truck, which she asserted was painful for Gemma in her divorce. Gemma, however, was noticeably absent.

In the absence of other witnesses, I testified on my own behalf and refuted the matters she raised. The judge listened attentively and, although it seemed from what we had been shown that day—me living on my own, hiring an attorney, appearing as required, and my sister with nothing but her bare statement of allegation to support her cause—we had demonstrated my complete sanity, he ordered that I be held in a psychiatric facility for seventy-two hours while an evaluation was conducted. That's how I came to be a resident at Broadmoor.

The hearing was held in the morning and I was transported to Broadmoor straight away. My sister arrived that afternoon, ostensibly to check on my condition. When she appeared in the doorway of my room I shouted for her to leave. She did not do so immediately and I threw a water pitcher at her. I was aiming for her head but she dodged it—the first nimble move of her life—and the pitcher sailed into the hallway. And that's how I came to receive regular doses of benzoquilamine—known to me as The Pill.

So, while I was sitting by the window in the warm sunlight staring at my hand, wondering when I would move it again, Homer came and got me and wheeled me to my room—even those of us who could walk were moved by the orderlies in wheelchairs. I assumed he was taking me to my room to receive the daily dose of The Pill. As I mentioned earlier, they gave it to me at that time every day. And always when they gave it to me, they took me to my room. I'm not sure why they did that. It was only a small pill and I could have easily swallowed it without any water at all, but they gave me a large glass to drink with it and stood by watching while I downed it all. Which made avoiding The Pill problematic.

The first time they gave it to me I swallowed it without question but then I noticed the way it made me feel and I did not like it. Rather like being myself but with another body wrapped around the outside, as if I had acquired an extra layer to live through. After that first time, I tried hiding The Pill beneath my tongue until the orderly left the room, which prevented me from receiving a full dosage—provided he left the room promptly and I could spit The Pill into the toilet. That method, however, allowed The Pill to partially dissolve and left a bitter taste in my mouth. Then I learned to distract the orderly with a cough during which I dropped The Pill into my opposite hand and placed it in my pocket. That scheme worked best and in the days that followed I perfected it until I could elude detection completely and avoid ingesting even the slightest amount of The Pill.

This subterfuge with The Pill went on much longer than I anticipated. The initial seventy-two hour hold on me was extended by a week, then by two. When Homer wheeled me from the day room as I sat staring at my hand, I had been confined at Broadmoor four weeks and I was beginning to wonder if I ever would be released, if I ever would see my home again, if I ever would sit by the window upstairs and gaze out at the neighborhood. And as I wondered about that, I considered that perhaps I should simply surrender to the inevitability of my circumstances, swallow The Pill, and yield to whatever might come next. Doing so certainly would have been easier than the constant vigilance I attempted to maintain.

But the thought of giving in to them—to my sister, to the Broad-moor staff, to the authorities—left me sad. I had lived in that house all of my life and for much of it I followed the same routine every day. The thought of being forced to live a different way left me hollow inside. As if the part of me at the center would be taken away and a void left in its place. Routine was important to me and maintaining the one I had was even more so. I abhorred change. Newness was not my friend. Constancy, regularity, rhythm, they were my friends. They kept me going and made life manageable for me. Even productive. Change threatened my existence.

Homer guided me down the hall to my room where I expected to see The Pill sitting inside its paper cup resting on the dresser. Instead, I saw Porter Fulbright, my lawyer, standing by the window on the opposite side of the bed. Homer left us and I moved myself from the wheelchair to the upholstered chair in the corner. Fulbright closed the door, propped against the foot of the bed, and then we talked.

"I located Julia," he said. There was a smile on his face when he spoke and I could see that he was satisfied with himself at finding her. She wasn't difficult to find. She lived just up the street from me and was always home. Though she, like me, preferred to sleep in the afternoon and sometimes into the early evening, which occasionally made getting her to the door between lunch and midnight difficult.

"The woman who walks her dog at night in her underwear." I don't know why I referred to her that way. In a third person sort of way. As if I didn't really know her.

"Yes," Fulbright said.

"What did she say?"

"She confirmed everything you said."

I had an expectant look. "And Margaret?"

"I found her, too." He seemed satisfied with that as well. "Right where you said she would be. One street over."

"She told you about Mrs. Washington?"

"Yes. She did." Fulbright still was smiling so I knew he had something else to say.

"And what else did you find?" I asked.

"The man with the little girl."

My eyes opened wider at the mention of this new information. "You found them?"

"Yes." Then he corrected himself. "I found the man."

"What did he say?"

"He said the little girl is his granddaughter. She stayed with him most of the time but in the afternoon she went to stay with a lady who lived a few blocks away. They cut through the woods because it was shorter and because it gave his granddaughter a chance to see some wildlife, which he enjoyed pointing out to her."

The way he described them seemed odd. "You're speaking in the past tense," I noted.

"They did that when the girl was younger," Fulbright said. "About six or seven. She's in college now. Which explains why you weren't been able to find them before."

Fulbright spoke as if everything were perfectly normal—a witness sought, a witness found—but for me, the news was quite troubling. I had seen the man and the little girl just a few weeks before I went to court. It was hot and sunny and they were walking through the woods. He in a dark gray suit with a hat. She in a summer dress. From the look of it, the dress was made of cotton. The fabric seemed very light. They were talking and smiling and laughing and I could almost hear their voices.

Was it real? Or was I asleep and dreaming? No. I couldn't have been asleep. I saw them through the window of the back bedroom. That's where I sat when I was awake during the daytime. The front windows were for nighttime. But I noticed Fulbright did not find any of what the man said to be troubling at all so I kept my thoughts to myself.

"They will come to court?" I asked.

"Yes," Fulbright said triumphantly. "They will be there."

"And what about the doctors who examined me here?"

"Other than the outburst you had when you arrived, they say

you have been incident free and are capable of taking care of yourself."

"Good." I said it with a soft voice that sounded distracted because my thoughts had moved on from the court appearance to the next topic. "Did my sister clean out my investment accounts?"

"No." Fulbright shook his head. "She hasn't touched them."

"You know this for certain?"

"Yes. I checked with your advisor. He didn't talk to me about the details but he said she had not contacted him since the day he met with the two of you."

This left me puzzled. "Then why all of this?" I had a bewildered look on my face and a troubled tone in my voice.

"Apparently," he replied, "she wanted access to your house."

My forehead wrinkled in a frown. "My house?"

"Yes."

"What for?"

"We're not sure. No one has seen her in several weeks."

I thought for a moment. "Several weeks would be about the time I was brought here."

"That's about right." Fulbright nodded. "That's about the last time anyone has seen her."

"Did you search my house?"

"I went over there, but I don't have any way of getting inside. Other than to break open a door. But that seemed a little extreme."

In spite of the way she acted, the news about my sister was troubling and I felt certain I knew where to find her. I was equally certain my keys were still in the pocket of the pants I had been wearing on the day we were in court. Those clothes were hanging in a closet by the bed. As Fulbright continued to talk, I thought of giving him the key to the house and asking him to check the attic. If she was in the house, she was either there or in her old room but I did not expect him to find her alive. There was no reason for me to think that, other than my knowledge of her as my sister, but the sense I had inside was that she was dead.

I kept quiet about it while we discussed our plans for the hearing that was scheduled to occur a few days later. All the while, however, my mind was torn between conflicting thoughts. If my sister was in the place I thought she might be, she would not be alive. Which meant she would not appear in court. If I kept that information to myself and she failed to show, the case against me would evaporate. Or at least be greatly weakened.

On the other hand, if her body was found after the hearing, the authorities might suspect I had something to do with her death, especially if I was the one who reported the discovery. The medical examiner could determine the time of death and it ought to be obvious that she died while I was being held in Broadmoor. Still, I did not feel comfortable being the one to find her and did not wish to trust myself to the medical examiner's call.

And then there was the matter of foul odor. When Mother died, I was away on a trip to Barcelona, one of the few times I left the country. Mrs. Langston, Mother's closest friend, was supposed to check on her daily but she went to San Antonio to see her daughter. Mother's body lay in her bed for ten days until I returned and discovered her. By then, decomposition was well along and the smell was horrible. I noticed it as I came from the car on the driveway beside the house and knew she was not alive. Gemma or Tony or Julia should have noticed it long before then but they didn't. Removing the odor required the services of a professional remediation company and a painting contractor who applied three coats of paint to the walls and ceiling. I even had the floors refinished and, of course, replaced the furniture. Though the furniture didn't matter. It wasn't old or important. We went through the same thing when Father died so nothing in Mother's room predated his death.

Whatever my sister did, she did of her own accord. I had nothing to do with it. And I had the best proof possible of that. I was confined in a psychiatric hospital at the time whatever happened to her might have occurred. But then I became concerned about Gemma. If something happened to my sister—as I suspected—then something might have happened to Gemma, too. Her family might like to know about it sooner rather than later. And for all I knew, she could be alive and languishing in a closet, her body bound and her mouth gagged. My sister was not above doing something like that if she took the notion.

When Fulbright and I finished our discussion about the case and he was preparing to leave I said, "I think you should check my house."

"For your sister?"

"Yes."

"I would be glad to," he said. "But I don't have a key."

I rose from my chair and crossed the room to the closet by the bed, then reached into the pocket of the pants that hung there and took out a key chain. The house key was on a small ring by itself and I removed it, then handed it to him. "This is a key to the back door. My sister's old room is a middle room at the top of the stairs. First room on the left. The windows look out over the driveway."

Fulbright had a puzzled expression. "She lived with you?"

I shook my head. "The house belonged to our parents. It's the place where we grew up."

"Okay."

"If you don't find her in her old room, check the attic."

Fulbright frowned once more. "The attic?"

"She often hid there when she was a child." It was one of her special places. I slept all day to avoid the light. She hid in the attic for the same reason. And for others, as well.

"You think your sister is hiding there now?" he asked.

"If you find her there," I explained. "You will likely find she is no longer alive."

Later that day Homer came again to the day room where I had returned to sit in the sun and continue my thoughts while staring at my hand. With little in the way of explanation, he placed me in a wheelchair and took me to the administrative office where Fulbright was waiting with a deputy sheriff at his side.

The deputy was a young man of Fulbright's height but with olive skin, dark hair, and even darker eyes. He was not particularly muscular and I judged by his long frame over which there was hardly any fat that he was a runner. There was a tension about him, too, that gave him a no-nonsense air. All business. No variation. Rigid. Which left me suspicious of why he was present.

They guided me to a conference room and the others followed but the deputy stood back when we reached the door. "I'll be out here," he said. Fulbright acknowledged him with a nod and my sense of suspicion grew to a state of apprehension.

Homer pushed me up to the conference table and then turned to leave. I took hold of his hand to stop him but he slipped it away. "You'll be alright, Hornwallace," he said. A tingle ran up my spine at the mention of it. That was the first time he or anyone else at Broadmoor had called me by my chosen name. It was an exhilarating experience but it told me something bad was about to happen.

The door closed as Homer left the room and when he was gone, Fulbright said, "I went to the house like you suggested."

"And you found my sister?"

"She was in the attic," he said.

"And not alive."

"No." Fulbright shook his head. "I'm sorry. She was dead. Had been for several weeks."

"And Gemma?"

"She is alive and well at her home."

I raised an eyebrow. "Alive?"

"Yes."

"That surprises you?"

"A little." I avoided his gaze. "Why is the deputy with you?"

"The court issued an order releasing you temporarily to our custody. They need you to identify your sister's body."

"At the hospital?"

"Yes," he said. "At the morgue."

When Father died I went there with Mother to claim his remains. I did not do that when Mother died as they came to the house and I told them the things they wanted to know about her while they were there. But the mention of the morgue revived a memory of being there with Father. And it revived a memory of the smell as well. The smell of the morgue was a problem for me. Something reminiscent of formaldehyde. The dull putridness of death. The cleaning agents they used. It gave me a headache and I was not looking forward to being there.

From Broadmoor, I rode in the deputy's patrol car to City Hospital, where the morgue was located. Fulbright followed us in his car, then accompanied us as we made our way across the parking lot to the hospital entrance.

The medical examiner—Robert Pouncey—met us in the hallway just inside the doorway and escorted us to his facility. Pouncey was a middle-aged man. Tall and slender with thinning hair. His sister was in my class at Amherst, though I doubt either of them remembered it. No one at Amherst remembered me, either.

When we reached the morgue, Pouncey took us to the far end of the room where several rows of cooler doors were located. He checked his file for the correct door number, then glanced over at me. "Are you sure you can do this? The body has decayed a good bit. It smells."

"Yes," I replied. "Go ahead." We were there. The smell was everywhere. There was no way out but to get it over with.

Pouncey unlatched the door and drew out a metal rack that held my sister's body. A wave of putrid morbidity gushed out with her. My stomach muscles revolted but I clinched them off and steeled myself against the stench.

The body was covered with a white sheet and when the rack was fully extended before me, Pouncey lifted the sheet from the head of the corpse. I recognized her immediately but when I didn't speak he said, "Do you know this person?"

"Yes," I answered. "That is her. That is my sister."

Pouncey quickly covered her body with the sheet, then pushed her back inside the cooler and closed the door. As he latched it in place I said, "How did she die?"

"Drug overdose," Pouncey replied. He took a can of air freshener from a cart nearby and sprayed it in the air. The fragrance was almost worse than the smell of my sister's body.

"What kind of drug?" I asked.

Pouncey checked his file again. "Lorazepam and amphet-amines," he said.

"I understand she was found in the attic."

"Yes."

"Was there any evidence of those drugs up there?"

Pouncey sorted through several pages of the file. "I was not at the scene but the detective who responded indicated there were two empty pill bottles near the body."

"Do you have those bottles?"

"No." Pouncey shook his head. "You will have to ask the detectives if you want to look at the bottles." Then his eyes opened wide and a sense of realization came over him. "But, there's a photograph in our digital file." He stepped to the far side of the room where a laptop rested on the counter. With a few strokes of the keyboard a file opened and a picture appeared showing two bottles lying on the attic floor.

I studied the image a moment, then pointed. "Can you zoom in on them a little closer?"

"Sure," Pouncey said.

The frame tightened and that's when I noticed one of the bottles was labeled for my sister. The other—the one that contained Lora-zepam—was in Gemma's name. "Any estimate of how much my sister took?"

"Based on the date the prescriptions were filled, the contents of her stomach, the blood tests, and the time of death, it appears she ingested about half a bottle of Lorazepam and a full bottle of the amphetamine."

That seemed like a lot to me. "She would have been able to swal-low all of that before passing out?"

"Yes."

"She would have needed a drink." My sister couldn't swallow a tiny allergy tablet without something to help her. "Any thoughts on what that might have been?"

Pouncey switched to a different page of the file on his laptop and pointed. "Whiskey," he said. An image of a bottle of Basil Hayden's appeared.

"Bourbon," I corrected, unable to let the discrepancy pass. The bottle of Basil Hayden's in the file wasn't one for whiskey. It was bourbon. A distinction my sister often noted with an odd, nerdy delight.

Pouncey seemed not to understand and responded with a wary nod. "Right."

"You mentioned time of death," I said, moving on. There was no point in explaining myself to him. "How long has she been dead?"

"As best I can determine, she's been dead about three weeks. Maybe four, but not any longer than that."

"Bodies are usually in this shape after three or four weeks?"

"They are if they've been lying in a hot attic."

Dead for about three weeks. Maybe four. The words rolled around in my mind and as they did the implications began to emerge. Based on that estimate, my sister had, indeed, died not long after I was taken to Broadmoor. And from the examiner's description, she died at her own hand. Which meant she had no intention of attending the hearing that would determine my ultimate end. She had no intention of following through with the proceedings she had initiated. She placed me at Broadmoor. Disrupted my life. Turned my world upside down. And intended from the beginning to rest my extrication on my own device.

Yet once again I had been victimized by her. It was nothing new. She had treated me that way all our lives. But this time seemed particularly cruel. She knew how I was and she knew what others thought of me because of it. The judgments they made of me at first sight. Opinions based on the shallowness of their minds but which prevented them from ever knowing me beyond their own myopic stereotypes. Sending me to Broadmoor only validated those opinions and I could hear their voices as plainly as if they were standing in the morgue with us.

"She always said he was crazy. Now we know it for certain."

"Wasn't he in a mental hospital?"

And that idiot Rankin with his arrogant tone, "He sees things and hears things, you know."

True enough, I did see things and hear things. Much of it not seen or heard by anyone else. But that was because I sat by the window at night long after everyone else went to bed and I saw what happened while they were asleep. And in the daytime, whether I was awake or asleep, I heard the sounds they made and recorded all of them automatically in my mind. They, on the other hand, knew nothing because they paid no attention to anything.

Unlike the experiences of others, the noises of life—a passing car, a door opening and closing, a bird flying overhead—were never relegated to contextual clutter for me. Instead, they were always in my ear. The delivery truck, the mail truck, the neighbor's car, the other neighbor's truck, the child pedaling past on a bicycle he received for his eleventh birthday, the voices from the party at which he received it. I heard each of them, separately and distinctly. Yet familiarity did not force the sounds of daily life to recede from the pale of my attention. My brain was never numbed to their existence. On the contrary, it was energized by them. My ears always attentive. My mind always at work. Never resting. Never ceasing to function. All day long. Questions. Answers. Questions. And more answers. Sorting. Resorting. Arranging the information that my senses gathered as I processed the world around me in a constant stream of detail, nuance, rhythm.

After a moment, I returned to the matter at hand and as I became conscious once again of my surroundings, I noticed that Pouncey and Fulbright were staring at me with a puzzled expression. I had no idea how long I had been standing in their presence without speaking, or even if I had not been speaking, but whatever I had been doing while lost in thought they seemed to take it as rather odd. A reaction I had grown accustomed to in others.

Without explaining myself I thanked Pouncey for his help, then looked over at Fulbright. "Is there anything else to do here?"

"No," he said. "I think we're finished here." He gestured toward the door and we started in that direction, then continued into the hallway. No one said a word as we made our way through the building with only the sound of our shoes clicking against the hard surface of the floor to occupy my mind.

As we neared the exit to the parking lot, the deputy took me by the elbow. "You'll have to come with me," he said.

I glanced over at him. "Any possibility we could go by my sister's house? We need to make sure it is secure."

"We need to—"

Before he could finish, Fulbright turned to me. "Are you in charge of her estate now?"

"I'm not sure." And I really wasn't. I had never seen my sister's will and wasn't certain she even had one. "But until that has been decided, we need to make sure the doors are locked and no one can get inside."

"Do you have a key?"

"No."

"I'll see that the locks are changed," Fulbright offered. "How about that?"

"Okay."

Securing the house wasn't all that I wanted to do, but I was certain the deputy was not going to allow me to visit the property, so I said no more. In spite of his appearance, which was almost as pleasing as Fulbright's, he proved to be a functionary by disposition and rigid by personality. Not the type for viewing situations creatively or for stretching the moment into an opportunity.

Almost on cue, he took me by the elbow again. "Come on," he said. "The court's order was for you to identify the body and go back to Broadmoor. We need to get you back there now." I offered no resistance as we made our way to the patrol car but I was worried, though not for the reasons I implied. Gemma might be living there and if she was I wanted to talk to her about the Lorazepam prescription that bore her name. That, however, like all my other questions, would have to wait.

We returned to Broadmoor without incident and I was wheeled back to my room, though not by Homer. I was just settled in place by the window when dinner arrived. They served all of the meals earlier than I liked, but once on their schedule I adjusted to it well enough. That day I was glad to have the food.

When I had eaten all I wanted I placed the tray in the hall by my door. The sun was still up so I returned to my seat in the chair by the window. Rather than staring at my hand, though, I gazed out at the lawn and thought of the events that had occurred that day, how my sister's death might affect the hearing that was scheduled in my case, and the way it might shape my life beyond that. I was alone now. No parents. No siblings. No offspring. No relatives of any kind from our immediate family. Just me.

For the next two days I kept to myself even more than normal. Each morning, Homer wheeled me to the day room where I sat by the window, but I had no interaction with anyone. There was little need for it. After the incident in the dining hall and after taking all of my subsequent meals in my room, most of the patients I had met when I arrived were either transferred to other facilities or simply forgot who I was.

At noon each day, Homer took me back to my room where I ate lunch. Afterward, I departed from my previous routine and remained there, sitting alone in the chair by the window, staring out at the lawn. Often I did the same at night, after dinner, and remained there until ten o'clock when the lights were required to be out. As that hour approached, I dutifully prepared for bed but when the building grew quiet I got up and moved back to the chair, sitting there for hours gazing up at the stars. Imagining what it might be like to be at home in the chair by the window in the front bedroom on the second floor, watching Julia as she walked by with her dog.

Finally, the day arrived for my appearance in court. The deputy who had come with Fulbright to tell me of my sister's death arrived at lunchtime and drove me to the hearing in his patrol car. We parked near the courthouse entrance and he escorted me up the steps and down the hall to the courtroom where I took a seat alongside Fulbright at the counsel's table. We hadn't been there long when an attorney for the county entered and took a seat at a table to our left.

Soon after that, the judge entered. Everyone stood while he made his way to the bench, and once he was seated we returned to our chairs. The bailiff announced our case and until then I had been calm, but as he said my name I grew tense and nervous. It sounded strange. My name. The courtroom. With the judge glaring over at me. Fulbright seemed to notice and I expected him to take my hand but instead, out of sight from the others, he rubbed the top of my thigh. At first I was taken aback by the gesture but then realized he had not wanted the judge to see lest he notice my nervousness and think it was related to my mental condition rather than to his presence.

While I struggled to maintain my composure, the attorney for the county stood and informed the court of my sister's demise. The judge already knew. Announcing it in court was merely a formality. All the same, everyone turned in my direction. I acknowledged them with an appropriate nod of my head but did not smile as might have been the custom on other occasions.

In spite of my sister's absence, the judge insisted on receiving a report from the doctor who evaluated me at Broadmoor. I assume he wanted a record of the doctor's opinion merely to protect himself should I later engage in some untoward activity. Despite my nervousness, I had every confidence that I was to be released that day. I had seen the people at Broadmoor. I was nothing like them.

Instead of accepting the doctor's report on paper, the judge called him to the witness stand and asked him to give an oral report as well. The doctor—an older man approaching retirement but still quite articulate—described his encounters with me in more or less accurate terms and summarized me as neuroatypical, a term I had never heard before but one I rather liked. Since childhood, many terms had been used to describe my personality and the manner in which I processed information, on the spectrum being the most frequent and also the one I disliked the most.

When I was eight years old, the school sent me home for being rude to a teacher. I wasn't rude. Blunt, perhaps, but not rude. Mother didn't allow us to act rudely. Officials at the school didn't agree with my assessment, however, and told Mother I should be evaluated before they would allow me to return to class. To satisfy them, Mother took me to a psychiatrist. It was my first experience with one, though by no means my last.

The psychiatrist—Dr. Malik, a crotchety man about the age of the doctor who evaluated me at Broadmoor, but with untrimmed nose hair that often was cluttered with residue of obvious origin—subjected me to a number of interviews. Interrogations, actually. Then administered a battery of tests, some of which I enjoyed very much and continued to repeat after Malik's assistants told me to stop. They tried to force me to quit but I resisted until they sent for Mother. She gave me a sip of Coca-Cola which slowed me just a little, then guided me to the window where I took another drink while I stared out on the traffic below. That was how she did it at home, too.

A few days after the final test, Mother and I went back for a consultation with Malik. The results of their work, he told us, indicated that I was brilliant in many areas, a fact that seemed to please Mother very much. "But," he added. "Your son showed considerable deficits in social skills. He also appeared unusually sensitive to light and sound."

"What does that mean?" she asked.

"It means that theoretical subjects are a simple matter for him but the normal auditory clutter that attends daily life poses an astronomical challenge to him. Has he always been this way?"

"No. When he is home he spends most of his day in his room."

"Room." Malik had a knowing tone and an accusative look in his eye. "Or closet?"

"He refers to the closet as his clubhouse."

"And friends?"

"Most boys don't have many, do they?"

"Most boys swim in a sea of testosterone," Malik replied.

Mother looked displeased. "You mentioned a social aspect."

"For one thing," Malik said, "he tends to be quite…blunt."

"Plainspoken," Mother corrected.

"No, ma'am." Malik shook his head. "Blunt. And while we were testing him, he had trouble keeping his shirt on. I think that was one of the things the school encountered as well."

"He does best when his clothes don't touch his skin."

"Yes, well." Malik defaulted to an arrogant disposition when he felt challenged. "That is rather unavoidable in some circumstances."

"That's all you found? He's brilliant but doesn't care for clothes? We already knew that."

"I'm trying to be kind," he said. I was sitting in the room while they talked and he glanced in my direction with that comment.

Mother seemed taken aback. "Why do we need your sympathy?"

"Because." Malik lowered his voice. "Based on the tests, interviews, and observations, I'm afraid I must tell you that your son is au—"

"No," Mother snapped, cutting him off. "You will not use that word over my son."

"Then what word should I use?"

"Brilliant will do just fine."

"Genius?" he said snidely.

"I'm the one paying your bill," she snarled. They appeared to have some sort of history between them but I knew better than to ask about it.

"Then let's just say, he's on the spectrum."

On the spectrum. I had no idea what that meant and on the way home I asked Mother. She smiled at me with the kindest expression of motherly love she'd ever shown. "It means, 'too brilliant for that damn doctor to handle,'" she said.

After that, I received my schooling at home through private tutors. Father arranged for it. Until I reached the ninth grade, they taught me from the comfort of my room and submitted reports of my grades to the school board. Father had friends there.

When I reached ninth grade there was a change in the school board. I was once again sent to school with the other students. It was a bit of a shock to my senses—the noise and light and the need for clothes that brushed against my skin—but I managed. And in the years that followed I heard many words used to describe me, but none of them proved adequate. And none of them as acceptable to me as neuroatypical.

That day in court, when we were there for the hearing in my case, I listened while the judge engaged the doctor from Broadmoor in a lengthy and elaborate conversation. At first he seemed really quite lost in the terms and distinctions, but slowly, incrementally, he came to an understanding of what the doctor meant by his description of me. "So," the judge said by way of summary, "he thinks differently from most people but he's not a threat to himself or anyone else." It was the closest thing to a compliment I had received from a stranger in a long time.

"That is correct," the doctor confirmed.

"Very well," the judge said. "I've heard enough."

Julia was present in the witness room that day. I caught a glimpse of her in the hallway as we arrived but Fulbright steered me away from her. She was wearing a red top with a black pencil skirt and high heels that accentuated her legs.

The man who walked with the girl through the woods behind the house was there, too. At least, Fulbright said he was that person. I wasn't certain he was the one I saw. The man at the courthouse that day was older and heavier than I remembered. Fulbright met with him while we waited for the proceedings to begin and when he returned he smelled of cigar smoke. I did not remember the man I saw ever smoking.

They were both present that day but neither of them was called to testify. After hearing from the doctor, the judge ordered me released and dismissed the petition that had been filed against me. The county attorney did not object.

When we were finished with the hearing in court and the judge released us to leave, Fulbright drove me back to Broadmoor to gather my belongings. Loading all of that into his car took longer than I expected—not even Homer offered to help—and processing me from their custody required a visit to the administration office, followed by a phone call to the judge's office, but an hour later we were on our way home. I sat in the passenger seat of Fulbright's car and stared out the window, watching as the landscape moved past. It reminded me of sitting at the window upstairs in the front bedroom of my house, only the images were brighter and everything went by much faster.

After weeks spent imagining the moment when I would finally be free again, the reality of it proved less exhilarating than I expected. The grass, it turned out, was as green from the window in the day room as it now was from the window of Fulbright's car. And the trees along the highway were the same as those on the lawn at Broadmoor. Still, I was glad to be rid of the place. Unlike the sounds from the neighborhood where my home was located, Broadmoor offered merely noise with no great purpose behind it. A cacophony devoid of rhythm, meter, or tempo save for the rise of the din in the morning and the waning of it in the evening. I found it very disorienting—even at night when the halls grew quiet and I could hear the sound of my breath again.

The trip from Broadmoor didn't take very long and soon Fulbright turned the car onto the driveway at my house. I glanced up at the windows on the second floor and they peered down at me like old friends welcoming me after a long absence. I smiled at them in return as we came alongside the house, then turned onto the concrete parking pad near the back door.

Father had the pad constructed when I was ten for the purpose of teaching me how to play basketball. I shot baskets with him for a while on two or three occasions, but each time we were out there I became distracted after only a few minutes—usually by my reflection in the window. I made a few attempts at the basket, halfhearted at best, then spent the remainder of the daylight hours standing before a downstairs window, noting the effect my position had on the shape formed in the glass, leaning this way and that and slowly moving across the plane of its reflective surface. Father, frustrated by my lack of attention to the matter at hand, gave up and went inside. After one or two sessions of that, Father stopped insisting we play and began parking the car there when he came home in the afternoon.

That day when we arrived from Broadmoor, Fulbright and I used the key from my keyring to open the back door. As I entered the mudroom, I expected to encounter the odor of my deceased sister still lingering in the air. To my surprise it was not, but scent from the cleaning agents used by the remediation company to scour the attic was strong. A sharp, chemical odor, in fact, and after only a moment my nose began to burn.

Fulbright accompanied me as I made my way into the kitchen, then walked through the downstairs rooms, raising the windows as we went. He seemed not to notice the smell and if he did, he was unaffected by it.

When we reached the hallway by the staircase I asked, "Were you able to secure my sister's residence?"

"Yes," he said. "And from what I could see, no one had been there in several days. Perhaps longer."

"You have a key?"

"Yes," he said, then he took a keyring from his pocket and handed it to me.

We climbed the steps to the second floor—I led the way—and continued through each of the rooms, raising the windows to air out the house. Fulbright stayed right with me. I think he wanted to make certain no one was lurking in one of the rooms. Or perhaps he wanted to judge my reaction to being back there and to being in the house where my sister had died. He didn't know the history of the place. Death was nothing new to it. Or to me. I didn't care that she had died there—my sister was the third person to die in the house during my lifetime. That sort of thing meant little to me and, in fact, served to deepen the experience of residing there rather than diminish it. I was at home where I belonged among the past and its memories, and I was glad to be there.

After we'd raised all the windows on the second floor and had gone through all of the house except the attic, Fulbright decided it was time for him to leave. I escorted him downstairs to the back door and waited while he made his way to the car, then watched from the front window to see that he really was gone. You can never be too sure about things like that. Sometimes people say they're leaving, then come back for one more thing they've forgotten they needed, or double back to look through the window and see what you're doing when you think you're alone. That's how my sister did me. Mother, too, sometimes.

In spite of my best effort to air out the house, the scent from the cleaning agents remained in the air so as Fulbright's car disappeared up the street, I moved away from the window, walked to the kitchen, and found a month-old package of bacon in the refrigerator. I switched on the radio that was tuned to the public radio station and the sound of an interviewer's voice filled the void in my mind. I listened to it while I fried the bacon.

Before long, the smell of rank bacon frying on the stove hung heavy throughout the whole house and succeeded in hiding the odor of the cleaning agents. When the strips of meat were thoroughly cooked and the fatty parts dry and crunchy, I poured the meat and grease onto a plate and set it outside by the back steps for an animal to eat. I left the greasy pan on the stove, however, which allowed the scent to waft into the air a while longer. Mother showed me that technique, though she preferred to use herbs and teas steeped in a pot of water that she allowed to slowly reduce until it scorched the bottom of the pan. "Bacon," she said, "is a measure of last resort." She wouldn't eat bacon for any reason. The animals that came to our back steps didn't have that problem, though. The meat and grease I'd set outside was gone in short order.

As darkness approached I went upstairs to the front bedroom on the second floor and sat in the chair by the window to look out over the neighborhood, as was my custom. One by one, lights came on in the houses up and down the street. A breeze came up from the south and nighttime slowly settled in place. My eyes were on the houses and the cars that passed my vantage point, then receded from view as the light melted away. All the while, though, my mind was on my sister and her demise. Not in a nostalgic manner—I wasn't lonely at all and we hadn't seen each other on a daily basis since she graduated from high school. The thing that occupied my thoughts about her was deeper than that and went to the heart of who we'd been, who we were, who I was. The thing that kept rolling around in my mind was the question of why she did it. Why did she kill herself and what did it mean?

No one in our family was particularly religious. Some would say, and some did say, that we were not religious at all. Once when we were at church, Mother declined to take Communion. Because she didn't go up, I refused to, also. That meant everyone seated on our pew had to move around us and that meant the entire church noticed—even though they were supposed to pay us no mind.

The following week, Mrs. LaRue, who taught my Sunday school class, let me know how deeply she disapproved of our action. When I suggested it revealed a serious view of the solemnity of the rite—a comment I might have delivered in a sarcastic tone—she became angry, recited her family's long history of providing priests to the denomination, and questioned the depth of our family's commitment to anything at all. I told her I didn't think we needed much of a commitment to the denomination, which she liked even less than our decision not to take Communion.

When I recounted all of that to Mother, she said it was alright if they didn't think we were religious. "Jesus wasn't religious, either." She said that often in response to many situations. Her friends—the ones who came to the house to play bridge and drink Chivas Regal all afternoon—laughed every time, but the people who attended the church where we sometimes went did not, Mrs. LaRue chief among them. They thought comments like that were sacrilegious. Mother thought their response merely confirmed that her observation hit too close to home for their comfort.

But, as I said, we were not particularly religious. Some of our Catholic acquaintances viewed suicide as a mortal sin. A sin that cuts one off from God entirely, unless it is followed by repentance and an act of contrition. Being dead, however, the one who commits suicide has no possibility of repentance and, presumably, is lost for eternity. We didn't believe that. I'm not sure what we believed, but we didn't believe that. Mother said Jesus didn't believe it, either.

Our lack of formal religious observance notwithstanding, Mother viewed self-inflicted death as a tragedy. Father saw it as a supreme act of cowardice. I saw it as the desperate act of someone who could find no other means of escaping whatever forces seized their mind.

None of us showed the slightest inclination in that direction. Even upon reflection that evening I could not fathom the notion that my sister did, either. But if that was not what happened to her, then what did? Try as I might, however, I could find no answer.

Sometime after midnight I remembered that my sister kept a diary. When she was living at home she wrote in it every night and hid it in a shoe box that was tucked in the back of her closet. I found it and read it every week. I suppose she realized what I was doing because when I looked for it later it had been moved and I found it beneath the mattress of her bed—she was that obvious about everything, though she thought she was being clever. After a while, it disappeared from beneath the mattress and I found it behind the grate that covered the heating duct in her room. Plaster dust had fallen on the floor when she removed the grate to hide it and she had not bothered to sweep it up. I was amazed she knew how to unfasten the grate but not surprised at all that she failed to notice the mess she'd created in doing so. Sometime later I checked for the diary in the duct and discovered it had been moved yet again. I never found it after that, though I suspected she placed it in the attic, but I did not care to go up there. The last time I read any of it she was beginning her senior year in high school.

Although my familiarity with my sister's diary practices ended when she left home after high school graduation, I was rather confident she had continued the habit in one form or another. She was that kind of person—an external processor who disliked conversation. Keeping a diary was her means of unburdening her soul, though from what I read when we were younger her burdens seemed quite light.

If my sister kept a diary up to the last days of her life, it might offer clues to why she did what she did—if, in fact, she had done what they said she had done. Finding her most recent one would be a challenge but she was so obvious in everything else, I was confident that if it was in her house it would be in one of her familiar hiding places—the closet, beneath the mattress, behind the grate that covered the opening to the duct in her bedroom.

Searching my sister's house, though, would have to wait until after the sun was up. I had the key that Fulbright gave me and I was my sister's sole heir-at-law. Getting inside her house would be no problem and I had every right to be there. But entering her house right then—in the middle of the night—would attract attention from her neighbors. Which undoubtedly would involve the police. Given my recent proceedings in court, I thought it best not to attract attention of any kind to myself right then. Finding the diary would have to wait a few hours.

While I waited, I continued to think and it occurred to me that she might have brought those diaries to my house. Or left them here when she moved on. I doubted either was true and certainly there would have been no reason for her to bring her diary with her on the day she came to kill herself—if that's how her life ended, about which I continued to harbor doubt, despite the medical examiner's opinion. Still, she might have brought them with her. My sister was fully capable of almost anything, a proclivity she had proven to be true many times. And if she did bring them here or keep them here, they almost certainly would be in one of the places she visited while she was living here—she was so unimaginative in that way. I might find them right now, right here, if I searched for them in the usual places. I might. It was a possibility. And besides, looking for them would give me something to do while I waited for the sun to come up over the trees.

From the chair by the window in the front bedroom I walked down the hall to my sister's room and searched inside the closet. Some of her clothes were hanging there—new ones, current ones, not clothing from her childhood—which told me she had been living there at least part of the time while I was at Broadmoor. But there was no indication Gemma had been there. That was curious to me because I was confident they had been romantically involved with each other right up to the end, though I had not seen either of them since the day the court took custody of me.

At least, I didn't think I had.

One day when Homer pushed me to my room and I sat in my chair by the window gazing out at the lawn, I became aware of a scent in the air that smelled like Charlie, a perfume my sister used to wear. It was popular back then among her friends. When they were at the house and the scent was particularly strong, Father and I used to sit outside until they were gone.

Once or twice he threatened to light up a Cuban cigar he'd brought back from the Cayman Islands where he'd been to meet with one of his advisors. He was as obvious about that sort of thing as my sister—going to the Caymans to talk to a financial advisor about an account created to avoid paying US taxes. His attorney tried to tell him he should meet his offshore advisors somewhere else—Rome or London or the Bahamas, even—but he didn't listen. He did, however, bring back Cuban cigars, which his lawyer was all too glad to accept when Father gave him a few.

At the time, Cuban cigars were illegal in the United States but they were readily available throughout the Caribbean. Father always purchased a dozen or so when he was down there and brought them back in his luggage. Customs officials never made an issue of them as long as he didn't bring back too many at once, like the time he tried to bring back three boxes only to have them seized at the airport.

Mother told us we should accept the heavy perfume scent as a gift and allow it to cleanse the house of the odors we created by living there. "A chance to change the air," she would say. But after my sister and her friends had been there a while, and the scent of perfume made Mother's head ache, and Father became impatient with sitting outside, she brewed a pot of her tea and herb concoction. "Better my herb than his," she used to say. An oblique reference to his Cuban cigars.

A check of the closet in my sister's room yielded nothing. Neither did the space beneath the mattress. I looked beneath the bed, too, just for good measure, but it was empty and void—except for a coating of dust on the floor, which I noted for later reference to the housekeeper. She'd been taking liberties with her work during my absence.

The air conditioner ducts did not appear to have been disturbed recently but just to be safe I used the flashlight app on my cell phone and checked inside. I found nothing there, either.

Only the attic remained as a potential hiding place for the diaries but my sister would have had no reason to hide them up there unless that's where they'd been all along and she wanted them to be discovered when her body was found, which apparently they were not. So I decided not to go up there. The attic was hot, even at night. But more than that, the items that were stored up there held memories from the past that did not like being kept there. Especially the ones trapped inside the musty sofa and the dusty boxes behind it. Every time I went up there those memories spoke to me and the sofa and other items that had been stored there complained about the noise they made, usually in loud and angry voices that I did not like to hear. The train set in the box at the far end was nice to me. And so was the airplane that sat atop the box. They got along well with their memories and did not mind being up there alone with just the two of them for company, though they often told me how much they missed seeing me and the laughter we shared in the past. The others, though, were not as polite and after all I'd been through in the past few weeks at Broadmoor and then in court, I didn't care to hear from them just yet.

When the search of my sister's room provided nothing except

the assurance that she had been living there at least part of the time while I was confined at Broadmoor, and that the housekeeper needed to pay greater attention to her cleaning tasks, I turned out the light and walked back to the front bedroom. My chair still was by the window so I took a seat on it, crossed my legs as was my customary posture, and, with my elbows resting against my thighs, sat hunched forward slightly while I once again peered out at the night view of the neighborhood.

As the hours ticked past I replayed in my mind the events of the past year. The pickup truck in Gemma's driveway, talking to Mrs. Washington by the mailbox, my sister's car replacing the pickup truck, Tony coming home early and catching them in the act. Then the trouble for me that followed. Again and again I replayed the sequence in my mind until finally it came to me. The pickup on the driveway was where the whole thing started. Until then, it had been just Gemma and Tony living next door with Gemma coming over in the morning for coffee, making obvious her desire for something more from me and, not getting it, returning home before lunch. But what if I had acted differently toward her?

What if I had relented and given her the attention she desired? The attention she craved? What if our rendezvous over coffee had become instead a rendezvous upstairs in my bed? Would I have avoided everything that followed my rejection of her? Would Gemma still be married to Tony? Would my sister still be alive? Would I have avoided Broadmoor?

Or were the seeds of the things that happened—Gemma and Tony, Gemma and my sister, Gemma and the divorce, Broadmoor— was that already planted in the soil of what had happened in the years before? Was this moment the result of events set in motion at my birth? Before my birth? Before my parents even met?

For the next several hours I stared out the window and reconstructed in my mind the events that sprang from my birth. Very quickly—much quicker than I thought possible—I strung together a series of events that led from my delivery to the time my sister graduated from high school. However, none of those events included

Gemma and for a moment I wondered how my sister came to be associated with Gemma—it seemed as though her car had appeared next door without provocation or antecedent—and then I remembered they'd been friends for a long time, but not in a way that led to anything else. Theirs was a friendship that arose over horses, which is where it faded, too.

When we were younger, my sister read a novel about horses—National Velvet or Black Beauty or something like that—and developed an insatiable desire to own a horse. At first Father resisted but finally gave in and found a stable near Round Rock that boarded them. He bought a horse for her and she kept it up there. Gemma had a horse there also and the two of them used to go riding together. Mother drove her to Round Rock on riding days, usually on Saturdays but sometimes on Sunday afternoons, too. I accompanied Mother once or twice. The drive up there was pleasant and I enjoyed the hum of the tires against the pavement. The sound of it eased my mind much the same as the voices on public radio now when I play it in the kitchen.

Horseback riding lasted about a year and as Gemma and my sister grew older, their lives took them in different directions but they never quite lost touch. Then, after Gemma married Tony and moved into the house next door, they saw each other slightly more frequently but solely on a social basis. That explained their acquaintance but it didn't explain for me how my sister came to be romantically involved with her. Or how the sequence of events that caused trouble for me—first the man in the pickup truck, then my sister, then my sister running naked from the house—came to be set in motion. To get answers to those questions I needed to locate my sister's most recent diary—if one existed. Barring that, I needed to locate Gemma. She could tell me what happened. If she would.

According to Fulbright, no one had seen Gemma since about the time my sister died. Perhaps she had engaged in some nefarious or explicit act that directly caused my sister's demise and fled to avoid the scrutiny of the detective's questions. More likely, though, she had grown bored with my sister, tossed her aside in exchange for a new romantic connection—just as she had replaced the man in the pickup truck with my sister—and become distracted by the bliss of that new paramour, which would have been very much like the Gemma I knew.

Regardless of what she'd done with herself, I wanted to know what had occurred to drive my sister to her death and Gemma was the one who could tell me. So I decided to go to my sister's house as soon as it was morning and search for the diaries, then find Gemma.

When the sun appeared through the trees behind Mrs. Washington's house, I rose from my place on the chair by the window in the front bedroom and went downstairs for a breakfast of Cheerios, toast, and coffee. Milk in the refrigerator was almost sour but I used it for the cereal anyway, though not in the coffee. Mother often said, "Sour milk is okay to cook with but you can't put it in hot coffee. It'll curdle with the first drop and ruin the whole cup." That morning, I drank the coffee black, though I added extra sugar.

About eight, I went out to the garage, raised the garage door, and got in the front seat of the car behind the steering wheel. The interior of the car smelled musty and there was a thin film of mildew on the steering wheel that rubbed off on my hand when I touched it. I found a wipe in the console and wiped away as much as I could, then placed the key in the ignition and turned it. The engine turned over once, then twice, then caught on the third try and sputtered to life. I allowed it to idle a while, just to be sure everything worked. Father taught me that. "Let it run a few minutes in the morning," he said. "To get the oil circulating through all the moving parts."

When the temperature gauge moved up from the bottom mark on the dial and the oil pressure light did not come on, I was satisfied everything functioned properly. I closed the driver's door, put the car in reverse, and backed it slowly from its place in the garage. It rolled out with no problems at all and I brought it to a stop directly opposite the post for the basketball hoop. The post still was standing by the parking pad, though it was rusted from exposure to the weather and the paint on the backboard was faded.

When the car came to a stop, I reached overhead to the sun visor and pressed the button on the remote control device that activated the garage door, then watched as it slowly lowered into place. The kids who lived up the street from me used to get in there and plunder through my tools when I left it open so I waited until the door was all the way down before continuing. As it banged into place, I removed my foot from the brake and backed the car to the street, then started on my way.

My sister lived on the opposite side of town, as far away from me as she could get and still remain a resident of the same city. That's what she told me. I'm not sure I ever believed that was how she really felt, but that's what she said. Word for word. I'm not making it up. Mother did not allow us to tell falsehoods.

The house, a two-story red brick federal with white trim, sat on a large lot that was covered with oak trees and azalea bushes. Being federal in style, it didn't have a porch—just a basic box for the center of the structure with matching wings on either side—and it wasn't as big as my house, but I liked the way it looked from the street. It had a nice balance and the landscaping gave it an elegance that reflected my sister's one strength—she had a wonderful sense of style.

When Mother was alive I used to go over there with her. After she died, my sister didn't want me around so I stayed away except to bring her some food once when she had the flu and couldn't get out. All of her friends were either at work or away and she had been subsisting on crackers and hot tea until that ran out, then she got desperate and that's when she called me. I was the last person on her call sheet. Which was alright with me. I didn't call her, either.

Why she wanted that house was a mystery to me. An apartment would have suited her need for space much better, but then she wouldn't have had the same degree of privacy. Neighbors sharing a common wall, as they do in an apartment, would have been too close for her. She always felt she was hiding more than her share of issues and an apartment would have put her too close to other people to feel like she was keeping those issues out of sight. Though most of the things she thought she was hiding were not of a nature anyone else would have bothered to obfuscate in the least. The few dark secrets she did have did not affect those of us who had experienced her presence at a greater depth. We already knew her for who she really was, not the person she wanted people to see. She couldn't hide from us and trying to hide from everyone else only caused her grief, though she never understood that.

The drive to the opposite side of town was uneventful and when I arrived at my sister's house I steered the car down the driveway to a place near the steps by the back door. Driving was one of my least favorite things to do and, despite the fact that I was at her house, I was glad when the car came to a stop.

With the car parked behind the house, I switched off the engine, then stepped out to the pavement and made my way to the back door. I used the key I'd been given by Fulbright to let myself inside but as I grasped the door knob I noticed he had changed the locks but used an inferior brand. Based on articles I had read, the ones he purchased were among the least reliable on the market and I made a note to have them changed again as soon as possible.

A stale odor inside the house told me Fulbright was correct in his assessment that no one had lived there in quite a few days. Certainly not since the locks were changed and probably not for a while before then. There was a heaviness about the air, too, and when I located the thermostat in the hall I saw that the air conditioner had not been set to operate frequently. I adjusted it to a lower setting and a rush of cool air swept through the house as the system turned on. I preferred the air cool and dry. That way, it didn't touch my skin so much.

As I made my way through the downstairs rooms, nothing seemed out of place. No dirty dishes cluttered the kitchen counter or sink; no newspapers scattered about the den; not even an open book or magazine lying beside a chair or resting on an end table. All of which raised my suspicions immensely. My sister was not a tidy person and she didn't keep a tidy house. A month's worth of dust on everything was not uncommon, but there was none of that. Only a light coating, as if the house had been cleaned recently—not real recently but more recent than my sister would have done. Which was contrary to my earlier assessment that no one had been there in quite some time, but still I whispered, "It's just too clean, though. And far too organized."

Upstairs I found much the same. The beds were made with the spreads stretched tightly and the pillows tucked in place. No clothes lying on the floor. No shoes out of place. Towels in the bathroom were hung straight, square, and even. And in the closet the clothes were organized with one size hanging to the left and another to the right. Gemma and my sister were not the same size. And that's when I knew Gemma and my sister had been living there together. I was certain of it. Gemma was the one who made sure it was put in order, too.

My assessment seemed all but undeniable and to test the notion that they had lived there together I leaned close to the bed and sniffed the pillows. One side smelled of Charlie, the perfume my sister had preferred since high school. The other side smelled like a scent from Lacoste, which Gemma preferred. I'd noticed her wearing it many times when she came to the house for coffee.

Assured by the clothes hanging in the closet that Gemma had lived there with my sister, and by the scent on the pillows that they had shared the bed, I sniffed the spread on both sides and found it only smelled of Gemma, then I checked the upholstery on a chair in the corner and sniffed around over the furniture. All of it smelled of Gemma. "She was the one who straightened this place." I knew it in my heart. "But why?"

Whether Gemma had been romantically involved with my sister made no difference to me. And the possibility that I might come to the house and discover evidence of their time together was a matter of no concern to either of them. They already knew that I knew they were together. Still, Gemma had gone to the trouble of straightening up.

Perhaps, I reasoned, she felt at least a twinge of guilt at the thought of someone besides me seeing the house the way it really was after one of their sessions together. Someone besides me who might see the disheveled bedding and the underwear strewn across the floor and conclude that the nature of their encounters had been quite passionate and even reckless.

My mind raced ahead—Gemma had rushed there after my sister died to straighten things up before anyone else arrived to have a look. Before the police arrived. Before the detectives arrived. Before I arrived. And after putting things in order, she disappeared to avoid answering questions that might pry beneath the surface of what appeared to be merely a suicide.

"This orderliness," I said softly, "is actually a cover-up meant to hide the truth of what really happened here." But what had happened there? Aside from two women making love, or having sex, or satisfying some inexplicable lust, what had gone on?

Answers to my questions could not come from the house. They could only come from Gemma or from my sister's diaries, if they existed. And there was only one way to locate the diaries, so I began searching for them, starting with the drawers of the nightstands on either side of the bed.

A search of the nightstands yielded nothing and working methodically around the room, I checked ever drawer in every other piece of furniture, every duct opening, and the space beneath the mattress. Still, I found nothing of the diaries. Then I moved on to the other rooms.

As I was lowering the mattress into place on the bed frame in the guest room, a woman's voice spoke to me from the doorway. "You won't find it there." At the sound of it, I turned to look in the direction from which it came and saw Gemma standing in the hallway. "Where is it?" I asked, without explaining myself.

"She took it to your house so she could put it with the others."

A frown wrinkled my forehead. "My house?"

"Yes."

Gemma entered the room and took a seat on the edge of the bed. "She didn't hate you, you know."

"She didn't like me, either," I replied.

"Maybe." She shrugged, then looked up at me. "Why are you here?"

"Did she have a will?"

"I don't know." Gemma shrugged again. "We didn't get that far."

My left eyebrow arched in a skeptical expression. "I think we both know how far things got."

"Yeah." A wisp of a smile came to her. "I guess we do."

"So what happened to her?"

"I don't know, exactly. We had a fight. She threw me out. I went to a hotel for a few days and then got an apartment."

I glanced around at the room. "Then you came back here to straighten up."

"No." She shook her head. "It was a mess when I left the last time."

That didn't fit with my understanding but her voice sounded genuine. "If you didn't do this," I said. "Who did?" I gestured to the room as I spoke.

"Did what?"

"Straightened up."

"She did," Gemma answered.

I shook my head. "Not my sister."

Gemma was insistent. "She kept it like this all the time."

"But you said it was a mess."

"Yes," she said. "It was always a mess after we were together. But she always put everything back in place."

"That's not how she used to be."

She had a knowing look. "You two never really understood each other, did you?"

I glanced away. "She didn't want me around."

"That's because you reminded her of your father."

I turned back to her sharply. "Our father?"

"He was all she ever talked about." Gemma gestured with her left hand. "That's why she kept the place so neat. She kept saying, 'What would Father think. He might walk in here any minute and see us.' At first I thought she was talking about the appearance of the room. Then I realized, she was talking about the two of us. Asking what her father would think about the way we were living."

My mind reeled at the suggestion of it. "She thought of him as if he was alive?"

"He was alive. For her at least."

"How is that?"

She pointed. "You were her father."

"Me?"

"It all got twisted up in her mind there at the end."

That wasn't what I wanted to talk about so I changed the subject. "Did you know she used your pills to do it?"

"Yes."

"Did you know she was going to do that, before she did it?"

She had a smart-ass smile. "I refilled the prescription so she could have them."

"Why?"

"It was what she wanted. I loved her. So I helped her do the thing that would make her happy."

"You think dying made her happy?"

Gemma rose from her place on the bed. "I think it put an end to the torment in her mind. One minute she's afraid her father will find out what she's really like. The next minute she's angry with you for finding such peace and being so functional." She took a few steps toward the door, then turned to face me. "Somewhere in all of that, you became Father in her mind and every time she saw you, she saw him."

"That seems impossible. We were hardly together at all after she moved out. She must have known I wasn't him."

"I think she knew. And I think she didn't know. And that was the problem. Knowing you were you and at the same time knowing you were him. And then realizing how crazy that was and that there was no way to stop it. That became more than she could manage and finally she just wanted to escape."

The words seemed to find a place inside me and as I thought about what Gemma had said I gazed down at a rug that lay on the floor just past the foot of the bed. It was red and black and gold with patterns of squares and triangles forming a background that was overlaid with the shape of a panther lying at rest on its side—a female panther from the look of it.

When I glanced up from the rug, Gemma was gone, but I found her downstairs. We resumed our conversation and I asked her about the man who came to her house in the pickup truck and then he was gone and my sister's car appeared.

When she lived in the house next door to me, Gemma needed help re-doing a bathroom. That's when she thought of my sister and thought she might be able to help. Why she thought of my sister, I don't know. Gemma didn't know either. My sister never really worked at a job or acquired credentialed skills of any kind, but she had a good eye for design and a number of people were aware of it. Perhaps that's how Gemma came to think of her.

At any rate, my sister agreed to help and came to the house to have a look at the project. They talked about colors in the bathroom, then about furniture and flooring in the downstairs rooms, then marriage and relationships and how things turned out for them and how different it had been from what they'd imagined it would be when they were young. At first they talked over a cup of coffee in the nook off the kitchen but before long they were talking about those things on the sofa in the living room and then on the bed upstairs. And just like that, an affair blossomed.

Not long after things turned romantic between them, the man in the blue pickup truck—who had been hired to do the work my sister envisioned—finished the job and was gone. But my sister remained.

"Yeah. She remained." Gemma had a wistful breathiness in her voice. "We were together in that house every day until Tony came home and caught us in the shower together."

I would have been fine without that much information about my sister's life but the question about how they came to be together bothered me and I asked and that's what Gemma said. So I was stuck with the mental images. But the part she said earlier—about me replacing Father in my sister's mind—that part still bothered me.

After a while I noticed Gemma was no longer in the room and my legs were tired from standing all morning so I took a seat in a chair by the window in the breakfast room and stared out at the lawn while I thought about my sister and how she could have confused me with Father.

"It was twisted," Gemma said from behind me. Once again I was startled by her voice and by her appearance in the room. "But that's the way she talked," Gemma continued. "Especially after you went to Broadmoor."

"After I was sent to Broadmoor." I felt the need to defend myself. Someone sent me to Broadmoor. I didn't go there on my own.

"She kept a diary of all that happened between us," Gemma continued. "I think it covers most of the past five or six years."

"Five or six years?"

"Yes," Gemma replied. "That's when this started."

A sense of confusion came over me and I didn't like the way all of this was going. Fulbright found the man who walked with the girl through the woods, but when I saw him in court he was old. He remembered walking in the woods but he said that was from years before. Now Gemma said her relationship with my sister started five or six years ago. I remembered it happening just last month.

Gemma kept talking. "I would find her at night wandering around the house, clutching that diary in her hand and saying, 'I have to hide this diary with the others. If Father finds it, he'll disown me.' When I reminded her that her father died a long time ago, she looked at me with the wildest eyes and said, 'Not him. The other one.' And once when I pressed her she took her wallet from her purse and showed me a picture in it of you. She jabbed it with her finger and said, 'That one. He will disown me.'"

"And that's why she filed the petition."

Gemma looked bewildered. "What petition?"

"The petition that sent me to Broadmoor."

Gemma shook her head. "You went to Broadmoor on your own."

"She told you that?"

"I was with her when you made her take you," Gemma explained. "We drove you out there to Broadmoor together. She tried to talk you out of it, but you insisted."

"That makes no sense," I sighed.

"None of it makes any sense."

It seemed that Gemma continued to talk a while longer but the things she'd said were overwhelming and confusing and I closed my eyes to think a moment and let them settle into the blank spaces of my mind. Slowly, imperceptibly at first, the confusion subsided, leaving only tension in its place. The tension of knowing but not knowing. Of time as a discontinuous jumble. First this. Then that. And the struggle of fitting it all in proper sequence. Had it been that long? Or was I merely…

Just then, I felt a hand touch my shoulder lightly and I opened my eyes to see the view from the chair by the window in the corner of my room at Broadmoor. Homer was standing beside me, his hand resting lightly on my shoulder.

"Mr. Dornblat." His voice was even and polite. "It's time for dinner."

At first I was confused but as I glanced around, the reality of the moment sank in on me with crushing devastation. The chair. The window. The lawn. I was in my room at Broadmoor.

Homer moved a portable table over to where I was seated, lowered it to a comfortable height, and set the meal tray on it. Chopped steak, mashed potatoes, green beans, and a roll. There was a bowl of congealed fruit for dessert and a glass of water with no ice, which was the way I preferred it. He tucked the corner of a napkin inside the collar of my shirt and stepped back, as if waiting to see what I would do.

At first I stared down at the table, wondering if I should eat. And if I should, when should I begin. After a moment, though, I lifted my head and my gaze fell on the nightstand by my bed. And I saw the paper cup for The Pill. And it was empty.

# Nora Mae

## *A Short Story*

In the afternoon, as the day wanes toward evening and a gentle breeze comes up from the south, I often sit on my back porch and drink ginger ale while listening to the doves cooing in the trees that grow throughout the garden that surrounds my house. A lush and verdant oasis, it is my refuge, my sanctuary, my place of peace and quiet, but it was not always so.

Despite the image conveyed by its present size and shape, the garden had an inauspicious beginning as a single daylily. One that arrived at my house in a plastic pot. The plant, given to me by my sister, came from the homeplace of a distant relative where my sister had been digging plants from the yard. She brought the flower to me and I named it Hemerocallis Dussie Moore, after the relative whose property it came from. Hemerocallis is the botanical name for daylily. Dussie was a long-deceased cousin from the maternal side of my father's family.

Whether my sister had permission to dig in that yard I do not know. She didn't say and I didn't ask. Mostly because I didn't care. Nor do I care now. The plant was a wonderful specimen and I was glad to have it, even if she stole it, which I am sure she did not. I just don't know for certain because sometimes my sister does things that surprise me. Not that I mind a surprise. And not that it diminishes my opinion of her. In fact, it has quite the opposite effect.

Things come to us from unexpected places—a co-worker's snappy comeback to a casual remark, the comment of a stranger uttered while waiting to cross the street, even the slogan on a t-shirt worn by a fast food patron you've never seen before. Seeing that daylily, with its deep orange bloom and dark green leaves, was just such a moment, and it brought back memories of my childhood that, though never far from my mind, often receded in the clutter of life.

After college I took a job as a staff writer with the *San Antonio Express-News*. Two years later, I moved to Atlanta for a job at the *Atlanta Journal-Constitution*. Most of my time was spent writing for the paper but I squeezed in a few hours each night working on a novel. When it was finished, I showed the manuscript to a friend. She knew an agent in New York and sent it to her. Four weeks later, I had an offer from a publisher. That first novel led to a second and then a third, and somewhere along the way I left the newspaper to write full-time on my own.

Life in Atlanta was fun and provided opportunities that were unavailable elsewhere in the Southeast. But after ten years I grew tired of the social stratification and the traditional Southern ethos. So, I packed up my belongings and returned to Texas, the land of my father and grandfather and many generations before them. The state where I grew up.

Our grandfather—whom we called Pop Pop—was a country lawyer who practiced in Brenham, a small town an hour northwest of Houston. When my father, Briscoe, graduated from law school, he joined Pop Pop and together they worked from an office located across from the county courthouse on Alamo Street. Most of their time was spent handling real estate deals, business transactions, and estate issues—wills, trusts, and probate disputes. Late in the afternoon, they could be found at a café on Baylor Street, regaling friends with stories, some of which were true.

Being lawyers in a rural setting, Pop Pop and Briscoe sometimes were paid by clients with eggs, butter, fresh vegetables, chickens, hogs, and occasionally a cow. Neither of them, however, showed any interest in gardening or animal husbandry, unless it involved a client and there was money to be made from it. Our mother, on the other hand, had a keen interest in all things related to plants and animals. Because of her, we had a lively herd of cows, an expansive flock of chickens, a large vegetable garden, and an even larger flower garden. And equally because of her, we learned to care for all of it. We also learned their proper biological and botanical names.

All of that came back to mind when my sister handed me the daylily and from that humble beginning, I immersed myself in gardening, adding to that single plant many others. Some of them found along the roadside or growing on a ditch bank. A few were discovered in ambiguous locations—that ill-defined zone between yard and highway—though some nearby residents seemed not to share my sense of ambiguity about the location and protested quite loudly when they saw me digging them up. Still others were rooted from cuttings that I pinched off plants while strolling through public gardens and the grounds of various institutions.

Gradually, the garden took over my entire back yard, then I let it slowly expand over the front yard as well. By growing it in an incremental fashion, I had time to think and change and rearrange. It also allowed me to avoid the yard police—those nosy neighbors who did not share my fascination with everything botanical and desired only that all the houses on the street have neatly trimmed lawns. With my stealthy approach, they either didn't notice the sprawling azaleas, camellias, sweat peas, nasturtiums and many others—the plants creeping up over time and becoming part of the existing landscape—or they enjoyed them too much to complain. I chose to think the latter—that they were mesmerized by the beauty and wonder of my creation—and took it as a compliment.

Hiram Gwinnett, who lived behind me, noticed my back yard, too, but, unlike the yard police, his was the notice of an open admirer. He often called to me over the fence that separated our property, usually with a question about the name or identity of a plant. Over the course of those conversations, I trained him to refer to them as plants, not weeds or flowers. The difference, as I often pointed out, was one of placement and enjoyment rather than an actual botanical distinction. Most of the desirable plants that people spend good money to buy today were once weeds of great disdain. A friend, for instance, spent much of his youth chopping lantana with a hoe from the family orange groves in Florida. Hiram spent an equal amount of time and energy mulching, watering, and otherwise caring for the clumps of lantana that grew as an ornamental near the corner of his house and his garage.

When I moved to the neighborhood, Hiram was already there and had been for quite some time, though no one seemed to know much about him. He was ten or fifteen years older than I—perhaps even more than that—and when I first met him, he seemed oddly aloof. However, once my garden began to expand, he warmed to me.

From comments he made in our over-the-fence conversations, I learned that Hiram was the only child of a farmer from Waycross, Georgia. He attended pharmacy school at the University of Georgia and apprenticed to a druggist in Sylvester, then bought the business. He never said how he came to live in the house behind me. I assumed he retired. We were a long way from Georgia.

A year or two after my garden overtook the back yard, Hiram died. No one knew he was gone until the mailman mentioned that mail was piling up in the box at his house and asked if I knew where he was. I went over there and collected the mail—we did that for each other occasionally—then walked to the back of the house and stood at a window near the kitchen with my hands cupped around my face to block out the light. That's when I saw him lying on the floor. At least, the body looked like it could be his. The light was gone from his eyes and his cheeks were sunken, leaving it to seem as if the carcass had been vacated from the inside and only the outline of a person remained.

A milk carton lay nearby and an empty glass was sitting on the counter. The refrigerator door was open and the light inside it still was on. And that's when I smelled the odor seeping through the windowpane and knew his body already was rank. I used my cell phone to call the police and took a seat on a lawn chair to wait until they arrived. Hiram had been a good over-the-fence friend and I preferred to remember him that way, rather than opening the door and confusing those memories with the putrid odor of rotten flesh. There was nothing I or anyone else could do for him then anyway.

Response time for a call about a dead body was a little faster than for other things, but it still took thirty minutes for a patrolman to arrive. I waited until he took my statement, then made my way back home. A neighbor from across the street was there and she said she knew how to reach one of Hiram's relatives, so I left her to see to the details. There was no reason for me to hang around and as I walked back home, I assumed that would be the end of the matter.

However, two weeks after I found his body, there was a knock at my front door and when I went to check I saw a man standing on the porch. He was dressed in a dark gray suit with a white shirt and muted tie. His hair was short and trimmed neatly around his ears and off his collar. He seemed not to pose a threat, so I opened the door and he identified himself as a lawyer.

"Our firm represents the estate of your neighbor, Hiram Gwinnett," he said. "You are his sole heir."

After the lawyer explained everything to me, and after I decided to accept Hiram's bequest, we still had to publish notices in the newspaper and gain approval from the probate court. We sent notices of the legal proceedings to every person the researchers thought might be related to Hiram and waited the appropriate length of time for them to respond, but only the lawyer and I appeared for the court hearings.

So, once all of that was finished and finalized, I became the owner of everything in the world Hiram Gwinnett owned on the day the milk carton slipped from his hand and he fell to the kitchen floor. House, pickup truck, financial assets. Even a second house at Apalachicola that I never knew he owned. All of it was mine, and I was overwhelmed.

At first, I didn't want to touch anything. I had seen him lying on the floor and I didn't really want to go inside the house after all of that. And even though his money and investments were in accounts that bore my name, they still seemed like someone else's property. But Nora Mae Gilbert, my next-door neighbor, insisted I had to check on things. "At least see about the house," she said. "You have to check on it. What if a toilet is overflowing? It might ruin the whole place and cost you thousands of dollars in water bills." So, after being upbraided by Nora Mae for a week or two, I finally walked over to Hiram's house.

Despite our many conversations, I had been inside Hiram's house only once before, when he called me over to look at a Camellia sinensis he was attempting to grow. He'd purchased it at one of the home improvement stores thinking he was getting a Camellia japonica. I told him to avoid those stores when shopping for plants, but he sometimes ignored my advice and what he got that day was not what he wanted. Japonica—the plant he wanted—is grown for its flowers. Sinensis—the plant he bought—is similar but grown for use in making tea.

"I don't care," he said. "I'll get a japonica somewhere else. I want to see what this one does now that it's here." And in one respect, he did precisely what I always told him he should do with his garden. Grow plants that fit a predetermined plan, but don't ignore the ones that show up.

After we looked at the bush that day and admired the leaves, Hiram invited me in for a glass of tea. At first I thought he was attempting a pun—look at my tea plant, have some tea—then I realized he hadn't noticed the connection. I enjoy tea, if it's brewed from real tea and not a concoction made from a mix, so I agreed to have taste of his. As things turned out, Hiram's tea was particularly good that day, so we sat at the kitchen table and drank an entire pitcher of it.

After we had our tea, we rode down to Stanton's and had a hamburger for lunch. That was one of the most enjoyable days of my life and we should have repeated it often, but we never did. The memory of that day was on my mind as I made my way to the back door and went inside the first time after Nora Mae encouraged me to do so.

Hiram's house key was on a ring with a medallion from the University of Georgia, the school from which he graduated. I took it from my pocket, placed the key in the lock, and gave it a turn. As the door opened, a rush of stale air greeted me full in the face. A cleaning crew scoured the kitchen floor and removed all traces of odor from Hiram's decomposing corpse. Still, the smell that day was very different from what it had been on the day we had tea together and I hesitated before moving inside.

A glance around the kitchen told me everything was okay in there, so I walked down the hall and checked the bathrooms to make certain none of the toilets was overflowing. I knew where the bathrooms were located. You can't drink an entire pitcher of tea in a single sitting without going to the bathroom at least once. After determining the plumbing posed no problem, I had a look in each of the other rooms, too.

Years before, I had been the executor of a cousin's estate in Tennessee, and I knew about going through things in an orderly manner and working methodically through the house to make certain nothing was overlooked. People have a way of putting important things in places that make sense while they are alive, but after they're gone and someone else takes over their affairs, locating those places isn't always obvious. Researchers from the law firm had already been through most of Hiram's belongings. That's how we knew about his investment accounts and the house in Apalachicola. Now, I needed to sort through it myself with an eye toward what to do with it.

The final bathroom that I checked was adjacent to Hiram's bedroom so as I came into the room and looked around, I thought about what it might be like to rummage through the drawers and closets. At once, the task seemed overwhelming and a bit too personal—the notion of sorting out his underwear drawer was more than a little off putting. But I was already in the room and I had to start sometime, so I avoided the dresser drawers and opened the closet door instead.

A bar ran from side to side across the closet, parallel to the door. Shirts hung on the left side. Trousers were in the middle. Suits, sport coats, and jackets were to the right. All of them laundered, pressed, cleaned, and in order. Shirts facing inward from one side. Jackets and coats facing inward from the other.

Grasping them four and five at a time, I removed the clothes from the closet and laid them on the bed, then checked the floor beneath. I found only a row of shoes arranged as neatly as the clothes, with casual shoes on the left and dress shoes on the right—I already knew his gardening shoes and clothes hung by the back door. In the corner of the closet to the right I found a double-barreled shotgun that I propped against the foot of the bed. A pole with a Georgia state flag attached stood in the corner to the left.

After making certain there was nothing else in the lower portion of the closet, I moved to the shelf above the bar. On the left side of the shelf was a cardboard box. I took it down and glanced inside to find it was filled with photographs. A cursory check of those on top confirmed what I already knew—none of the photos meant anything to me. And that was the difference between what I had done on behalf of my cousin's estate in Tennessee and what I needed to do for Hiram. I knew my cousin. I was one of her people. Faces in the photographs she owned were familiar to me. The names mentioned in her letters and documents were people I knew. Going through Hiram's belongings, none of it meant anything except as the remains of a friend's life.

After checking the box to make sure nothing important was hiding at the bottom, I set it on the floor and turned back to the closet. Next to where the box had been was a camera—the kind that took film—but a check of it showed there was no film inside.

Beside the camera was a thick binder with a leather cover. I took it down and leafed through the pages to find it was a wedding album with pictures of a very young Hiram standing next to an equally young woman who was very obviously the bride. She seemed vaguely familiar but I could not recall ever knowing anyone who lived in Georgia, other than Hiram.

Behind the last photo of the album was a marriage license and I glanced over it quickly to find that Hiram Gwinnett married Judy Lingo on June 17, 1964, at the Episcopal Church in Vidalia, Georgia. "Hiram was married," I whispered. "And I never knew it."

After working through Hiram's bedroom like that—going through the closet, his dresser drawers even though I didn't want to, and the nightstand beside his bed—I moved on to the next room down the hall. On the shelf in the closet was another box of photographs and beside it was a box of papers. Funeral home bills. Hospital bills. Doctor bills. At first I thought they were for Hiram's wife—which would have explained why I never knew about her—but when I checked the names, they all were for different people.

Beneath the shelf, two winter coats hung on the bar and on the floor beneath them was a box with an electric train set inside. From the age of the engine and rail cars, it appeared to be a toy from Hiram's childhood. Other than those few items, there was nothing else of much importance in the closet or the room

Earlier, as I approached the house, I was ill at ease about going through Hiram's belongings and aggravated at Nora Mae for pushing me to do it—and aggravated at myself for allowing her to coerce me into doing it. Once inside, though, the tension lifted—until I thought of opening the dresser drawers. Concentrating on the closet got me past the anxiety of the moment and made it easier to look through the room's contents. But when I entered the second bedroom, the sense of unease returned and standing there, facing the closet with only the photographs, receipts, and toy train, I was confronted by an overwhelming sense of emptiness. Almost despair.

Not the uneasiness of looking through the belongings of another. I was beyond the awkwardness of plundering Hiram's possessions. This was a profound sense of hollowness welling up from deep inside me. An emptiness at the thought that this was all that remained. An emptiness that asked, "Did Hiram really live, and die, and leave behind only boxes of photographs of people no one knew? Copies of bills with names that no one recognized? A childhood toy unused for decades? Is that it?"

Once when I was in an automobile dealership, I saw a display case that contained trophies won by a race car driver. From a distance, the trophies appeared interesting but as I approached the case, I saw that they were cheaply made of inferior wood and metal. Not only that, the metal was tarnished and the finish was gone from the wood in almost every place. The driver was deceased and I wondered then, as I did in Hiram's second bedroom, "Is this all there is to life? To live and die and leave behind only a few relics that mean nothing to anyone?"

As I stared at the box of receipts, those thoughts tumbled through my mind and I descended into the morass of dark emotion. More than gloom and doom. The bottomlessness of nothing. The emptiness of a void. The blackness of the abyss.

Rather than continuing through other rooms in the house, I returned the box of receipts to the closet, made my way to the back door, and stepped outside. Sunlight filtered through the canopy of trees that sprawled overhead—mostly live oaks and ash. And as I gazed across the back yard, a breeze swept over me. As the air brushed across my arms, I looked up to see the roof of my house rising above the fence that separated my property from Hiram's and I thought how nice it would be to have a gate in the fence so I could walk straight over, rather than being forced to make the block.

After a moment spent contemplating how to build a gate without losing the entire fence, my mood lightened, somewhat, and I started toward the street for the trip home by the long way around the block. Before I reached the first corner my mind had moved on to consider what I could do with the things in the house. Particularly the photographs. Someone in Hiram's family might like to have them. "I should contact someone," I said to myself. "And see if they're interested."

One of the people identified by the law firm as Hiram's cousin was Karen Richardson. According to the lawyers, she lived in Sylvester, Georgia. I located an address for her and wrote her a letter offering her the pick of the photographs and family memorabilia. Two weeks later I received a response indicating she would be glad to have them. Her sister, Linda, was interested in them, too. With another round of correspondence, arrangements were made for them to travel out from Georgia to see where Hiram lived and collect a few of his things.

Before they arrived, I sorted through the boxes of photographs one more time, just to make sure nothing of importance escaped me and then I set them on a table in the middle bedroom. I was glad for the cousins to come but I didn't want them to think they had the run of the place and could take whatever they wanted.

On the appointed day, Karen and Linda arrived at my house and we walked around the block to Hiram's. All the way I was wishing I had gone ahead and cut a hole in the fence so we could go back and forth easily, but my garden wasn't designed for that and I didn't want to merely hack a way through it.

When they said they wanted to come for a visit, I assumed they would glance through the boxes, giving the photos a cursory review, then proclaim their interest in them all, take a brief tour of the house, and leave. The cousins thought otherwise, preferring to discuss each photograph in detail, remembering the person or event depicted, then recalling other incidents and people brought to mind by their conversation. I brought a chair from the living room and sat to one side, listening.

By noon that first day, they had made their way through only the first box and seemed content to sit and talk and look. I, however, was famished and suggested we break for lunch. They were agreeable and I took them to Stanton's. While we ate, I told them about the day Hiram and I came there. They were particularly amused that we drank a pitcher of tea at the house before coming. Afterward, we returned to the house and they spent the remainder of the day looking, remembering, and talking. Always talking. I don't think that house ever had heard so many words as it did from those two.

At the end of the day, I was exhausted from listening and suggested we should take a break until morning. The cousins agreed and went off to a hotel. I went home and collapsed on the bed, fully clothed. I didn't awaken until sunlight came through the bedroom window the next morning.

After another day of looking and talking, the cousins decided they wanted all of the photographs. I was glad for them to have them and gave them two other items as well—a chair they said had been made by Hiram's great grandfather and a pitcher that had belonged to his grandmother. Later when Nora Mae heard what I had done, she thought they manipulated me into giving them those things, but even if they did, I didn't mind. He was their cousin, not mine. I had no sentimental attachment to the chair or pitcher. And being gracious is never a bad thing.

On the morning of the third day, we loaded the boxes of photographs into the trunk of Karen's car and placed the other items on the back seat. The chair was a tight fit, but we made it work.

As they prepared to leave, I remembered the box of receipts that I found in the second bedroom and I showed it to them. They looked through a few of the papers and then Karen said, "I know or knew all of these people, but I have no idea why Hiram had their receipts."

"So, some of them are still alive?"

Karen picked up the receipt for the funeral home that lay on top. "Well," she said. "This one's not. This is an invoice for Luther Adcock's funeral. He died before Hiram moved out here."

"We went to the service," Linda added.

"Half the town went."

"I liked the preacher's sermon."

"I hate that man."

"Let me move over a little," Linda said, I think only partly in jest. "Just in case lightning strikes."

"I'm not the only one."

"I know," Linda said. "But still. He is a preacher."

"Doesn't give him an exception."

There was a hint of coldness in Karen's voice that I couldn't resist. "What about the preacher?"

A darkness came over her. "Get me started on that and we'll be out here another three days."

An awkward silence settled over the room, then Linda took a paper from the box. "This is a doctor's bill for Mitzy Preston. She lives up the street from me."

Everyone seemed to relax. "All of them are marked, 'Paid,'" I noted.

"Yes." Linda nodded. "They are."

"Do you think Hiram paid them?"

Karen spoke up. "There's no way of knowing."

"I can ask Mitzy," Linda offered, still holding the bill in her hand. "She and I are pretty good friends."

"You mean acquaintances.," Karen needled.

"No," Linda countered. "It's more than that."

"Not after that thing with the cat."

"Well," Linda conceded. "There is that... But I'm curious about these receipts. I'll ask her anyway. It might give us a chance to clear the air."

I was curious, too. "What's the thing with the cat?" I asked.

Karen grinned. "Linda ran over one of Mitzy's cats."

"That's what she says," Linda quipped. "I never knew I hit anything, and I still don't think I did."

Karen smiled. "But?"

"But I might apologize if she'll tell me about this bill."

The thing about the cats stuck in my mind. "Cats? How many does Mitzy have?"

"Lots." Karen sighed. "Mitzy has lots of cats."

"Too many cats," Linda noted.

"Her place smells like a litter box."

"She smells like a litter box."

"Maybe we should leave it at that."

"Good idea," Linda said. "But I'm still asking her about these receipts."

Karen gestured to the box. "Do you think we should take them with us?"

Something inside me bristled at the idea. People—especially the well-intentioned—have a way of taking a thing and running with it. If you let them, they'll take over your entire life. I wasn't sure if Karen and Linda were like that, but I didn't want to find out. The photos, the chair, the pitcher—that's all they could have of me. And of Hiram. But I remained curious to know what they might discover about the receipts. Better to write them about it, though. Later. After they were gone. "No," I replied. "I'll keep them here."

As they walked out to the car once more, I remembered the wedding album and asked about Judy. They both looked at me with blank expressions. Karen finally said, "I have no idea what you're talking about."

"Me, either," Linda added. "We've never known Hiram to be married to anyone."

They waited while I retrieved the wedding album from the closet and brought it to them at the car. Neither of them said a word as they leafed through the pages until they reached the license that was tucked in back. Karen pointed to the first witness signature. "Randy Starnes was Hiram's best friend from high school."

Linda pointed to the second one. "That's Pete Whiteside. Another of his high school buddies. I saw Pete at the grocery store the other day."

"So, who is Judy Lingo?" I asked.

"Maybe she was someone he knew from college," Karen suggested. "According to this license, they got married in 1964. Hiram would have been about twenty years old."

"Twenty-two," Linda corrected.

"Yeah," Karen agreed. "So maybe that's what it was."

Linda frowned. "But then, she would have been with him when he came to Sylvester."

Karen nodded. "Maybe."

The way they talked left me wondering how they knew so many details, but I decided to let it pass. They were leaving. I was ready for them to go and didn't want to chase down one more rabbit hole of who-was-where and what-was-what.

"Well." I reached out for the album and Karen handed it to me. "When you get back to Georgia, maybe you could find out about Judy, too."

"Yes," Karen replied. "Maybe we can."

"We'll put her on the list," Linda added. "It'll be like homework."

We said goodbye once more, then they got into the car and started back to Georgia. When they were gone, I went inside the house and returned the box of receipts to its place on the shelf in the closet of the middle room, then checked to make sure the lights were off and locked the door on my way out. But I brought the wedding album with me to my house.

# 2

Almost every afternoon when I went out to sit on my back porch to enjoy the view of the garden, and listen to the doves cooing in the trees, Nora Mae appeared at the corner of the house, mail in hand, fresh from her walk down to the mailbox by the street. Naturally, I could not shoo her away and, having a cold bottle of ginger ale in my hand, I could not ignore the fact that she had none in hers, so I always offered her one. I kept them in a cooler on the porch. It was no difficult matter to say, "Grab a bottle from the cooler, Nora Mae." And she always did.

Sitting there on the porch together, we talked about whatever came to mind, and when she finished her ginger ale and it was time for her to go, she rose from her chair and started for the steps. But just before going down she always glanced in my direction and said, "I might be gone by morning. When they come to get my body, make sure you tell them who I am."

At first it bothered me that she talked that way—an obvious allusion to death—but after she'd said it a dozen times I realized all she wanted was to make certain someone noticed her presence. To be sure someone marked her down as in attendance that day and noted that she was yet among the living. Being the most recent addition to the neighborhood—and the youngest—I was the designated recipient of her daily entreaties, others on the street having long since written her off.

Layton, who lived on the opposite side of her, said she was crazy and refused to answer the door when she came over. Augusta, who lived across the street, stopped returning her calls long before I arrived. And Harry, who lived on the opposite side of me once shot her dog, so they had nothing to do with each other except to exchange complaints with the police.

As for me, I always enjoyed a good story. Which meant Nora Mae and I spent many hours together on the porch. Talking. Listening to her was much easier than listening to Hiram's cousins. I didn't know them. Or any of the people they mentioned.

Nora Mae grew up in Euless, a town that eventually became a suburb of Dallas. When she was a girl, it still was a long way from anywhere. Oliver Hale, Nora Mae's great grandfather on her mother's side, moved there with his family when he was ten years old. Not long after they arrived, Elisha Euless, for whom the town was named, built a cotton gin. Oliver went to work there the summer he turned twelve. He worked at the gin—and later at Euless' sawmill—until he was twenty, then he met Delia Northcutt, the woman who became Nora Mae's great grandmother.

After that, Oliver didn't want to be anywhere Delia wasn't, so he opened a blacksmith shop in a barn not far from the cotton gin and went to work for himself. With the profit from the shop he bought a house on Main Street and married Delia. Not long after that, they started producing children. As Nora Mae described it, "One child per year for the next twelve years—almost—there was a break in there between some of them—but they all survived to adulthood."

When she told me that part about all of them surviving to adulthood, I wanted to call bullshit on it. Times were tough back then. Many children did not even survive delivery. But Nora Mae showed me clippings from the newspaper to prove it. Several years earlier, a reporter from the *Euless Times Democrat* heard the story and was as skeptical as I, but he had the time to research it and he wrote an article for the paper about how it was absolutely true. I read the article.

The lives of Oliver and Delia—and, by extension, Nora Mae—might have followed a different path but one day Moses Watson brought his two-horse surrey to Oliver's shop. The surrey needed a new axle and the horses needed to be re-shoed. While Oliver did the work, Moses got into a card game and lost big. So big, he couldn't pay for the work on the surrey or the stable fees for the horses. Eventually, after several long and heated arguments, Moses surrendered the surrey and horses to satisfy the bill.

Every Sunday after that, Oliver and Delia tooled around town in that surrey with their children seated behind them. They were a sight to see and the talk of the town, with everybody asking on Monday, "Did you see the Hales on their ride yesterday?" And people reckoning the quality of their Sunday afternoon by whether they did or not.

Finally, Harold Barnett decided he wanted Oliver's surrey and horses as a present for his wife. "She wants to ride around like that on Sunday afternoon and you're the only one in town with a surrey that nice."

At first, Oliver was reluctant to trade, but Barnett kept offering more and more until finally Oliver said, "I tell you what, Harold. I'll swap you that surrey and the horses that go with it for that forty acres you own out by Denham's Creek." No sooner were the words out of Oliver's mouth than Barnett thrust his hand toward Oliver to shake on it and said, "Deal."

For six months after that, there was no Oliver and Delia riding around town on Sunday afternoons with the kids seated behind them. And there was no peace in the Hale household, either. Delia was mad.

In the seventh month, a man by the name of Quarrels came to town riding in a two-horse surrey with a leather top and fringe hanging from the edge all the way around the top. He stopped at the train station where he found a telegram waiting for him. It seemed he'd been traveling for two weeks, making his way east from Albuquerque and stopping at every station along the way to telegraph his wife in Slidell. She was pregnant and due almost any day. When he checked at the Euless station, he learned that she was in labor. "Get here quick," was all the message said.

Needing a ticket on the afternoon train, Quarrels asked around town about a loan or a deal or a handout or anything to help him on his way. "It'll take a week to get there from here by carriage and I can be there tomorrow on the train." The storekeepers and the banker were sympathetic to his situation but unwilling to advance any money. Only the Methodist minister was willing to help, but he had no means by which to do so.

The minister, however, knew the inside story on almost everyone in town and brought Quarrels to Oliver and soon a deal was struck. Forty dollars for the horses and the surrey, with Quarrels having the right to buy them back at the same price plus ten dollars if he came through town again and wanted them. "Provided," the minister added on Oliver's behalf, "the horses are still alive."

"Deal," the man said.

Money changed hands. The horses were stalled, watered, and fed in the barn at the blacksmith shop. The surrey was parked outside for a fresh wash. And Quarrels made the afternoon train headed east as fast the locomotive would go. The fireman, Oliver's first cousin, kept the firebox stoked with extra coal and they highballed it all the way.

The next Sunday after that, Oliver was once again at the reins of a two-horse surrey, this one even better than the first. Delia, looking proud and dignified, was seated next to him with their children all around, laughing and carrying on like they had good sense.

Soon after, Oliver and Delia began having children again and before long, they were riding in that surrey with twelve children seated beside them and behind them—and the extra ones hanging off the back. The youngest of those children was Hubert, Nora Mae's grandfather and the last child Oliver and Delia ever had.

Hubert grew up in Euless and eventually took Oliver's place as the town's blacksmith. By then, however, smithing wasn't as profitable as it had been, but Hubert had seen the end coming and opened the town's first automobile dealership—Hubert Hale Motors—in a building next to the barn where the blacksmith shop had been.

Hubert had hoped for a son to take his place but had three daughters instead and learned that women could do anything a man could do and sometimes do it better. The youngest was Ida, Nora Mae's mother. She was the first in the family to attend college, doing so in Austin where she met Tommy John Gilbert. Tommy John was a man of vision and ideas. "Entertainment is the thing of the future," he often said, and he envisioned a string of movie theaters reaching from Amarillo to Houston. "Even all the way to New Orleans," he sometimes added.

No one paid much attention to Tommy John or his ideas, but Hubert thought Tommy John might be onto something. Yet even using rudimentary math and figuring with a pencil on a writing tablet at the kitchen table Hubert came to a serious obstacle. "A venture like that would require capital we don't have."

And that's when someone suggested Hubert find out more about the black slick that formed from time to time in a low spot on the forty acres that Oliver received from Harold Barnett when they traded for the original two-horse surrey a hundred years before. And that's when they found oil. Lots of oil.

Not long after that, movie theaters started showing up in towns and villages across south Texas. They attracted lots of attention, too, and with all of those people standing around waiting for the next show, Tommy John saw another opportunity. "We need to sell them something," he said. And soon after that, shopping centers sprang up next to the movie theaters. As time went by, many of those centers became malls. Some of them quite large. All of them very valuable.

Tommy John was a man of vision and insight. Hubert knew a good thing when he saw it. And Nora Mae never lacked for money a day in her life.

When she told me that story I was quite entertained but it sounded too much like a typical Texas tale, which made it a tall tale and just another of the many fabrications that made Texans interesting. Except, in this instance, the movie theaters actually existed and so did the shopping malls. I knew where five of the original theaters were located. Nora Mae's sister, Louise, ran the company that managed them. And Hubert Hale Motors was right there on Main Street in Euless for anyone to see, along with the five others opened in Fort Worth by Nora Mae's sister, Irene.

Nora Mae talked to me about that sometimes—the trust that held the rights to the forty acres, the way the dealerships and the malls and the movie businesses were owned. About the wily nature of her sisters and how just because you have relatives doesn't mean they all know how to relate.

Even from our first conversation on the back porch, I sensed there was more to the story than just sisters who couldn't get along, but Nora Mae didn't elaborate and I didn't push the issue. Secrets come out best when they come out in their own time and I assumed hers would too, eventually. Most afternoons we just talked about the flowers in my garden or the birds in the trees or the noise from the highway we heard in the distance.

Things remained that way between us, following a comfortable rhythm. She came over in the afternoon, we sat together on the porch enjoying the garden view. But not long after Hiram's cousins returned to Georgia, I mentioned to Nora Mae that I had found a wedding album in the closet at Hiram's house. That's when the secrets began to emerge.

"Did you know Hiram had been married?" I asked the question as a conversation starter, thinking she probably had no idea whether he had or not—though she had lived on our street longer than any-one and there was always the possibility.

Nora Mae was silent a moment, then she looked over at me. "Yes," she said softly. "I knew."

My eyes opened wide. "How did you know that?"

She cleared her throat. "Because I had an affair with his wife."

Her response left me astounded and for a moment I didn't know what to say. Nora Mae noticed the look on my face and gave me a coy smile. "Rather shocking, isn't it?"

"You had an affair with Judy Lingo?"

Nora Mae nodded her head. "She and I met during freshmen orientation."

"So, how did she end up with Hiram?"

"Judy knew she was attracted to women, but she felt guilty about it. She'd struggled with it since puberty. Maybe even before. I'm not sure. But she tried to be the person everyone wanted her to be, but she just didn't care for boys that way. So, when she got to college, she decided to live the way she really felt. But after our first year, she told me she couldn't do it anymore and that's when she started seeing

Hiram."

"And they got married."

"Yes," Nora Mae replied. "The next summer."

"But I'm guessing you and Judy couldn't stay away from each other."

She took a sip of ginger ale. "And you would be correct," she said.

"And Hiram found out about it?"

"Judy told him."

"He didn't know about her…situation before that?"

She seemed amused. "You find this difficult to discuss, don't you?"

"No," I said. And I really didn't. I just didn't know the correct terminology. I sipped from the bottle in my hand, then said, "You can be whomever you want to be. And you can be with whomever you choose. I just don't know the correct terms for the topic."

"Hiram knew nothing about her being lesbian," Nora Mae said.

"And how did he take it when he found out?"

"Not as well as you are."

"What happened?"

"He tried to live with it, but she didn't want to be a man's wife and she couldn't make herself enjoy it."

"So, she tried coming out, then she tried being straight. Then she gave up and just went back to being…who she really was?"

Nora Mae grinned. "I like watching you squirm."

"I'm not… Well." My shoulders slumped. "Okay," I admitted. "I'm squirming, but not because the topic offends me."

"Just makes you feel awkward," she quipped.

"Yeah." I took another sip. "Awkward."

We sat in silence a moment, then I said, "What happened to Judy?"

"She moved in with a friend of ours. A girl named Rita, from Tallahassee."

"She didn't move in with you?"

"No." There was a hint of disappointment in her voice. "We

weren't together very long. I didn't even know she'd left Hiram until after they divorced."

"Is this why your sisters don't come around? Because you're lesbian?"

She waited a moment before saying, "That's a complicated story."

I smiled in her direction. "Need another ginger ale?"

"Something stronger than that," she replied.

"Wait here."

I went inside and found a bottle of Jack Daniels whiskey in the cabinet, dusted off two glasses, and added a couple of ice cubes to both, then brought them out to the porch. "There's a Coca-Cola in the cooler," I said as I returned to my seat.

She pointed to the bottle. "I take mine straight."

I poured a glass half full and handed it to her, then reached in the cooler for the Coke. As we settled into our first sip, I said, "Okay. You have something stronger. Tell me about the complications."

Nora Mae took a sip from her glass, held it on her tongue a moment, before letting it slide slowly down her throat. Finally, she said, "My daddy wanted a boy but all he and Mama got were girls. Mama died giving birth to me, so I was the youngest, which meant Daddy and I spent a lot of time together. I grew up wanting to please him. He was going through a tough time with Mama dying and all."

"Is this going to get really awkward?"

She whapped me on the arm and snapped, "Not like that!"

"I don't mean anything against your daddy. I'm just checking to see what's coming next."

"Do you want to hear about it, or not?"

"Yes," I said. "I want to know."

Nora Mae took another sip from her glass, but didn't say anything, so I prompted her. "Your father dressed you as a boy. Then what?"

She took another sip. "He dressed me as a boy." She seemed to force the words from her mouth. "And he called me Johnny. Everyone thought it was cute."

"Was it difficult?"

"No." She seemed to relax again. "I actually found it exceedingly comfortable and even after Daddy got reconciled to Mama dying and he didn't spend so much time with me, I kept dressing like a boy."

"Even after you started to school?"

"I lived that way from the time I can remember until the summer I graduated from high school. Everyone in Euless knew me as Johnny Gilbert."

"No one harassed you over it?"

"One or two tried, but I put them in their place. Everyone else was smart enough to keep their opinions to themselves."

"And they called you Johnny."

Nora Mae nodded. "Even my sisters called me Johnny."

"So, they were supportive?"

"At first. When they were young, they thought it was funny but after they got old enough to understand things like that, they were embarrassed." She looked over at me. "I had my hair cut about like yours and I wore men's clothes."

"And they didn't like it."

She looked away. "We haven't really talked much since I graduated from high school."

Something in her voice made me suspicious. "And I'm betting there was a reason for that besides what you've told me."

A smile turned up the corners of her mouth. "My oldest sister, Lucille, had a friend."

"A boyfriend?"

"No." She shook her head. "A girlfriend. She was several years older than I was, but I thought she was the most beautiful person in the world. She seemed to think the same of me."

My eyes opened wide once more. "Oh."

"Yeah," she sighed. "That's when I learned how two women give each other...the pleasure of a physical relationship."

Her cheeks turned a darker shade of pink than normal and I grinned. "Now who's feeling awkward?"

Her voice took a sarcastic tone. "Despite the way they talk about sex on television, most people—gay, straight, or indifferent—don't like talking about the intimate details of their lives."

"And Lucille got mad about that? About the way you felt toward her friend?"

Nora Mae sighed. "Someone saw us together."

"You and Lucille's friend?"

"Yeah."

"Together as in...together?"

She scowled. "We were naked in the backseat of her car. Okay?"

"And that's how you became a lesbian?"

"No." Her scowl changed to a look of disdain. "You think it was a choice?"

"I don't know."

"Did you choose to prefer women?"

"No." I shrugged. "I don't think so."

"That is your preference, isn't it? Women?"

"Yes," I replied.

"Do you remember a time when you thought it through and decided that's the way you would be?"

"No. It was just there." That was the truth. I remembered that much. When I reached puberty, sexual awareness sprang up inside me. Leapt up, actually. Exploded, to be more exact. There was no time for choosing or deliberation. Almost overnight, my sense of being was oriented in every way around an inexplicable urge toward members of the opposite gender.

"Okay," she said. "That's the way it was for me. At puberty, when all the other girls were interested in boys, I was interested in girls. That thing you feel when you see an attractive woman, that's how I feel when I see them, too." She shook her head in dismay. "Choice," she scoffed. "It's not a choice. When people come of age, sexuality is on them before they know what's happening. It's just that, for some people, it appears one way and for others, another."

"So, Lucille was angry because you were with her friend, or because you were with a woman?"

"She was mad because the boys who saw us were people she knew, and they talked about it. A lot."

"And she was embarrassed."

"She was many things." Nora Mae looked over at me and held out her glass. "Give me another shot of that Jack Daniels." That's when I noticed her glass was empty and I reached for the bottle. "Two fingers," she said, indicating how much she wanted. I put a little more than that in the glass, added some to mine, then set the bottle beside my chair.

"So," I said after a moment. "Why was Hiram living here, right in your back yard?"

"He didn't know I was here when he bought the house."

"When did he find out?"

"About a year later."

I gave her a perplexed expression. "It took that long for him to find out you were his neighbor?"

"I don't go around to that side of the block, as a normal thing. And he didn't come over on this side, except once or twice when I saw him over here with you."

"What did he say when he found out you lived here?"

A smile turned up the corners of her mouth. "He just shook his head and said he'd come all the way out here to get away from everyone who ever knew him, and here I was. Someone who knew his secrets."

"Did you?"

"Did I what?"

"Did you know his secrets?"

"Not many. But I'll tell you one thing." She paused long enough to sip from her glass. "Those cousins you had over there looking at his stuff, they didn't know him, that's for sure. They knew him after he graduated from college, but they didn't know him before then. They only knew him after he came to Sylvester to run that drug-store."

"So, Hiram was okay living that close to his ex-wife's lover?"

She avoided my gaze. "Whatever happened between us happened a long time ago."

"Why didn't you say something to me about this before?"

She looked over at me once more. "My life's not an open book, you know."

"But you knew I was wrestling with what to do about Hiram's belongings."

"This isn't a part of my life I like to talk about."

We sipped and rocked in silence for a while, then I asked, "Is Judy still alive?"

Nora Mae stared ahead, her eyes focused on the garden, and took another sip. "She died."

"When?"

"A few years ago."

"How did you find out?"

"Rita called me."

"You two are still in touch?"

"Yeah."

The tone in her voice said Nora Mae was through talking about her past, so I said, "Do you think I made a mistake giving those photographs to the cousins?"

"It was alright," she replied.

"Did you want them?"

"No." She shook her head slowly. "I wouldn't have known any more about the people in those pictures than you did."

"What would you have done with them?"

"Burned them, probably."

"Why?"

"Those pictures are all from the past," she said. "Nothing good can come from dragging the past into the present."

"We've been talking about the past."

"I know."

"And I think some good has come from it."

"Maybe so. But we know each other. We don't know anything about the people in those pictures. We'd just be dredging up shit we don't understand. Pardon my language."

"Do you really think that?"

"No telling what we'd find if we started digging around in that box."

"The whole thing seems sad."

"What whole thing?"

"To live all your life, and die, and all that remains is a house full of furniture no one wants and photographs of people no one remembers."

"Life is a fleeting thing."

"If we had burned all those photographs and destroyed the remaining papers, there would be nothing left of Hiram's life."

"You think there should be more?"

"Yes."

"I don't know what good holding on to a bunch of photographs does for him."

"But who will remember who he was?"

"We would remember."

"And after we're gone?"

"Like I said, do you think it should be different?"

"I think a person spends their life looking for meaning and significance, and with great effort they noodle out a little bit of it, and then they die and everything around them dies, too. And in a generation, the memory of them is gone."

She had a knowing smile. "We still remember Mark Twain."

"But not his brother," I responded.

She raised an eyebrow. "I didn't know he had a brother."

"And that's my point," I said, gesturing with my glass.

By then, afternoon had faded into evening and darkness was coming on. Nora Mae tipped up her glass, drained the last drops from it, and handed it to me. "This is a depressing conversation," she said.

"Maybe we should sing a song or tell a joke."

"Huh. I have things to do." She stood to leave, then paused and looked back at me. "You remember what to do?"

"Tell them who you are."

"And?" She elongated the sound of it for emphasis.

"Pull you out before you start stinking." After the way we found Hiram's body on the kitchen floor, she had added that to her good-bye litany. She didn't want her body left to rot in the house like his.

"Be a good neighbor," she said, "and don't forget." Then she pushed open the screened door, plopped down the steps, and disappeared into the night.

# 3

After Nora Mae went home, I sat on the porch and watched while nighttime slowly enshrouded the garden with darkness. As the evening cooled, mosquitoes appeared, but the screens on the porch kept most of them at bay. There was a ceiling fan overhead and I turned it on for good measure. The breeze it generated felt pleasant and bugs that wriggled through the screen were quickly whisked away.

As I settled into my chair once more, I poured the last of the Coca-Cola from the can into my glass and added more Jack Daniels. Then added a little more.

The conversation that afternoon was, as Nora Mae pointed out, depressing. To think that we live and die and all we leave behind are the things we collect. Bits and pieces of this and that. A generation, perhaps, to remember us. And in a hundred years, all is forgotten and gone. No trace of us or anything we did remains.

Even in my own experience, I knew the names of the people who owned my house before it became mine—Maude and Simon Barnett—but who owned it before they? And who owned it before anyone thought of adding streets and houses? What were they like? What were their hopes and dreams and how much of it did they achieve? Did they make a meaningful contribution to the human conversation? To advance us forward even a little? Did they try? I doubted anyone knew or would ever know. Not now. Not after so many years passed and so many memories were lost.

And who would know about me? Would I sink beneath the ocean of time, my entire life submerged in the expansive void of the past, leaving no trace of my presence? No hint that I ever had existed?

As I sat there on the porch, an odd sense of disconnectedness came over me and I felt myself becoming distant from myself—and from reality. As if I was, right then, sinking into the abyss. Buried alive in an anonymous grave. With no one on the surface above me to know or care that I was trapped below. No one to hear my cry for help. No one to come and find me. No one to even think that I might exist deep down, below, far below, in the darkness of nothing.

With the glass still in my hand and those thoughts tumbling one after another through my mind, my heart rate quickened. Sweat formed on my arms and back. My shirt stuck to my wet skin. And my mind raced faster and faster.

Was this a heart attack? Was I thinking those thoughts because I had reached the end? Would my next breath be my last?

One thought cascaded onto the next and I felt as though I were trapped. First in a grave. Then in a box. And a darkened room, groping for the light switch, the door, the way out, anything to restore a sense of relevance to my mind. To see. To know. To relate.

In desperation, I stomped my foot and felt the impact of my heel against the wooden floor. The concussion of the impact vibrated up my leg and reverberated through my body and somehow jarred my mind into an instant of self-awareness. In that sliver of clarity, I spoke aloud to myself. "Calm down," I said. "Think. Just think."

Hearing the sound of my voice expanded my sense of self-awareness and I used the moment to make an inventory of my body. There was no pain in any of my extremities. None down my left arm. None in my head. And the thought came to me that I should stand up, leave the porch, and step out to the garden. I did and made my way up the path that ran through the center of the garden as far as the fence that separated my property from Hiram's.

Now and then a mosquito buzzed around my ear and I felt one or two strike my legs near the ankles, but the relief of being in the open, with the sky above me, the night air against my skin, and the flowers all around, made the annoyance of the bugs seem a small thing.

At the fence, I looked up at the sky, spread my arms wide, and took a deep breath, allowing my lungs to fully inflate. I held it there a moment, then exhaled and repeated the same process.

Slowly, the distance between me and myself shrank and I returned fully to the moment. The sound of the night became clear again. A cricket chirping. An owl warbling in the tree that stood in Nora Mae's back yard. A peacock calling for its mate—someone who lived three streets over had four of the birds that wandered the neighborhood. Listening to the chorus of nature, the panic that had seemed on the verge of overwhelming me just moments earlier faded away and my body relaxed.

With my body at ease, I lowered my arms to my side and my thoughts returned to the earlier questions of life and death and meaning. While Hiram was alive, his house, the gardening, our conversations over the fence, were things of purport. They had substance.

That sounds like I knew him well, though I did not. Or that we meant more to each other than I've made it seem—and perhaps we did. But going through his belongings had been a far deeper experience for me than I had expected. I was a stranger to his past and in sorting through the things he left behind, I realized just how lifeless they were without his presence. How gone he really was. And how gone I will be when I die.

When Hiram died, the life that infused our conversation and our interaction ended. Without him, the things he left behind appeared much the same as his corpse had seemed when I saw it through the kitchen window—a hollow, lifeless shell of what once had been. Resembling him, but not really him any longer. The essence that gave vibrancy to whatever we shared was gone and the emptiness left behind by its absence was obvious.

And that's when I realized that whatever Hiram and I experienced—whatever Nora Mae and I experienced, whatever I experienced with anyone else—the vibrancy of it was in the interaction. The mutuality. The relationship.

Our relationship, however imperfect it might have been, was the thing that brought value and meaning to the moment. Without that relationship, the objects left behind were little more than lifeless remnants. Corpses of individual occurrences. Skeletal remains. The once vibrant body having lost the meaning and purpose that gave it life.

As I mulled those thoughts around in my mind, I remembered Hiram's cousins. Photographs in the boxes meant nothing to me. They were, in effect, a collection of dry bones from a past I knew nothing about. But the cousins knew the faces and the context from which those images sprang and instantly infused them with life once again. Giving away those photographs was the best thing I could have done. Had I kept them, they would have remained lifeless and, eventually, would have been thrown out with the trash. Or burned, as Nora Mae suggested. Hiram would have been lost forever.

And it occurred to me that by leaving Hiram's house and the remaining contents untouched, I was merely preserving the sense of death that invaded it when he died. Giving away his things was the only way to reverse that.

"Give away the parts that have no meaning to me," I said. "Keep the ones that do and fold them into my own experience."

The part that meant the most to me was the garden Hiram attempted to create in his back yard. Our conversations, our interaction, our relationship was focused on that and I knew instantly what to do with it. I would combine his garden with mine.

Rather than waiting to test the thought or consult an expert on whether keeping Hiram's property was the best and wisest course of action, I returned to the house, found a notepad at my desk, and made a sketch of the two yards as they existed. Then I made another sketch of how they might be transformed into a single garden.

Designers say that a first idea is often good but it's an idea any-one could imagine. So, I set that first sketch of the combined space aside and pushed my idea to the next level. Then I pushed it to the one after that and finally, sometime after midnight, I had a plan that I liked.

When I awakened the following morning, I waddled into the kitchen, brewed a pot of coffee, and sat at the table with a cup while I reviewed the many versions of garden plans that I had created the night before. The final one still seemed the best, so I resolved to begin working on it that day.

After a second cup of coffee, I retrieved a hammer and crowbar from the tool shed and walked up the path to the fence. In only a few minutes, I had pried loose enough boards to create an opening and before long the only thing that remained of the fence were the posts that once held it in place.

By the time I gathered and stacked the boards from the fence, it was almost noon. Before returning inside for lunch, I walked over to Hiram's house and wandered through the rooms, mentally inventorying the furniture. One or two pieces seemed interesting to me and he had several lamps that were serviceable. The rest appeared rather common and I decided to ask Nora Mae if she wanted any of it.

That afternoon, when Nora appeared at my back porch, I suggested we take our ginger ale and walk over to Hiram's.

"What for?" she asked. I could tell from the look on her face that she didn't really want to go.

"I've had another look around," I replied. "And I think you should, too."

"There's nothing over there I need to see."

"Have you ever been inside the house?"

"No."

"Then how do you know there's nothing in there you'd be interested in."

"Call his cousins back if you're interested in giving it to someone who cares."

Rather than concede the point, I handed her a bottle of ginger ale, took her by the arm, and ushered her down the steps to the garden path. "Come on," I insisted. "I'll be with you every step of the way."

When we reached the back door of Hiram's house, I took a key from my keyring, inserted it into the doorknob, and gave it a twist. Just then, Nora Mae grabbed my wrist to stop me. "Does it still smell?" she asked.

"It smells like Hiram," I replied. "But not like his dead body."

She relaxed her grip on my arm and I pushed open the door.

Nora Mae sniffed the air as we entered the kitchen. "You're right," she said. "It smells like Hiram." I wanted to ask her more about that but thought I should keep the focus on her and the house, rather than on the recent nature of her relationship to him and how she knew what he smelled like.

As we moved through the kitchen, she opened the cabinet doors and glanced inside. At first, I thought she was merely curious but then I realized she was searching for something. I kept quiet and let her look, curiosity doing more to calm her emotions than I ever could.

In the dining room there was a china cabinet, one of the few pieces I liked. When Nora Mae opened the doors to look inside, her face lit up. "That's his mother's china," she said.

"Hiram's mother?"

"Yes."

"You knew her?"

"Not well. They took me to eat at his parent's house twice. Before Hiram found out why Judy and I spent so much time together. Both times, his mother used this china."

"His parents lived in Waycross?"

"Yes."

"Would you like to have it?"

"The cousins didn't want it?"

"I didn't show it to them."

"They weren't close," she said. "I doubt they ever met Hiram's mother."

"You shall have it," I said. "We'll bring some boxes and carry it to your house."

She seemed pleased with that idea but reluctant to follow through. "Why me?"

"These dishes have meaning and purpose for you," I replied.

"And not to you?"

"To me, they are merely nice dishes. But with you, they have life."

She gave me a look. "You're a philosopher now?"

"Just a man, wrestling with the scars of life."

"Okay," she said, finally. "I know right where I'll put them."

From the dining room we moved down the hall and checked the bedrooms. Nora Mae shared my opinion of the furniture. "Pedestrian," she said. "Although the lamps might be useful."

"Do you want them?"

"No." She shook her head. "What are you going to do with this house?"

"Use it as a guesthouse, I think."

"Then the lamps might find a place here," she noted. "Are you sure you don't want to keep the furniture?"

I shook my head. "It has no meaning for me. And I don't care for the style."

"And with the money he left," she suggested, "you can buy whatever you want."

"Exactly."

There seemed nothing more to address and I was thinking the afternoon was about to end, until we came to the living room. As we entered the room, she put her hand to her mouth, and I noticed her eyes were full. I followed the focus of her gaze and saw that her eyes were fixed on an end table. It was made of dark wood—aged mahogany or oak, perhaps—with a leather top. The leather had been polished and worn and used and had a beautiful luster. It was one of the few pieces I admired.

"You recognize the table?" I asked, knowing full well that she did.

Nora Mae nodded her head. "Judy bought it at Cardwell's Furniture Store in Augusta not long after they married. I helped her pick it out."

"Then we will carry it to your house right now."

Tears trickled down her face as she looked over at me. "You don't mind?"

"Not at all. I want you to have it. It's yours."

"But you've already given me the china."

"Do you want the china cabinet to put it in?" I asked.

"No," she answered. "I have a place for the dishes but not for a china cabinet."

"Then come on." I picked up the end table and started toward the door. "Let's take this over to your house and find some boxes for the dishes."

Packing the dishes took an hour or so and then Nora Mae brought her car around and we loaded the boxes in the trunk, rather than making multiple trips lugging them to her house on foot.

Later that week, a recycling center came for the mattresses and boxed springs that were on the beds. The Salvation Army took the furniture. Only the lamps, china cabinet, and kitchen table remained. I decided at the last minute to keep the table. It meant something to me.

With the house emptied of its contents, I turned my attention to the yard. A teenager who lived at the end of our block came to help me and we removed the fence posts. Then we went to work deconstructing and reconstructing what had been Hiram's back yard. Redefining the space from his to mine. Giving it a new sense of life. Transforming it from Hiram's yard to my garden.

Most of Hiram's property was covered in shade. Grass grew only in two small patches near the garage. The rest of the area behind the house was bare dirt, which he always raked clean and swept smooth. Because it couldn't grow a lawn, he made sure not a single sprig of grass crept in. The ornamentals he grew were chosen for shade tolerance, mostly, and were held in pots or raised beds. Some of his pots were quite large and expensive to replace, so we took care not to damage them as we moved them from place to place.

The raised beds were bounded by four courses of used railroad ties that gave the area a very urban feel. Amateur came to mind, too, but I don't like that word. People who have credentialed education tend to use it in a derogatory manner when referring to those of us who have no need to be taught how to do what we do. I learned gardening on my own, but I was no amateur. And I wasn't a dabbler. Hiram was.

Still, I didn't care for the use of railroad crossties. They did not fit my personal aesthetic. I also didn't like the positioning of several of the beds. There were five in total but two were used for vegetables, a kind of gardening that did not interest me. So, we eliminated the vegetable beds completely and confined the raised bed feature to one side of the yard

For the beds that remained, we removed the crossties as the border and replaced them with walls made of brick that had been salvaged from an old store in Navasota. We set the brick on a concrete foundation that was eight inches thick and tied the bricks to it with rebar. The bricks were laid in two rows—creating a border with an outer wall and an inner wall that went all the way around each bed—each row about six inches apart with the rebar up the middle between them. For added stability we included a cross-course every four feet, tying the outside row to the inner. When the mortar between the bricks cured, we filled the space between the rows with concrete and added a cap course on top to finish it off. It was more than was required to contain the raised beds, but visitors sometimes like to sit on garden walls. I didn't want these to collapse when they did.

Adding brick walls to contain the raised beds expanded their size—we didn't remove the crossties until the brick walls were completed so as to not disturb the plants that were growing there. The sweat and time expended in doing that went a long way toward converting Hiram's back yard into my garden. The transformation took on an additional aspect when I reviewed the plants he'd had placed in the beds.

One bed was filled with nothing but ferns. Another had only caladiums and coleus. The third held impatiens—lots and lots of impatiens. Most people plant impatiens as an annual bedding plant and remove them after they stop blooming. Hiram planted the perennial kind and allowed them to seed. As a result, they returned each year. It was one of the few things that I thought he did correctly, and I liked it. So, I left the impatiens undisturbed.

Rather than trying to continue entirely with shade plants, though, I had a tree service remove the largest tree—an ash that was long past its prime. They also pruned the others to allow more sunlight. Doing that allowed us to change the mix of plants and we added phlox, heliopsis, hosta, and ligularia along with Sweet William, bottle brush buckeye, and a Japanese maple for extra color, especially on the side that did not have the raised beds.

Late that summer, I built a brick wall where the fence between the yards had been. The wall, however, only went part of the way across from either side, leaving an opening in the center for a path. And not a finished wall, either, but one with the middle crumbling down, as if the wall was old, had fallen into disrepair—as if a path opened naturally through a place where the wall had deteriorated. And then I made the path.

While we worked in the garden, a painting crew repainted the house, inside and out, and a contractor added working shutters to all the windows, screened porches to the front and back, and replaced the air conditioner. When the work was completed, I furnished the interior with antiques and collectibles that I liked, stocked the closets with fresh linens, and dubbed it my guesthouse.

Gradually, the garden became seamless except for the outdoor rooms we'd created with the wall and the raised beds. And slowly, it moved around the ends of the house to overtake the front yard. I helped it by planting ivy on one side and confederate jasmine on the other. After a few seasons, the guesthouse became an ornament in a tangled green morass. For good measure, I added wisteria in two or three places. The lavender flowers in the spring were especially striking.

When I asked Nora Mae what she thought, she said, "You have a guesthouse, but no guests."

And I had an idea for what to do about that.

# 4

If I had learned anything from my experience in settling Hiram's estate, and in redefining the property that once had been his, it was that meaning and purpose in life come from relationships. Physical objects and professional accomplishments meant very little apart from that. It was my relationship with Hiram that gave meaning to the conversations we shared and the gardening we did together. And it was my relationship with Nora Mae that made our conversations on the back porch meaningful.

If relationships were the key, then repairing relationships was an act of supreme kindness. An act of ultimate purpose and meaning. I knew from my conversations with Nora Mae that her parents were dead and that she and her sisters had not spoken to each other in years. And so, I decided to help Nora Mae repair her relationship with her siblings.

After the two yards were combined into a single garden, the wall constructed, and the house renovated and furnished, I wrote to Nora Mae's sisters—Lucille, Irene, Louise, and Lois—and invited them to celebrate Nora Mae's birthday at my guesthouse. I wasn't sure any of them would respond, much less attend, but a week after I contacted them, Lois accepted my invitation. Louise answered a few days later, followed by Irene after that. Only Lucille was left to respond and when another week went by with no word from her, I telephoned her.

"I received your invitation," Lucille replied when I explained the purpose of my call. "But I'm not interested in Johnny's birthday. And I'm sure as hell not interested in a party for her. She's had parties enough."

"Why do you say that?"

"It's a long story," she said.

"She's your sister," I said.

"That's right." There was a nasty edge to Lucille's voice. "She's my sister, not yours."

"Doesn't that mean something? That she's your sister."

"It meant something to Daddy." The inflection on that last word spoke volumes. "It doesn't mean much to me."

"Your father cared for her."

"My father cared for all of us."

"But you said, Nora Mae meant something to your father, not to you."

"And?"

"Was there a problem with that?"

"He facilitated her craziness. Look, I'm not comfortable talking about this with a stranger."

I ignored her comment. "He dressed her as a boy."

"Look, after Mama died, things got a little lopsided, if you know what I mean. It was humorous at first, but then it got a little out of hand."

I knew what she was avoiding so I pressed ahead. "In what way?"

"Well, the flat top haircut, for one."

This was a new detail. "He let her get a flattop?" I inflected my voice to sound more surprised than I really was.

"Took her to the barber himself," she announced triumphantly.

"And that was too much for you."

"The jeans. The t-shirts. The caps. All of that was fine," she said. "But the flattop went too far."

"And that happened after your mother died."

"Yes. Once she was gone, there was nothing to curb his need for a boy."

"Nora Mae thinks the reason you won't talk to her is because she had a fling with one of your friends."

"She told you about that?"

"Yes."

"And that's what she thinks this is all about?"

"Isn't it?"

"No," she snapped, and she ended the call abruptly.

Later that day while I was in the garden, my phone rang and I saw from the screen that it was a call from Lucille.

"Look," she began, when I accepted the call. "I'm not angry with you. And I'm not trying to be rude. It's just, there's a lot to this that you don't know and I'm not comfortable talking to you about it. I don't even know you."

"I understand. And my point wasn't to get you to talk to me. I just thought that it would be a tragedy for you all to live your lives and not try to find a way to get along."

"We get along."

"By avoiding each other."

"Well. Yeah."

"Your sisters are coming. And my invitation to you stands. I have plenty of room for all of you in my guesthouse. The five of you can stay over there and shout and yell and argue and say all those things that need to be said."

There was silence for a moment, then she said, "I'll think about it." And she ended the call abruptly once more.

Two weeks before Nora Mae's birthday, I decided I should tell her what I had done. When she came over that afternoon for ginger ale, I told her. She wasn't happy. "This is a big mistake," she said.

"Why?"

"It's too much," she complained.

"Nonsense," I replied. "We'll have the meals catered. And if you decide you want to eat out instead, I'll make the arrangements and cover the cost. It's no trouble at all."

"I didn't mean that."

"Then what did you mean?"

"I mean, too much time has passed. It's too late. And it's none of—"

I cut her off before she could finish. "All of them are going to be here."

She looked over at me. "All of them?"

"Except for Lucille," I said.

Her shoulders slumped and she looked away. "That figures." There was a note of resignation in her voice.

"What do you mean?"

"Did she tell you why she wasn't coming?"

"She tried."

"Then, I assume she told you it had to do with Daddy and my obsession about being a boy."

"Yes. And his obsession about having a son."

Nora Mae shook her head. "That's what she always says."

"Well," I said with a hopeful tone. "She's not mad about you being with her friend."

Nora Mae frowned. "Her friend?"

"Yeah. In the car. And the boys saw you. And—"

"You talked about that?" Nora Mae's eyes were ablaze.

"I asked her about it. Was I not supposed to?"

"You don't know her. You've never met her." Nora Mae was angry. "And you were talking about the intimate details of my life."

"I'm sorry. I thought—"

"Who else have you told about that?"

"No one." I was feeling defensive. "Why would I talk to anyone else about it?"

"You didn't share it with your buddies down at the café?" Nora Mae had a biting edge to her voice. "Get a good laugh about two lesbians in the back seat, doing the—"

"Stop it," I snapped.

"Just like those boys who saw us that night in the car."

"I haven't told anyone." Now I was angry. "And I only mentioned it to Lucille because you said that's the reason why she was mad at you. But when I asked about why she was mad, she didn't say anything about that incident. She only mentioned the part about you and your father." I sighed and leaned back in the chair. "Come on, Nora Mae. You know me better than this."

"You should stay out of things that don't concern you."

"But this does concern me," I replied.

"I don't think so."

"You're my friend," I insisted. "And this thing with your sisters has gone on long enough. Too long, in fact."

"So, now you're a counselor?" Her voice was heavy with sarcasm.

Condescension always made me angry, but I pushed the feeling aside. "I've learned a few things I think can help you."

Nora Mae stood and handed me her ginger ale bottle. "You need to learn one lesson real good."

"What's that?" I asked as I took the bottle from her.

"Stay out of other people's business."

And with that, Nora Mae shoved open the screened door, moved quickly down the steps, and disappeared around the end of the house.

Despite the reaction I received from Nora Mae and Lucille, I was determined to follow through with my plan to help the sisters reconcile their differences and restore their relationship. As the date for their arrival drew near, I hired a cleaning crew to make sure the guesthouse was in order, stocked the refrigerator and cabinets with food and drink, and readied my house, just to be prepared.

The event for Nora Mae was scheduled to begin on Friday. The sisters arrived late in the afternoon. Lois and Irene came together. Louise arrived separately. They gathered at my house first and then I rode with them around the block to the guesthouse, which let me know that, in addition to the path I had created between the two properties, I also needed a driveway. Space for that, however, required one of the adjoining houses, of which I made a mental note.

With Irene, Louise, and Lois settled into the guesthouse, I

returned home. Nora Mae's absence at the guesthouse had been obvious so I walked across the driveway and knocked her door. She called to me from behind it. "Go away."

"Open the door," I said. "We need to talk."

"I don't want to talk," she replied.

"Your sisters are waiting for you."

"I didn't ask them to come and I don't want to see them."

"They drove here just to celebrate your birthday."

"Not all of them."

"It's a start."

"I appreciate your concern, but I would rather not see them."

"You're treating them rudely," I said. Then I added, "And me, too."

"I didn't ask you to do this."

Rather than argue, I returned home and made coffee, then sat alone at the kitchen table and enjoyed it. Before I finished the first cup, there was a knock at my front door. I thought it might be Nora Mae so I quickly made my way up the hall and looked out a window. Much to my surprise, the person at my front door was Lucille. We had never met but I recognized her from photographs Nora Mae showed me once before.

As I opened the door, Lucille said, "I smell coffee."

"Would you like some?" I asked.

"Please."

She followed me to the kitchen and I gave her a cup, then we walked out to the back porch and sat in the rocking chairs while we drank.

"That's the guesthouse," I said, pointing across the garden. "You can drive around the block and park over there. Or, you can leave your car at the end of the driveway here and walk over."

"Is the guest of honor over there?"

"No," I replied. "I haven't been able to convince her to attend."

"She's angry with us still?"

"She's angry with someone. Me for doing this, I know. I'm not sure why she's angry with y'all."

"I'll talk to her," Lucille offered. "Maybe I can coax her off her high and mighty pedestal." She rose from her chair and pointed. "This is her house over here?"

"Yes," I said.

"Care to join me?"

Given Nora Mae's response to me not quite an hour earlier, I didn't think my presence was a good idea. "Might be better if you go alone," I said.

"Alright." She pushed open the screen door, walked down the steps, and headed across the driveway toward Nora Mae's.

At my usual time, late in the afternoon just as daylight was beginning to wane, I walked out to the porch and sat alone with a bottle of ginger ale in my hand. Two hours had passed since Lucille went over to Nora Mae's house and the thought came to me that perhaps I should check to see if Lucille was safe. I dismissed the notion almost as quickly as it arose, but the idea had traction and didn't quite go away.

A few minutes later, though, I heard them as they came down the driveway and walked past the end of my house. They were chatting and laughing and arm-in-arm and never once looked up to see if I was present. I kept quiet and did nothing to alert them but watched them from my place in the chair on the porch as they made their way up the garden path to the guesthouse and disappeared inside. Through the back window, I saw the sisters cross the room to greet them and they embraced in a group hug. The sight of it left me full and warm inside.

# 5

The following Tuesday, after Nora Mae's sisters were gone, Nora Mae appeared at my back porch. Mail in hand, she made her way up the steps and took a seat beside me.

"Have a ginger ale," I said.

"Don't mind if I do."

"Lucille and everyone made it home safely, I assume?"

"Yes." Nora Mae reached over and gently rubbed the back of my hand. Our eyes met and she whispered, "Thank you."

"You're very welcome," I replied.

We sat in silence a good long while and watched as the afternoon gently dissolved into twilight. As we were nearing the bottom of the ginger ale bottles, Nora Mae said, "Lucille was mad at me because I got Mama, and then I got Daddy, and then I got do to whatever I wanted."

"Because your mother died giving birth to you?"

"Yes. And because Daddy dressed me as a boy. I told her he only did that at first. After that, it was my idea. I liked living that way. But it's true, he never made me stop."

"That was when you were a child, too."

"Yes. But she said when I got older and I came out as a lesbian, I got to do that, too."

"Your father didn't try to make you stop?"

Nora Mae shook her head. "He never said a word about it. Never changed the way he treated me. Never said anything about it, one way or the other."

"And Lucille saw that as acceptance."

"It was acceptance. The best kind of acceptance. The kind where you make no judgment about the other person at all."

"And your father never said anything about it?"

"The only thing he said was, 'Nora Mae, if you aren't romantically interested in boys, don't ever let anyone persuade you otherwise. Marriage is a relationship that requires all you have and if you're with a man and you'd rather be with a woman, everyone will be miserable.'"

"Good advice."

"I thought so, too."

"So, Lucille thought you got it all? Your mother, your father, and the life you wanted to live?"

Nora Mae nodded. "She said I got to do everything I ever wanted to do."

"And she didn't?"

"Not in her mind."

"What did she want to do that she didn't get to do?"

"She didn't get to be a ballerina. A professional one."

A frown wrinkled my forehead. "To be what?"

Nora Mae smiled. "Lucille wanted to be a ballerina."

"Why didn't she do it? Even now, it's rather obvious she had the body type for it."

"She had the perfect body for it. And the perfect feet for it, too."

"Then why didn't she?"

"She danced at a small studio in Euless after school. But to be more than that, she needed to go to Dallas and join a professional company. Dallas or Houston. And Daddy wouldn't let her."

"Why not?"

"He thought nothing would come of it."

I shook my head. "How many times have I heard that."

"She's not sad about the way her life turned out," Nora Mae continued. "I mean, it's been a really good life for her. Great husband. Great kids. And life has been good for all of us. But…"

"But none of that speaks to the dream she had."

"Exactly."

"Houston Ballet has a performance every few months," I offered. "I think they have one that starts next week."

"Lucille lives in Dallas."

"Don't they have a ballet company up there?"

"Yes. They do." Nora Mae smiled. "That's why we're meeting up there next weekend to take Lucille to a performance."

My eyes filled with tears at the thought of how things worked together to bring us to that point. Hiram talked to me over the fence. I answered back. We became friends. When he died, he left me his house and all that he owned. Sorting through his belongings brought me to a crisis of meaning and purpose. Found the answer in relationships. Gave away the remainder of his things—most of them—redefined the property that had been his. Infused it with life and purpose once more. Extended that life and purpose to Nora Mae and her sisters. And now they were extending that life to Lucille. It was almost more than I could accept. And the emotion it brought inside me was almost more than I could control.

Nora Mae leaned closer and touched the back of my hand again. "Are you alright?"

"Oh, yes," I whispered. "Quite alright."

We sat in silence again as we emptied the ginger ale bottles and after a while, Nora Mae stood to leave. "You remember what to do?" she asked.

"Pull you out of the house before you stink."

She turned toward the screened door. "Don't forget."

Just as she was about to start down the steps, I said, "Mind if I make a call or two about your trip to Dallas?"

She looked back at me. "What for?"

"I know a couple of people with connections to the arts in Dallas. They might be able to get you backstage."

Nora Mae grinned. "That would be wonderful."

Other novels by Joe Hilley

*Sober Justice*

*Double Take*

*Electric Beach*

*Night Rain*

*The Deposition*

*What the Red Moon Knows*

For more information, please visit www.JoeHilley.com.

9 780999 781333